The Destiny

Nataly Adrian

The Destiny Book

Matador
9 De Montfort Mews
Leicester LE1 7FW, UK
Tel: (+44) 116 255 9311 / 9312
Email: books@troubador.co.uk
Web: www.troubador.co.uk/matador

ISBN 1 904744 93 1

Cover illustration: Sibila Jaksic

Typeset in 11pt Stempel Garamond by Troubador Publishing Ltd, Leicester, UK
Printed by The Cromwell Press, Trowbridge, Wilts, UK

Matador is an imprint of Troubador Publishing

"Each of us has a golden coach that appears to us once in our life. It is often covered with dirt and awfully smelly, but everything depends on us whether we're going to recognise it as our special golden coach and enter inside."

My grandmother Elena
(10.09.1911–08.03.1974)

Seasons and Time in Destin

There are thirty flower years in the town of Destin. The Rose Year indicates the beginning of the new cycle.

There are three seasons: the Season of Birth, the Season of Growth and Maturity and the Season of Decline.

There are nine months and every month has eight weeks. Each week, which is one moon-phase, contains five days.

Every week has five days.

The numbers indicate hours, minutes and seconds.

Contents

CONTENTS

To:
Marie-Louise Kane, who gives so much and never expects anything in return

Goran Kelecic and Yasmine Boucetta, who are always so close to me

Parick Gremy and Yvon Cauchois, for their kindness and their support

Christal Olivier, the mother of the Glimmer race

My family – my eternal love

How the Story was Born

When I was about twelve years old, I was so curious that it was very difficult to follow and control me. If I wanted to know or see something, there was no way of stopping me from doing it. And above all, I wanted to travel. As I was little, I couldn't go very far away by myself, but I would sit on the bus and let it take me in any direction it pleased. I lied to my parents that I was going to see my friends, but instead, the bus would take me far-off for somebody who was that young.

So, one day I decided to go to Pula, a picturesque town situated in Istria, in Croatia, rich in history. I didn't know much about the place, but I would stop people in the street and ask them to teach me more about it. There was the Arch of Sergians that I really liked so I would pass underneath it several times, imagining myself to be some kind of a female Caesar, even though I was just a disobedient little girl. However, what enchanted me the most was the Roman amphitheatre, which we called Arena. I thought it was the most magnificent site I had ever seen and therefore returned to Pula several times afterwards just to see it again. I recall getting myself some food and then sitting in the middle of the Arena in order to observe it better. Most of the times I visited it I was its sole visitor, but that never bothered me. While I sat there, my head would be swamped with the images that I had developed in my mind thinking about the Arena's history. It was the place where the slaves came to entertain the Romans who were deciding on their sort – who had complete power over those slaves. The slaves were their merchandise and the affluent Romans could do anything with them; sell them or let have them killed. "How horrible", I thought, "that such a superb monument bears such a morbid history". And since my first encounter with the Arena this idea has dwelled in my head not wanting to leave me alone.

I once spoke to my mum about it and she told me the legend, which has been passed down from one generation to the next. If the legend is to be believed, fairies decided to build the Arena one night. They carried stones from the mountain Ucka and the whole of Istria all through the night, rushing to finish their job before dawn. Suddenly they heard an unexpected morning cock-crow, and frightened by the sunlight left the Arena uncompleted. As it is today – without a roof.

Then one day, many years later, the idea came to me about the *The Destiny Book*. I was just about to pass my metro ticket through the machine to catch my train thinking about my life and all that it had reserved for me, when the little discovery lamp switched on in my head and told me: "Nataly, I have an idea for your book." This is exactly how it all started. Given that the Arena inspired me, I decided to personify it and name the girl who had saved the town in my book after it. But then, I needed to think of a name for the boy who was going to help Arena and save her from the Queen and the Creatures, and I just couldn't bring any name to mind. I was desperate to find her saviour, so I went on reading the Arena's history and then came up with this very captivating story. At one point in the sixteenth century, the Romans decided to destroy the Arena and use its stone to construct another amphitheatre in Rome. However, there was a senator called Gabrielle Emo who disagreed with this idea and put his foot down about the proposal. Through this, he saved the Arena and in a way allowed me to get inspired about my book. In order to thank him for doing so, I decided to use his surname as a name for the boy who saves Arena in my book and becomes her husband later on. So, Emo saves Arena in reality and in my book too.

I've always believed that if we have been sent to this planet, it is because we need to complete a precise mission, which is not revealed to us (like the Sudba Creatures never unravel the mystery of their decision about the child's destiny), but we need to figure it out alone during our lifetime. Some people say that there are gods who throw dice when creating our destiny; others argue that our race has been conceived in a laboratory....

I personally don't like to look at things that way; I prefer to concentrate on the mission that I have been entrusted with and make it a good one.

And I would like to believe that part of this mission is to give life to the *The Destiny Book* and entertain my readers with it.

The Legend

The town of Destin was a small town in the county of Amazeshire, set in a valley of outstanding beauty, where everything appeared quite neat and perfect as well as unusual. Destiners paid great attention to the image of their town and were proud of their imposing architecture. For that reason, the town seemed almost idyllic and very pleasant to live in. Even its people looked somewhat different for they were either very fat or very thin, and they all had one thing in common – extremely red cheeks. Apart from that, there was another odd thing about this town – it didn't have any trees, only flowers that were as high as trees. However, Destin wasn't famous either for its appearance or for its people, but for a legend passed down from one generation to the next.

Legend had it that the Amphitheatre, which was situated right in the centre of the town, had at one point belonged to a certain Ranna, the hideous Queen of the "Sudba" people – Creatures whose role it was to create a destiny for each person born in the town. Indeed, when a woman became pregnant, she was obliged to report her pregnancy to Queen Ranna and further to this announcement, the Sudba Creatures would gather to decide on the baby's fate. The inhabitants of Destin knew when these Creatures were holding their meeting for they would cover the Amphitheatre with a thick sheet of iron. Besides, it was impossible to approach it given that a kind of magnetism protected the site so that nobody could enter. Each Creature was held responsible for a particular human quality; there was a Love Creature, an Intelligence Creature and so on – yet the destiny was kept strictly within the walls of the Amphitheatre and was never revealed to a soul. As you can imagine, Destiners were more than respectful of the Sudba Creatures and extremely careful in their dealings with them as their childrens' lives were in the Creatures' hands. Therefore, they had the tradition of leaving presents in front of the Amphitheatre when something nice happened to their child, whereas if the contrary occurred, they avoided having to speak to the Creatures when meeting them in the street.

The Creatures were each about seven feet tall, their stocky bodies were draped in cloaks and their faces hidden behind masks. It was said that they were possessed by the spirit represented by the mask and each mask was so lifelike that it was easy to see from their exuberant expressions which spirit they were possessed by. It also soon became clear from their behaviour which quality they embodied. Walking along the street, the Suspicion Creature would be the edgy one looking over its shoulders every few minutes and the Laziness Creature was the one dragging its huge flat feet. The Creatures lived in plush rooms under the Amphitheatre and if they went out, they did so for a very short time and only during the day as their powers progressively weakened with the coming of night.

However, in spite of the Sudba Creatures' rule and unbeknown to everyone, two newborn babies, Arena and Emo, did in fact escape this law and were thankfully able to change things in the town. The peace and quiet that the present day Destiners enjoyed was all thanks to what happened in those days – all thanks to the "Legend".

Indeed, the mystery surrounding the disappearance of the Creatures and the role of both Emo and Arena in saving the town baffled the Destiners greatly. Nobody actually knew exactly what had become of the Creatures. The red-cheeked Destiners often puzzled over it together on afternoon walks in their flower-lined avenues.

Some people even believed the Sudba Creatures were only biding their time and would come back one day.

Visit to the First Circle

Irian Horvats was among the smallest but also the loudest people in Destin. If he wanted something it meant that he needed to have it on the spot and if anybody ever dared to oppose his will, he would climb to the top of a flower, making it impossible for his parents to get him down. Nobody understood how he managed to climb flowers so well, their stems being very slippery and their petals more than unstable. Given that the people in Destin were either very fat or very thin, he was obviously a member of the second group and this he used to his advantage.

He was nine and a half years old and small in size; the only thick and solid-looking part of his body was his crop of hazelnut hair, which appeared heavier than the rest of him. It was also particularly straight as if somebody had ironed it, and if Irian didn't keep it tied back in a ponytail, it would have been difficult to see his small handsome face, which was in perfect proportion to the rest of his tiny body. Nevertheless, the face was illuminated by two restless shiny button eyes, aquamarine to turquoise in colour, which dominated his face and which often moved faster than hummingbirds' wings. His cheeks were scarlet, a real contrast to his translucent skin, so that when he was angry it looked like they were burning up. His grandmother used to say that she could even spot the steam coming through his skin, though that of course wasn't true! But what was true was that Irian knew how to attract attention and he did indeed receive a lot of attention because nature had given him a good sturdy spirit.

It was the Growth and Maturity Season of the Jasmine Year and the first day of the Fifth Month. A warm temperature had begun to settle in the air and deciduous flowers started to grow new leaves and petals after the cold period, making the town look more colourful and lively. In Destin the New Moon was always recommended for new starts, and it indicated the beginning of the new week, month, season as well as the new flower year.

It was the first day of the school holiday and on that day Irian woke up in a very good mood because he was going to spend the day with his Uncle Tattoo, who was one of his favourite people. Uncle Tattoo lived in the First Circle of the town, which was right next to the Amphitheatre, and Irian loved hearing stories about the Amphitheatre legend.

The town of Destin was divided into circles and there were ten circles altogether. From the air, the town looked like a target-practice board – with the Amphitheatre as a bulls eye in the centre and then around it a first, smaller circle, surrounded by a second and somewhat bigger one and so on. Irian lived in the Tenth Circle and his school was in the Fifth. To walk from one circle to another took about ten minutes so, as you can see, Destin wasn't a big town. It was easy to walk around but if somebody for some reason wasn't in the mood for walking they could travel by hot air balloon instead. In each circle there was a hot air balloon lift-off station and every circle had its own colour so, for instance, if you wanted to travel to the First Circle you needed to take the yellow hot air balloon on the yellow line – which was always the busiest so one had to be patient. However, if you were to go to the last circle, there were always fewer passengers waiting for the blue hot air balloon.

That day Irian was flying with his mother. Surprisingly the yellow balloon wasn't busy at all, which meant that they didn't have to wait for another one. It was clear that Irian's mother felt relieved, as it wouldn't put Irian into a bad mood.

At the First Circle stop, Uncle Tattoo was already waiting for them. He was called Tattoo because of his job, which was to make tattoos, although he didn't have any himself. Every time Irian came to visit him, Uncle Tattoo had to draw a small tattoo on one of Irian's arms or else Irian would race up one of the flowers again. Well, it was just a fake one, but to Irian that didn't make any difference as long as the tattoo represented one of the Creatures from the Legend.

4

If you hadn't known that Tattoo and Irian's mother were brother and sister, you would never have guessed it. While she was slim and small in stature, Tattoo was tall and well-built appearing older than her, although she was in fact the older one. A few nasty wrinkles had appeared on his face a while ago and the black in his hair seemed to be fighting a losing battle with the white.

'I am so pleased to see you, Irian' said Uncle Tattoo breezily, opening his arms to greet his lively nephew who was already running towards him.

'So am I Uncle Tattoo. If only we could move in with you in the First Circle ' he said, shrugging his shoulders.

'You haven't been here for quite a while. I think you'll be nicely surprised' said Uncle Tattoo.

'Surprised?' Irian raised questioning eyebrows.

'Yep' replied Uncle Tattoo. 'A new tavern has just opened right next to the Amphitheatre. I'm sure you'll like it. It's called *The Old Times*.'

'Really? I can't wait to see it!' exclaimed Irian.

The First Circle was the smallest but liveliest in the town. It was connected to the Amphitheatre by the many small bridges of the river Eneo, which circled twice around the Amphitheatre and then flowed out southwest along Sunny Avenue. As it was the first day of the school holidays, the bridges were packed with stands selling all sorts of things – it seemed as if every single child had come there to spend his first day of vacation and his pocket money. The air was filled with screams of excitement as people stood in admiration before the new tavern, which truly did look appealing as well as unusual.

The Old Times overlooked the Amphitheatre and it was vast in comparison with the other taverns in the town, which could sometimes hardly cater for a dozen people. It looked like a teacup with an immense terrace in the shape of a saucer. Its chairs were either very small or very big and there was a proportionate number of them to fit the varying sizes of its customers. The handle of the teacup served as a staircase to the first floor, which gave a magnificent view over the town of Destin.

Obeese Esteam whose great, great grandfather, Sir Esteam, had been mayor and one of the most eminent historians Destin had ever known, had set up the tavern. The late Sir Esteam had been very famous in the town and regarded by everyone as a kind of local hero. When he had passed away, Destiners raised a statue to him and placed it before the Amphitheatre. The reason for his popularity was that he had opened the Amphitheatre to the public and introduced balloon transport in the town. Apparently, he had been a mysterious man who hid his private life far from the public eye. According to one story, regarded by Obeese and many other Destiners as malicious gossip, he had belonged to the Sudba Creatures though, of course, nobody really believed this. However, he had been one of the more portly members of the town, so the statue never went unnoticed even if you knew nothing about him. His great, great grandson and present benefactor of the tavern, Obeese, resembled him in many ways.

Obeese was unmistakably one of the fattest people in Destin, just as portly as his great, great grandfather, Sir Esteam. In a way he resembled a giant because he was so tall, which wasn't common in Destin, and he also had a very hoarse voice. Obeese was in his thirties and a bit of a character. However, people loved his ready wit and he never seemed to be in a bad mood. He had a habit of pulling his socks up while talking to somebody, particularly when he was embarrassed, so the children used to imitate him whenever his name was mentioned.

When Irian, his mother and Uncle Tattoo arrived in *The Old Times*, there was a carefree crowd enjoying a balmy sunny day, as well as a considerable number of people queuing to get in. Obeese was sitting right at the entrance engrossed in a book. Irian liked Obeese and was glad to see him again.

'I bet you're going to order "Queen Ranna's Choice" – I know you' said Obeese once when they had all sat round the table. As usual, he was wearing a shirt that was too tight for him, therefore revealing all his bulges while the shirt's seams seemed ready to burst at any moment. Given the heat, he rolled his sleeves up, allowing everybody to see the tattoo on his arm. Obeese was used to it, as if the tattoo was just another part of his body. Its hues had faded a bit, but not the memories of the day it was done, when he had first met Tattoo. The tattoo was like a stamp confirming their friendship and his admiration for Tattoo's talent.

'What is "Queen Ranna's Choice"?' asked Irian.

"Queen Ranna's Choice" consisted of fries and vegetarian sausages. All Destiners were vegetarians and they believed that you would turn into an animal yourself if you ate meat – they could also afford to be vegetarians given that nature had endowed the area with a perfect climate, which provided them with luscious fruits and vegetables. Not long after the meal, Irian's mother had to leave, but Irian didn't complain as he was going to stay with Uncle Tattoo and Obeese.

During his meal, Irian just couldn't take his eyes off the Amphitheatre. There was a kind of magical attraction about it, and it always seemed to Irian as if somebody was calling him from inside the Amphitheatre to enter and unravel its secret. He kept thinking about its inner quarters where the Creatures used to live and wondered if anybody had ever visited them.

'Obeese' said Irian spontaneously, 'why do you think the Local Council doesn't let anybody enter the inner quarters of the Amphitheatre?'

'I presume because they want to avoid any trouble' replied Obeese, pulling his chair closer to the table.

'Why would there be trouble? It is only a legend after all' commented Irian.

'Well, that's what they teach us when we're little.'

"What they teach us when we're little" repeated Irian to himself. "What does he mean by that? That all this might not just be a legend after all?" thoughts whirled through Irian's mind too rapidly for him to take anything in.

'But, why do they call it a legend then?' asked Irian at length.

'I guess because they have scanty evidence and therefore can't prove it used to be the truth.'

'Do you think that somebody knows the truth and is trying to hide it from us?'

'I wouldn't put it that way' said Obeese. 'I would rather say they're trying to be careful.'

'But there isn't any danger. Even if the Creatures are hiding, their powers have been destroyed.'

'Irian, that is only the rumour of the Legend.'

'Yes, but we don't have any real evidence,' commented Irian 'Or, do we?'

Obeese didn't reply. Instead, he started to fiddle with his beer mat. Irian could see that Obeese was pondering the question seriously, his piercing blue eyes fixed on the beer mat. However, he was almost convinced that Obeese's eyes were visualising something else in his secret thoughts. Something was niggling at him.

'Has anybody ever visited the inner quarters?' asked Irian with great interest.

'Yes, my great, great grandfather, but he thought it would be better to keep it a secret from everyone.'

'Why?'

'Listen, Irian!' said Obeese seriously, his eyebrows raised and his voice lowered. 'There is something I've been meaning to tell you for a long time but first, you must promise never, ever to tell anybody.'

Irian was now exploding with curiosity, imagining what Obeese was about to tell him that nobody else could ever know. He had spent countless nights trying to work out what was hidden behind the guarded doors of the mysterious inner quarters, and now the biggest secret that had ever existed in that part of the universe might be revealed to him.

'Before my great, great grandfather died, he told my great grandfather that the Sudba Creatures hadn't completely disappeared. Apparently, they are only biding their time to come back.' Obeese looked straight into Irian's eyes that were now larger than a house. Irian could hardly breathe with excitement.

'But how can they possibly come back? Haven't their powers been destroyed?' pressed Irian, astonished.

'My guess is that their powers are only hidden and they are now trying to regain them' explained Obeese.

Uncle Tattoo, who hadn't participated in this conversation having bumped into a friend sitting at the bar, then came back to the table. However, before he approached, Obeese had managed to whisper into Irian's ear: 'Hey, this is our secret, ok?' And Irian nodded his agreement feeling proud of this secret conversation "between men".

'Irian, your friends Floria and Nuro are here. Why don't you go and say hello to them?' suggested Uncle Tattoo.

Floria and Nuro were brother and sister and Irian's dearest friends. They also lived in the Tenth Circle so Irian spent practically all his free time with them. Nuro and Irian were in the same class, whereas Floria, who was a year younger, attended different lessons. Nuro and Irian got on very well together thanks to Nuro's compliant nature. Nuro wasn't very bossy, he would let Irian be responsible for setting up the rules of the game and simply follow his ideas. Actually, Nuro was rather timid so Irian was a kind of a social bridge for him connecting him with the rest of the world. Both Nuro and Floria were small and quite introverted, but they had a soft and serene personality. Their father, a very well known opera singer, had lost his voice at one point in his rather successful career, so Floria had learnt to lip-read to help improve communication between them. She had tremendous brown eyes that were full of life and always on the look out.

When Irian got to their table, Floria was completely immersed in her thoughts, which was rather unusual for her. Her mind seemed to have floated away for a moment, but then, when Irian called her name, she came back down to earth, so to speak. She was called Floria because her mother had an incredible passion for flowers. Their house seemed more like a botanical garden than a place to live because of all the flowers they had. It was common to hear Floria's mother calling her "my little bud" or by various flowers' names as well as buying her clothes with flowery patterns.

'Hello Floria. Penny for your thoughts? You didn't even notice me when I first said hello!' remarked Irian obviously surprised by her uncharacteristic behaviour.

'Oh, hello Irian' she muttered. 'I, I was just thinking...'

'Irian!'exclaimed Nuro, whose dark hair was as tousled as usual as if he had just woken up. 'When did you get here? This place looks great, doesn't it?'

'Yeah, you're right. I've been here for a while' replied Irian. 'Uncle Tattoo and I were thinking of visiting the Amphitheatre. Why don't you join us?'

'That's fine with me. I just need to check it with my dad' answered Nuro.

His father, Mr Cardolito, was actually in the middle of conversation with Uncle Tattoo. Mr Cardolito was communicating with his hands, although Uncle Tattoo didn't seem very comfortable with this technique.

'Nuro!' exclaimed Uncle Tattoo. 'I was just suggesting to your father that we all go to the Amphitheatre.'

'You've taken the words right out of my mouth' said Nuro.

Irian went to say goodbye to Obeese who winked at him as if to remind him of their secret and Irian winked back. The Amphitheatre being literally next to *The Old Times* it only took them a few seconds to get there.

The Amphitheatre was a spacious open-air building, oval in shape and made of stone, it was built on three levels and, strangely enough, it was still in perfect condition. For security reasons there was only one entrance, which was protected by two fat guardians who always stood in two separate guardrooms. They were clad in black uniforms and on their feet they wore white boots, which were so high that they covered half of their thighs. They had black gloves and white masks hid their faces to keep them anonymous. The guards were not allowed to speak to anybody – not even to each other! Between the two guardroom doors stood the main entrance bearing the emblem of the Sudba Creatures above its arched door. The emblem was made up of an open book, held by two white hands containing on the right page an image of a man and on the left page an image of a woman. A marker in the form of a golden key divided the two pages. The entrance door beneath was large with a notice board to the right, though there was nothing written on it. Rumour had it that the Creatures used transparent pencils to write with; necessitating a drop of special liquid to reveal the writing on the board. There were many boards like that whose signs were invisible within the building and this appeared to be as much of an enigma to the

Destiners as was the Legend itself. A ticket office was to be found directly after the entrance door and at the beginning of the sunray passage, which led to the heart of the Amphitheatre.

From the inside the building appeared to be considerably larger than it seemed from the outside. It had been set up to accommodate a large number of people. The centre itself was an empty surface with a picture of the sun spreading its rays all around, with a circle of tribunes rising to the summit. Anyone suffering from vertigo would never, ever have managed to climb to the last row of seats. The seats were medium-sized, indicating that in comparison with Destiners, the Creatures didn't have such radical weight-differences. Destiners used to say it was impossible to count the seats as the number changed each time you counted. According to one story, the Creatures were pretty lazy, therefore when they wanted to skip their duty of creating a child's destiny; they would simply cast a spell on their seat to make it invisible. That way, Queen Ranna couldn't get angry with them, unless she somehow noticed their absence. The circle representing the sun was Queen Ranna's podium, but it was also the door hiding the famous underground corridors where the Creatures had lived. The door was now locked and nobody in the town knew who possessed the key. In the past it had been entrusted to Sir Esteam but later on, everybody had lost track of it.

'I heard that somebody tried entering the corridors the other day, but was stopped by the guard' declared Nuro while walking towards the Amphitheatre.

'Really' said Irian, flabbergasted. 'Who was it?'

'No idea' replied Nuro. 'Apparently, there's something very precious in those corridors. I wonder what it could be...'

"That's it. Maybe the Creatures are hiding their powers in the secret passages" thought Irian. However, the identity of the person who had tried to enter the forbidden corridors bewildered him. It meant that somebody apart from Obeese and himself knew what was going on.

'How do you know about that?' asked Irian.

'Actually, I was eavesdropping on a conversation between two men in *The Old Times*' replied Nuro in a rather low voice.

'Two men?' repeated Irian. 'Which two men?'

'I don't know. I've never seen them before. They seemed rather weird to me. What do you think, Floria? You saw them as well.'

Floria was standing just behind them and was staring at something in the distance.

'Unfortunately, I didn't really pay much attention to what they were saying' replied Floria.

Suddenly a thought occurred to Irian.

'Actually, I think I did see them. Weren't they sitting at the bar?' Irian remembered seeing two men sitting a few chairs away from him. He had spotted them because they were loud and uncouth. One of them, with reddish hair, kept wiping his hand across his mouth during his meal, whereas his friend belched so loudly that at one point everybody turned their heads towards him.

'That's right!' answered Nuro.

'Now I remember. One of them kept looking at Obeese and I didn't like his eyes. There were scary' remarked Irian.

'Maybe we should ask your uncle about them. He knows everybody in Destin' suggested Nuro.

'I wouldn't do that. You know perfectly well that he doesn't believe in the Legend, so he'd only say we're wasting time on something that he thinks is a complete invention' answered Irian, trying to imitate his uncle's voice.

It was true that Uncle Tattoo didn't pay much attention to the Legend. He was very down-to-earth and not at all superstitious, which was uncommon for somebody born in Destin. In his opinion the Legend was a pure myth – something for people to natter about when they had nothing else to say.

Mr Cardolito went to make a half tour around the Amphitheatre with the children while Uncle Tattoo queued to get the tickets. Once they were all together, they entered the Amphitheatre. The moment they got in Irian, Nuro and Floria ran towards its centre.

'Irian, look, you can still see that the door has been forced' said Nuro. It was obvious that the yellowish door had been slightly damaged around the lock, clearly showing that some-body had tried to force it open.

'But however did they manage to avoid the guard?' Irian scratched his head and tried hard to figure out what was going on.

'I guess the answer isn't as simple as that. I think we should look in *The Destin Times* first to get an idea. I'm sure Mr Tappin could help us' suggested Nuro.

The Destin Times was the local newspaper and one of their neighbours, Mr Tappin, worked on it. Besides, Mr Tappin's daughter, Armianda, attended the same class as Floria.

'I can check that out tonight when I get home' said Irian. 'You know my dad never throws newspapers away. If you want to, you can both come and help me look.'

It was true that Irian's father had piles and piles of newspapers in his study, which irritated his wife, but it was an old habit that Irian's father just couldn't get rid of. Just as people have books, Irian's father had shelves stacked with newspapers. Whenever he was asked why he kept them all, he couldn't think of an answer. He probably just didn't have the heart to throw them away. His fingers were always black because of the ink, which would then become smudged on his face and Irian even thought that his father smelt of newspapers, which were made out of dry petals.

That day they didn't stay very long at the Amphitheatre because Mr Cardolito had something important to do. Floria and Nuro left with their father, so Irian stayed with Uncle Tattoo. He felt almost guilty about not sharing the secret with his two best friends, but he didn't want to break his promise to Obeese. He also wondered whether Obeese knew about the break-in, but when they passed near *The Old Times* on the way to Uncle Tattoo's house, he wasn't there.

'Which character do you want on your tattoo today?' asked Uncle Tattoo, patiently.

'Let me think' replied Irian. 'This time I'd like one of the Creatures. Can I have the Intelligence Creature?'

'Well, this is a turn up for the books!' exclaimed Uncle Tattoo. 'So, you're not interested in Queen Ranna anymore?'

'Yes, I am, but it's good to change things sometimes.'

'You're right.'

'Oh, I wish I could draw like you' sighed Irian.

Uncle Tattoo's house wasn't very far from the Amphitheatre and was only a few yards on from the pet shop *Your Best Friend* where Irian liked to pop in. Mrs Petsome, an elderly lady, worked there and she allowed Irian to come and play with the animals. The earliest memories Irian had of Mrs Petsome were the times she had spent teaching him animal sounds, which she did with such patience that it was as if she were teaching him to speak. He thought that she hadn't changed much over the years – she still had a slight moustache under her flat round nose, and mousy-brown hair that she swept back from her face. Even her black nail polish was as impeccable as always, covering her long, slightly curled nails.

Passing by her shop window, Irian was suddenly aware of being stared back at by a pair of button-round dark brown eyes. They belonged to the most enchanting white and chocolate-coloured puppy which had been born the previous month and Irian fell for him immediately.

'Can I have him, Uncle Tattoo?' asked Irian.

'I think we'll have to check that with your mother first.'

"Why do people always have to check things with someone else" wondered Irian, frustrated.

'What would you call him, Irian?' asked Mrs Petsome.

'Hmm, that's a good question' said Irian pensively. I would call him Ogi like my favourite storywriter. Can you keep him for me?'

'Of course I can. Anyway, I couldn't give him to you right now because he's still too little to be taken away from his mother' replied Mrs Petsome.

'I'll come and see you later on with my mum. If she agrees, we'll come and take the puppy when he's ready.'

The puppy really was a cute little thing and Irian could already see himself playing with him in his garden.

After the pet shop, they finally arrived at Uncle Tattoo's. Uncle Tattoo had a special flair for creating things, which made his house very original. There was an irregular-shaped clay gate, which looked a bit like mountain slopes. Behind it, there was a garden where Ginimma, Uncle Tattoo's wife, grew fruit and vegetables. The garden consisted of two circles separated by a path, which led to the house. Its front door was wide because both Ginimma and Uncle Tattoo were large in size. Uncle Tattoo used to joke that it would be less of a hassle to leap-frog over the top of him than to make the long journey around his huge body, given how fat he was.

When Irian and Uncle Tattoo arrived, Ginimma was reading in the garden.

'Look who I'm bringing you!' exclaimed Uncle Tattoo.

'Is that Irian?' she asked, taking off her glasses. 'I was just talking to Petalber about you. He might call in later on.'

Petalber was their son who had just got married and moved away with his bride, Maia, to the Third Circle. Irian didn't really like Petalber perhaps because he didn't like playing with him. Petalber was quite snooty and only chose to be with people with whom he had, as he would say, "something in common". Irian couldn't understand this behaviour because neither Uncle Tattoo nor Auntie Ginimma were like that. And they thought the same on the quiet, but of course Irian didn't know that.

'What were you saying about me?' asked Irian.

'Well, I don't know if you've heard. They're organising a big party in the Amphitheatre for Legend Day' said Ginimma, who was so soft-spoken that it was hard to hear her.

Legend Day was a bank holiday dedicated to the town of Destin.

'Oh, it had completely slipped my mind. Of course I'm coming' replied Irian. 'When is it?'

'Tomorrow evening' answered Ginimma.

Uncle Tattoo went to get drinks for everybody and they all sat in the garden. After a while, he took his colouring pencils and drew a small tattoo on Irian's right arm. It was the Intelligence Creature, as Irian had asked.

'When I'm older, you'll give me a real tattoo, won't you?' said Irian.

'I think we'll talk about that when you've grown up' replied Uncle Tattoo and Irian frowned.

Irian, Uncle Tattoo and Auntie Ginimma spent a very pleasant afternoon together, playing different games. A couple of hours later, Irian's mother came to collect him. On the way home, Irian managed to persuade her to pass by the pet shop to see the puppy.

'Look how sweet he is!' exclaimed Irian, once they had arrived at the pet shop.

'Would you really be ready to look after him? You know that puppies need a lot of attention' pointed out Irian's mother.

'Sure' answered Irian. 'I can have him, can't I, mum?'

'As it is your birthday very soon, I suppose the puppy could be your birthday present' her resistance crumbled in no time at all.

Irian was very excited at the thought of having a puppy. However, he needed to wait a full month before he could realise this idea. The little puppy was having his milk. Mrs Petsome promised to take good care of him until Irian came to collect him. On the way home they took the blue balloon back to the Tenth Circle.

It was already bed time when they arrived home, so Irian couldn't look in the newspapers about the Amphitheatre incident. Instead, he closed his bedroom-door behind him and went to bed.

That night he had a strange dream. He dreamt that he had found a special book where he could find a description of everybody's destiny. However, when he started reading it there was everybody else's destiny in it apart from his own. He desperately looked for the description of his own destiny, but it was nowhere to be found. He had been on the verge of tears, when Obeese had appeared and told him: "You're so stupid. Don't you understand?" And Irian kept on asking: "Understand what?", while Obeese just laughed. A tall thin man with a moustache standing behind Obeese had also laughed. Irian had obviously screamed during the nightmare because his mother rushed in to wake him up.

'Are you ok?' she asked in a gentle voice, imprinting her tiny lips on his forehead.

'Yes' he answered, hesitating.

'What were you dreaming about?' said his mother, concerned.

'I can't remember' he lied, not wanting to upset her.

Irian couldn't get back to sleep. Instead, he tiptoed to his father's study to look for the article on the Amphitheatre incident. He lit a candle and started his research. His father's study was a big, messy room, overflowing with musty old newspapers and only Irian's father could find his way through the piles. Irian had already begun to think he would never find the right one, but then, after about an hour of constant searching, he found a recent pile. Leafing through each newspaper to find the article, he eventually came across the one he wanted. It had been written by Mr Tappin:

"UNSUCCESSFUL BREAK-IN ATTEMPT IN THE MYSTERIOUS CORRIDORS

Last night G.C. (31) attempted to enter the Amphitheatre's mysterious corridors but was foiled just in time by the guard.

G.C. from Amazeshire used a cunning plan to deceive the guard. By starting a fire not far from the building to attract attention, he was able to penetrate the Amphitheatre. It took several minutes for the guards to realise what was happening before they intercepted him and prevented his entering.

Police are detaining the man for questioning and it is not known when he is to be released."

Irian was trying to puzzle out the identity of G.C., though the initials rang no bells. He carefully tore the article out of the newspaper and returned to his room. He had gone through the article again and again before he finally turned the lights off.

It was almost morning when Irian fell asleep at last. Usually, he was the one who woke everybody else up, but that day his parents managed to enjoy a quiet breakfast without facing the barrage of questions Irian had prepared to ask. So his mother could quietly savour her coffee and his dad could read his newspaper in peace. It truly was an unusual morning for Irian's parents.

Legend Day

The streets in Destin were crowded. Even though the mayor had introduced extra balloon schedules, everybody was sauntering towards the First Circle because it was impossible to get on a yellow balloon. However, nobody seemed to mind walking, on the contrary, there was a pleasant sort of atmosphere. Irian was heading towards the centre with Nuro, Floria and their father. Despite sleeping in until late, Irian still felt very drowsy and couldn't stop yawning. Normally, he was always ahead of everybody, leading the way, but this time he was finding it difficult to keep up with his friends.

'Come on, Irian' said Nuro. 'At this pace, we'll never get there.'

'I can't go any faster' replied Irian. 'Anyway, I don't see why we have to rush around so much.'

'Well, you said yourself that you wanted to go to *The Old Times* for a pudding. I'd be extremely surprised if we get a seat by the time we get there' said Nuro.

'Look!' exclaimed Floria. 'There's Armianda.'

Armianda was Mr Tappin's daughter and one of Floria's best schoolmates. She was very much like her father in that she always had a lot of questions. She simply had to know everything that was happening around her. Irian sometimes found her too nosy, though that was just part of her nature. She wasn't trying to be nasty on purpose, but questions were her way of leading a conversation.

In Destin, close friends stroke the side of each other's faces twice when saying hello. So, Armianda and Floria performed this gesture, which was a common sight to Destiners.

'Are you by yourself?' asked Floria.

'No, my parents would never let me go to the First Circle alone. I'm with Mrs Verlic, but she's met somebody too. She's talking to a man down there. Can you see her?'

Mrs Verlic, an elderly woman, was their neighbour from the Ninth Circle and she looked after Armianda whenever her parents were busy.

'Aren't your parents coming?' asked Floria.

'Actually, my mum isn't feeling very well, but my dad's already there. As far as I know, he's supposed to be interviewing somebody.'

'Do you know who?'

'Not really, but it must be someone important because dad's spent quite a few days preparing for this interview' replied Armianda.

Nuro and Irian who were not very far from Floria and Armianda now caught them up. Irian seemed to get his second wind when he spotted Armianda, hoping that she knew something more about the mysterious G.C., knowing how curious she was.

When they finally arrived at the First Circle, the place was swarming with people so that they could hardly make their way around. A multitude was gathered in front of the Amphitheatre waiting for the mayor to declare the celebration officially open. Irian, Nuro, Armianda and Floria tried getting in *The Old Times* though that was practically impossible. Irian took the opportunity to look for Obeese who was nowhere to be seen.

During the Legend Day, the Local Council usually launched new projects such as theatre openings, new playgrounds, generally speaking, things to improve the Destiners' quality of life in some way. This time they were introducing a new communication system, which seemed to amuse people. It was a tiny gadget, approximately two inches in size which looked a bit like a lipstick, called – a talkastick. Its usage was very simple – all you had to do was turn the lower part of the talkastick – just like pushing up your lipstick, and this would push out the microphone to the top. After this the bottom part was detached and you had to stick it in your ear and pronounce the name of the person you wished to speak to. If the person had his talkastick handy, the connection was instantly established.

'This looks great' said Nuro, taken aback by the invention.

'I hope my parents get me one for my birthday' sighed Irian.

'I thought you wanted a puppy' said Floria.

'I do, but I could have a talkastick too' replied Irian.

They all approached the stage for a better view of the mayor who was presenting this new gadget. It truly was fascinating for children and adults alike. Following the presentation there was a competition with a talkastick as the prize. The aim of the game was to say aloud "she sells sea shells on the sea shore" ten times without making a mistake. Nuro was too shy to take part, but Floria, Irian and Armianda decided to give it a try. However, they had to hurry as many other people had the same idea. There were ten participants chosen to go up on the stage. A lady in a yellow dress, who had a go first, got so confused when hearing the tongue twister that she just muttered something which was completely wrong. After her a stocky man had a go, but when he let out his tiny voice, which was completely disproportionate to his huge appearance, the audience just burst into laughter. This probably embarrassed him so much that he lost his tongue and spoilt it all. It was then Irian's turn and he started off really well but then, at the fifth repetition he got tongue tied on the third word of the given phrase, which happened to Floria as well. The situation got really tense when the man after Floria got the phrase right nine times, but failed on the last attempt. Finally it was up to Armianda to play and she managed to pronounce them all correctly.

'So, the winner is Armianda!' exclaimed the mayor, and the audience applauded loudly.

'Here we are my dear; you can have a talkastick. Which colour would you like?' asked the mayor.

Armianda chose pink, shook the mayor's hand, and they all left the stage.

'Can I see it?' asked Nuro.

Our group of friends gathered round to get a better look at the pink talkastick, when suddenly Irian noticed that somebody was pulling his sleeve. When he turned round, Obeese was standing next to him.

'You looked just the part on stage' said Obeese.

'Hello, Obeese' said Irian in surprise. 'I passed by *The Old Times* earlier on, but I couldn't see you.'

'I've just arrived actually' replied Obeese.

'You know I've been thinking a lot about yesterday.'

Obeese stepped closer to Irian.

'Have you heard about the break-in in...' Irian continued.

'Let's talk about that later on' Obeese interrupted him, sinking his voice to a whisper and looking around suspiciously. 'This is not a good place for a conversation.'

Just then, Irian heard a strange sound behind him coming from Armianda's talkastick as the mayor called her to check if it was working.

The celebrations continued until dawn and parents didn't seem to mind their children staying out late that night. Even Irian somehow managed to stay awake, but he just couldn't find the right moment to speak to Armianda or Obeese. Besides, Obeese had to leave to get up early the next morning, so he had to wait for another meeting with him. On the way home, however, he managed to grab a moment to talk to Armianda.

'I think you'll have to wait for a while before using your talkastick' said Irian. 'None of your friends has one yet.'

'I know, but I suppose it won't be for very long' replied Armianda. 'Did you see all those people interested in it?'

'You're right.' There was a small pause before Irian went on. In his head, he was looking for the right words to ask her about the break-in. 'How did your father's interview go?'

'Well, I reckon.'

'Who did he interview?'

'The mayor. As far as I know, dad wanted more details about the break-in in the Amphitheatre.'

Irian was all ears.

'Yes, I read his article the other day. Does he know who the man is?'

'Well, I'm not supposed to tell you because I'm not supposed to know myself, but I heard dad talking to a police officer on the phone, and he mentioned the name Gadious Cheater.'

This name rang no bell at all for Irian.

'What are they going to do with the man?'

'Look, Irian, I just heard his name, okay, but that's all I can tell you. By the way, why are you so interested?'

'Because it just sounds extraordinary that somebody could do such a thing' this was the best excuse Irian could come up with on the spot.

They soon arrived at the Tenth Circle and everybody went home. His mother was still awake reading so they quickly exchanged a few words before going to sleep. His room was on the second floor on the right, and Irian wished it were on the ground floor – he was simply too exhausted to make the slightest effort. He took off his clothes and snuggled down into his bed but left the little lamp on. His wall was like a picture gallery of all the Creatures he liked looking at, but that night he felt as if they were in fact looking at him, although that of course could not have been true. He started to believe that there was something far more complex about all this than just a pure legend.

A Day with Grandfather

Not far from Irian's house was a playground, which Irian often used with his friends, after which he would visit his grandparents, on his mother's side, who lived in a small house nearby. It was literally only fifteen minutes walk from his house, so Irian could go there whenever he wanted. Destin wasn't a dangerous place to live, but people were exceptionally superstitious and believed that the Creatures hid all around the area. This was why they didn't want to leave their children out alone in the street except for short distances. Irian's parents were somewhat more flexible, but he still had to ask their permission whenever going somewhere by himself, which of course, annoyed him excessively.

When he arrived at their house, Grandmother was just about to leave. She was going to the Flower Fair, so Irian stayed with Grandfather. After a few rainy days, the weather was wonderful, so they decided to stay outdoors. Grandfather had been a hot air balloon pilot, but was now retired. However, hot air balloons were still his passion in life and he would always get excited when a new type was introduced to the public transport system. He always wore a golden medal that he had won for being the best hot-air balloon pilot years ago, and he made sure it stuck well out so that everybody could see it properly.

'We could take the Old Lady out.' This is how he referred to the hot air balloon he had bought many years ago and which was extremely old-fashioned in comparison with the models currently seen in the town. 'She likes being taken out.'

Irian would chuckle whenever he heard Grandfather talking about a balloon like this. His wife, Irian's grandmother, didn't really like it when he flew his balloon, and particularly when it was a question of taking Irian with him. However, given that she had left for the Flower Fair, there were no restrictions on them to the relief of both grandfather and grandson and the complicity between them made it seem an even greater adventure.

'Perhaps we could go for a panoramic flight of Amazeshire. I know a good place that's a treat for the eyes and there's also a nice little lake where we could go for a swim. How do you fancy that?' asked Grandfather.

Irian felt almost embarrassed but he couldn't stop laughing, so he was hiding and blocking his nose, so that Grandfather wouldn't hear him. Grandfather was a funny old man who was always ready to tell a joke or go off on an adventure. Despite his age, he hadn't lost that youthful springy step. His wife used to say that she had two sons, Tattoo and her husband. He and Irian got on like a house on fire.

He kept his balloon in the shed, so they had to take it out and get it ready for the flight. When he had started flying hot air balloons, they had not been very safe, so he always wore a helmet. Irian had to wear one too to please him and no matter how ridiculous he found it he didn't want to offend his doting grandfather. They finally got on the balloon and a few minutes later were flying high up in the air. In Destin, flying hot air balloons in the town was forbidden as the traffic there was already quite heavy. This time, Grandfather decided to fly south-west.

It was early afternoon and the bird's eye view was stunning. Amazeshire hadn't been given its name by chance; the county did look truly amazing. Its fields were never the same and were of every possible colour and shape, strewn around with houses. It took them about half an hour to arrive. The spot was simply perfect for relaxing, with its picture-postcard atmosphere. They parked the balloon not far from the lake and sat in a shady nook under the star-shaped flowers. The clear blue lake beckoned and as it got hot after a while, Irian climbed one of the flowers near the lake and dived in.

'I wish I could do that, but I'm far too fat' Grandfather sighed.

'Look, there's a big stone. You can jump from there!' exclaimed Irian from the water.

That is exactly what Grandfather did producing a big splash

in the process. Irian couldn't help bursting into peals of laughter. They stayed in the lake for quite a while but then Irian started shivering with cold.

'It's time to get out, young man.'

They dried themselves and lay quietly in the sun. Irian enjoyed spending a little time away from Destin, but found it very difficult to relax. Since his conversation with Obeese, he couldn't think about anything else but the Creatures and their hidden powers. And then, there was this Gadious Cheater who represented a real enigma to Irian. His mind seemed like a stuffy room chocked full of so much furniture in so many different styles, nothing matching.

'Grandpa, do you think the Legend of the Sudba Creatures and Queen Ranna is really just a legend?' asked Irian tearing away at the piece of leaf that he had previously found in his pocket.

'Well, I've asked myself that same question many times. But you know what they say: "there's no smoke without fire".'

'What does that mean?'

'It means that if people talk about something, there must be a grain of truth in it. Just look at the Amphitheatre, how can it be in such perfect shape after so many years? I believe that's one sign already that it can't just be a legend.'

Irian had never thought about it like that, but totally agreed. The Amphitheatre always appeared ship-shape, despite the years and the fact that it had never been renovated.

'There is one person who could probably help you better than I can' he said finally.

Irian felt like a human question mark.

'A little after you were born, on a day just like today, I went on a balloon ride. It was a beautiful sunny weather; everything just perfect for flying and that day I headed west. I stayed out for quite a while because I fell asleep in the sun. When I woke up, it was a bit cloudy so I decided to hurry home, you know grandma and all that, but it was already too late. Despite being up in the air I couldn't control the balloon. I didn't have the faintest idea where I was going and I knew your grandma would be worried stiff, that's why she doesn't like me taking the Old Lady out now

– that day scared her so much. So, as I said, the balloon kept on going in its own direction driven by this horrific wind. I even blacked out at one point because I hit my head against something. I couldn't tell you how long it lasted but when I woke up I didn't have a clue where I was. There was just the Old Lady, the fields and me. Then, much further away, I spotted a house. The Old Lady was a bit worse for wear, so I had to walk to it, which was a tall order because I was worn out with a few aches and pains, but that house was my only hope. On the way I had to keep resting but despite the pain I managed to get there. It was a small house with peeling walls, badly run-down and seeing that the door was open and nobody answered, I simply went in. I noticed that somebody must live in the house but was out, so I started to look around. It was very strange and everything was exceptionally old. After a while, I didn't know what to do, so I sat on the sofa and decided to wait for the person to come back. I didn't know who would turn up; I just know I felt completely lost. I was also starving and tired, and it was so comfortable on that sofa despite its pitiful state, I somehow managed to doze off. I might have slept for an hour or for a day, I just couldn't and probably will never be able to tell you, but when I woke up there was this old woman sitting next to me in her armchair. She was looking at me but I realised she was blind because when I looked at her she didn't move her eyes. She reacted only when I said hello. I apologised for bothering her and explained what had happened. She answered that I could stay as long as I wanted, and then made me something to eat. I learnt that her name was Peena. She was an exceptional woman because even though she couldn't see, she knew perfectly well how to find her way around the house, and she prepared a hearty meal. When I started to feel a bit better, I went to get the balloon back, but another storm was approaching so I couldn't go anywhere. In the evening we sat down to a cup of tea and had a chat while heavy rain splattered on the roof. Peena told me she'd lost her sight about ten years before when she had seen the Water Castle. I didn't understand what she meant by that, so I asked her to explain and she told me this very far-fetched story.

One day she was out for a walk and got lost, just like me. She was wandering around trying to find her way back when suddenly everything started to change around her. The night suddenly turned into day, the fields started to disappear under the water and in the blink of an eye there was a massive lake in front of her. She couldn't believe her eyes – she could still use them then, of course – and the most amazing thing happened; the water that had been calm for a while suddenly began crashing about in huge waves. She saw two hands appear out of thin air and start to create the most beautiful Water Castle, which looked like a waterfall that was turned upside-down. The moment the Castle was finished, she saw that the same hands had created a watery path in front of her leading up to it. She was so stunned that she could think of nothing else but to follow the path which disappeared behind her, as if somebody was erasing it as she walked. The path led her to a big steep staircase to the entrance of the Castle. Inside, everything was made of water: the chairs, the tables, the beds... It all seemed like the craziest and most extravagant dream. Then, my dear Irian, it turned into a nightmare, because when she went into the great hall in front of her she saw the Sudba Creatures. Queen Ranna was sitting on the throne and the Creatures were walking up and down. She was all of a panic, but she couldn't run away. You know, the Creatures and the Queen have become even more evil since they lost their power over creating destinies and, apparently, Ranna threatened that they would return to Destin one day and control us once more. The Water Castle is their hiding place, in fact, and it's visible to people only once every twenty years, providing somebody somehow manages to find its location. Queen Ranna decided to blind poor Peena so that she couldn't show the whereabouts of the Castle to anybody and she was sent away. Without her eyes, she couldn't find her way back but she's lucky she got away with her life, I think. One of the villagers helped her to return home. She told the people in the village about it but nobody believed her and thought she had gone crazy, so she had to move away. This is when she moved to the house I'd come across.'

Irian was almost angry with Grandfather for keeping this story a secret from him for such a long time. But his anger was overwhelmed by great excitement flowing through his entire body. In a way, Peena's experience was the link connecting his imagination with reality.

'Do you think she's still alive?' he asked.

'I don't know. She was already quite old when I met her.'

'Could you take me to her?'

'If you really want me to, but it can't be today because we have to get back. If your grandmother arrives home before us, we'll be in a big trouble. Ever since that storm, she always panics if I'm out in the balloon.

'Does grandma know about your encounter with Peena?'

'No way! She would think I was completely nuts to believe in such things.'

'And did you believe the woman?'

'Well, she was very convincing, but it's hard to say. I'll tell you what; I'll be very busy this week because I'm helping Petalber with his new house. As soon as I get that done, we can go and look for her together.'

'Oh, thank you, grandpa' said Irian gratefully. 'I can't wait to meet her.'

They went for another swim, had a walk around the lake for a while and then, finally, got on the balloon. Not long after they had arrived, Grandmother arrived too. She brought several kinds of seeds from the Flower Fair, so Irian helped her plant them. Their garden was already full of different types of plants because Grandmother was very fond of gardening. Whoever passed near their house would stop and look at their garden, which was a real masterpiece.

Irian stayed with his grandparents until the evening when Grandfather walked him home.

'Grandpa, you promise to take me to that woman?'

'I promise. But, what are you going to do if we find her and she tells you herself about the Water Castle?'

'Well, I'll ask her to take me there.'

'You're such a dreamer. Your grandmother would have my guts for garters if she knew I was telling you all this.'

'Don't worry, I won't mention it to anybody. Mum's the word.'

'I'll come and see you when I find some time for our trip.'

When Irian got home, he went straight up to his room. All he could think about was the Water Castle and Peena. He decided not to say anything to Obeese or anybody else.

It seemed as if he was slowly starting to fit the pieces of his puzzle together. The Water Castle cancelled out the last of his doubts about the Creatures' existence.

Irian's Birthday

In Destin, a birthday was very significant. It was a rite and every-body celebrated his or her birthday. The day before, it was important to have a good rest because the person celebrating had to stay awake throughout the whole of the day. Irian was thrilled about it as he was going to be given a great deal of attention and he was also curious about his presents. Well, he knew that he wouldn't get his puppy yet, because it was too early to separate him from his mother. However, there would be other presents but he had to wait before discovering them.

So, at precisely midnight, his parents came into his room to make sure he wasn't asleep. This was always the case with younger children because it was crucial not to let them sleep, which was par-ticularly hard with babies. Therefore, family or friends would help the exhausted parents, but as Irian was older now staying up wasn't such a problem. Actually, until the children were twelve, parents got a day off work, and as Irian was only ten years old that day they could stay with him the whole day. In fact, the reason why it was so important to stay awake on your birthday was that you were draw-ing energy from other people around you and from nature itself. This is why spending the day with people who loved and cared about you was recommended and it was good to go into the coun-tryside to get purer energy. So if you fell asleep you would miss all this intake of both human and environmental energy. Irian had a lot of ideas about what to do for his birthday, so that was already a good thing. From midnight until very early in the morning, they played different games, and then his grandparents came round at about seven o'clock so Irian's parents went for a quick nap.

'So, are you excited about going to the Birthday Cave?' asked Grandmother.

'Yes, I am but I hope I'm not going to be told off like the last time' answered Irian.

'Well, everybody gets what he or she deserves. It's definitely better than having the Creatures decide about your life' answered Grandfather.

'Stop filling his head with that Legend! How many times do I have to tell you!' exclaimed Grandmother crossly, who didn't believe in the Legend at all.

The Birthday Cave was the place where everybody had to go on his or her birthday. Situated outside the town, the Cave was beehive-shaped, right in the middle of a blue field. The person was to enter it alone at the exact time of his or her birth, which in Irian's case was midday. That day, his parents and grandparents accompanied him to the Birthday Cave and left him ten yards in front of it as the rule demanded. Irian had to hurry because it was already midday, so he ran to the entrance door.

When he entered, the only light in the room was spilling in through the cracks in the door. Therefore, he didn't know whether to go in further or wait for some kind of sign, but he decided to wait. After a while, something seemed wrong as nothing was happening until finally he heard a husky Voice saying: "Welcome Irian!" Just then the lights went on and Irian noticed that not a thing had changed since the previous year. The place was called a cave, though it was nothing like one really. It was a sumptuous room in many shades of blue, creating a unique kind of harmony. Blue was the protective colour of the town of Destin, and Destiners connected it with the night. Given that the Sudba Creatures dreaded the night because it weakened their powers, Destiners had adopted it as their principal colour. Every detail in the Birthday Cave symbolised something. The floor, for instance, which was made of little shiny pearls glued together, represented the town. These pearls were arranged in ten circles, each indicating one circle of Destin. Around the sides, within the thick crystal walls, a wax-like liquid flowed slowly in all directions forming different shapes and symbolizing the defeated Creatures. There was no sunshine coming in, however, light emanated from the stalactites. As the ceiling wasn't very high, some of them were almost touching the floor.

Irian was asked to approach and enter the space in the middle of the room, which was surrounded by glass. Within the glass space was a kind of a chair that looked just like a hand on which he had to lie down. It had been placed in the centre to represent a new concept of life, no longer defined within the walls of the Amphitheatre. The Voice led him through the whole process and Irian had simply to obey it.

'So, Irian' said the Voice, 'you're waiting to receive everything you have attained throughout last year?'

'Yes' replied Irian fearfully.

'Let me think, what have I got for you? You've learned to be more patient, which is very good. What do you expect from your tenth birthday?' inquired the Voice.

'I'd like to do something very unusual and challenging' answered Irian earnestly.

'Something unusual and challenging' repeated the Voice. 'What do you mean by that?'

'I'd like to experience a great adventure, something nobody has ever experienced before' said Irian with great enthusiasm, his fear forgotten.

'You've always been ambitious, haven't you? And a little impetuous. Anyway, it is up to you to create that adventure. Ask yourself what you want, and your mind will give you the answer. Now, close your eyes and let's work on both your new mental and physical strengths.'

Irian did as he was told and felt smoke spreading within the glass capsule. Suddenly, it had become so hot inside that he started sweating, but he mustn't move. He felt a slight tickle in his body each time a different colour of lightning appeared from the stalactites and struck him. The lightning was actually a new life quality and, given the different life qualities, there were various colours for each quality. Irian had the feeling that these qualities were never-ending; though in reality, the whole thing didn't last that long.

Finally, the glass opened on one side and Irian could finally get off the hand-chair.

'How do you feel now?' asked the Voice.

'I must admit I like the feeling of being ten years old. There is a great deal of positive energy inside me. It's wonderful, actually' Irian replied.

'I'm glad to hear that. It means you've learned a lot during your ninth year. Now go to your family and happy birthday.'

When he came out of the cave, the daylight dazzled him, and he had to shade his eyes with his hand. He had a quick thought for poor blind Peena.

His family was waiting outside impatiently, and Irian ran towards them.

'Look how he's grown' remarked Grandmother.

'You seem a bit maturer, I'd say' added Grandfather.

'How did it go?' asked his mother.

'It was ok but I don't like being stuck on that chair' replied Irian.

'Well, we all have to go through that' said Irian's father.

'What would happen if we didn't go to the Birthday Cave?' asked Irian.

'Well, you would miss out on everything you'd learned during the previous year' answered Grandmother. 'Remember what happened to Didoo?'

Didoo was one of Uncle Tattoo's neighbours and when he turned four years old he was on holiday with his parents, who were a bit careless and who hadn't taken him to the Birthday Cave. Therefore, he was always behind everybody else among his peers and would probably always remain so.

'Let's go home now. Everybody's waiting for you' said Irian's father.

'I can't wait to see my presents' said Irian, impatiently.

They walked home from the Birthday Cave, as it wasn't very far from the Tenth Circle. When they were leaving, there was another group of people waiting in front of it to enter. However, Irian was glad that it was all over for him.

His friends had already arrived and were waiting for him in the garden. Not long after they'd got back from the Birthday Cave, Uncle Tattoo and Auntie Ginimma arrived. Everybody was very excited to see how Irian had changed. Irian went to check himself in the mirror and was pleased to see that he was almost two inches taller and he noticed that his cheeks were somewhat less red. While he was observing himself in the mirror, he heard his mother calling him. It was time for his birthday presents. At last!

In Destin, you couldn't just send your present to somebody by post; you had to hand it over yourself. In return, the person to whom you gave the present could thank you with a little rhyme. If it was a little child the parents could help. This gesture was not obligatory, but it was practised by many people.

When Irian got to the sitting room, there was a huge bag full of presents and his friends and family were waiting to see his reaction. He was beaming all over, curious to see what he had been given. The first present out of the bag was very small and Auntie Ginimma and Uncle Tattoo's names were on it. Irian shook it slightly, but couldn't guess what was wrapped up inside, so he opened it.

'A blue talkastick!' he exclaimed 'It's wonderful! Thank you so much Uncle Tattoo and Auntie Ginimma. It's exactly what I wanted!'

Apart from a talkastick, he received many other presents such as games, a new desk from his parents, two books *How to Make a Puppy Happy* from Nuro and Floria and *The Truth about the Legend* from Armianda, etc. As he was unwrapping the last present, Floria came in singing the birthday song and carrying a cake that Mrs Cardolito had made for him. It was a gorgeous creation in the shape of the Good Mood Creature with ten candles on it. Before blowing out the candles, Irian chanted a little rhyme to thank his family and friends for his presents.

> *"I may seem young, I may seem small*
> *But give me a chance and I'll surprise you all*
> *With you by my side and with you in my heart*
> *There's nothing in this world that can tear me apart!"*

Everybody applauded the rhyme and Irian blew out the

candles. He had managed to blow them out all in one go before his mother cut the cake and gave a piece of it to everybody. The cake was made of various fruits and was so scrumptious that it very soon disappeared.

Irian spent a lazy afternoon playing with Floria and Nuro in his room where they tested out all the games he had been given.

'Irian' said Nuro after a while 'you know those two men we saw in *The Old Times*?'

'Yes' replied Irian, obviously curious.

'I spoke to my dad the other day and he said that they used to be friends of Obeese' said Nuro.

'Really? How does he know that?' asked Irian.

'Dad told me that Obeese had had another tavern many years ago before he opened *The Old Times*, a tavern that the two men visited very often and so that's how they became Obeese's friends. Nobody knows exactly why, but they argued a lot and now they've started to go to *The Old Times*. Apparently, Obeese owes them something.'

'I wonder what it could be. Who knows, maybe Uncle Tattoo knows something more about it? But I guess he wouldn't tell me anyway. Do you know their names?'

'The man with black hair is called Zlob and the other one, with reddish hair, Vrag. As far as my father knows, they live somewhere in south Amazeshire.'

'I hope Obeese isn't having too much trouble with them' said Irian.

'You've always liked Obeese, haven't you? I don't like him' said Nuro.

'Neither do I' said Floria, who was listening to their conversation and observing Nuro and Irian, her eyes wide.

'I've never understood why you two don't like Obeese. He's never done anything bad and he's Uncle Tattoo's best friend. Uncle Tattoo wouldn't choose just anybody as his best friend.'

'I adore Uncle Tattoo, and his friendship with Obeese baffles me. There's something about Obeese, as if he had a secret life. It's hard to put it into words.'

'How does your father know about those two men anyway?' asked Irian.

'One of them, Vrag, worked with my dad in the theatre, but he lost his job because he got drunk. Apart from that, he used to see them a lot in the other tavern Obeese used to have.'

'And what about Zlob?'

'Dad doesn't know him.'

'How could Obeese be friends with such people?'

'No idea. But, they aren't friends anymore.'

In his mind, Irian was trying to remember the two men. It was true that Obeese looked at them from time to time, but Irian didn't really pay attention to that. No matter what Floria and Nuro thought about Obeese, he couldn't say anything bad about him. He was trying to recall their conversation about the Creatures, "why did he choose to confide such a big secret in me? Why didn't he tell Uncle Tattoo if they're best friends?" Irian had been thinking about that over and over again since their talk in *The Old Times*, but then he had found all kinds of explanations. He thought that the reason why he chose to share the secret with him was because Uncle Tattoo didn't believe in the Legend at all. Therefore, if Obeese had said something to Uncle Tattoo, he would just have laughed at him. In any case, this was definitely the best explanation Irian could come up with although, deep inside, he found it difficult to believe. There was something mysterious about Obeese, but Irian was confused over defining it. Never ever before had he suspected Obeese of anything, however, he could not remain so positive towards him after this conversation with Floria and Nuro.

The Hot Air Balloon Fair

The Balloon Fair always took place during the school holidays and it wasn't only for children but for everybody who liked balloons. It was held in the Fifth Circle where the biggest balloon station was and that day transport was free of charge for everyone. There were many balloons displayed, new and old models in all possible colours, and everybody could get on the balloon or ask the pilots questions. Grandfather proudly took part, and his Old Lady was there too. It was amazing to see all these everyday balloons and the ones that hadn't been in use for ages. One of the balloons displayed used to belong to Sir Esteam who, at that time, had been the only person allowed to fly above Destin. His balloon was made of gold with many precious stones so it drew the biggest crowd because everybody wanted to see it up close. However, it was also the only balloon that nobody could get on as it was too delicate; the director of Balloon Transport thought it wouldn't be a good idea to let anybody step onto it. Apart from that Sir Esteam's balloon was kept under glass in order to protect it from grubby fingers. There were some other interesting balloons like new models that hadn't yet come out which were really peculiar in shape. Many older Destiners didn't like these newly designed, snazzy balloons, while children looked on at them, fascinated. Most of the balloons were only exhibited so that people could have a better look at them, but some of them there were on sale. Of course, they were very expensive as was the balloon licence, and not many Destiners could afford one. However, many people in Amazeshire had private balloons, as this was the best way to travel around if you lived in a remote place. If they couldn't afford it, there was always the Public Balloon Transport everywhere in Amazeshire.

'I wouldn't mind this one' said Armianda, who was visiting the Fair with Floria, Nuro and Irian, as they stood in front of one of the older balloon models.

'You wouldn't get anywhere in it. Look how old it is' commented Irian.

'I'm not in a hurry. If I had my own balloon it wouldn't be to rush somewhere but to fly for pleasure whenever or wherever I want, and with whomever I please' retorted Armianda, somewhat annoyed at Irian's way of looking at things.

'So, where would you go for example?' asked Irian, a bit sarcastically.

'Probably where you wouldn't' replied Armianda, readily.

'Come on you two, we're not going to argue over balloons. There's no accounting for taste. I suppose you both know that' said Floria.

That day the Local Council introduced an intensive balloon course for children. It was actually held in the Balloon Station and any child could attend this short class. The first part of the lesson was about balloon construction, while the second part dealt with flying. Children of all ages had crowded into the room, all of them with their eyes wide open in order not to miss a single detail. After the lesson, the children could ask questions or even get on the balloon.

'Who knows what helium is?' the instructor had asked.

'It's a gas that helps the balloon fly' answered one child.

'How can helium make the balloon rise?' asked another child.

'Because during the day sunlight heats the helium causing the balloon to rise' replied the instructor.

'And what happens at night?' asked another child.

'Well, at night the colder atmosphere makes the helium shrink, and the hot-air bag below is heated to warm the helium and maintain altitude.'

'Can hot-air balloons go up to the stars?' asked a wide-eyed little girl and everybody had laughed.

Nuro wanted to be a hot air balloon pilot, and he probably had the best score to the questions, but he didn't dare to say his answers aloud. He was also very interested in balloon construction, and his father promised to take him to the hot air balloon factory for his birthday. Nuro was very much into technology just as Irian was interested in the Legend. His room looked like a laboratory where he experimented on things. His father even helped him construct his own little hot air balloon model, but of course, it couldn't fly.

That day different trips were organised for anybody interested in visiting any of the towns in Amazeshire. The choice included a trip to Sakarin, a little village situated only a few miles from Destin, known for its delectable sweets. Irian, Floria, Nuro and Armianda couldn't pass up this opportunity, so they all got on the balloon to go to Sakarin accompanied by Grandfather, who had a very sweet tooth too. They were lucky to get seats on the balloon, as this trip was particularly popular. Mr Integger, their mathematics teacher, was also on the balloon with his younger daughter and it was obvious that he felt embarrassed to find himself on the same balloon as his pupils.

'You've changed, Irian. Was it your birthday recently?' asked Mr Integger smiling though his features were not naturally intended to wear a smiling aspect.

Irian wasn't very good at mathematics, therefore he wasn't very pleased to see Mr Integger. He answered the question and then very quickly looked in the opposite direction.

'I hope you're going to do better at mathematics next year' Mr Integger continued, though Irian wasn't looking at him anymore.

Nuro, who was sitting next to Irian couldn't stop laughing and Irian found it very annoying.

'I don't find it funny at all' said Irian angrily when they got off.

'I'm sorry. I wasn't really laughing at you' replied Nuro.

'He means it, Irian' said Floria. 'I don't know if you've noticed that Mr Integger had a wig on which wasn't well stuck down on the right hand side. I was laughing too.'

Mr Integger was not well-liked by his pupils or colleagues. As a teacher he wasn't even that bad, but he always needed to say something offensive that would spoil the whole atmosphere in class. This behaviour was very strange because he wasn't a dim-witted man and he came from a very respected family in Destin. There were many different stories circulating about him and his past. Apparently, he worked for the Mask Heads in Amazeshire, the secret organisation that supported the Sudba Creatures' return and that wanted to seize control over the mayor and the Local Council. Nobody knew who the leaders of this secret organisation were or how many people were members. However, every so often, they would send threatening letters to the mayor, the contents of which were never revealed to the public. Well, nobody was really sure about Mr Integger's participation in this organisation but, for some reason, people directly linked his name with it.

'I can already smell the cakes' said Grandfather, who simply adored sweets and couldn't help eating them although his middle was already so vast that it looked like he had been entrapped in a huge sugary doughnut years ago.

'I've heard that they've introduced some new recipes' said Armianda.

'The last time I came here there was a hot air balloon made of chocolate. It's incredible how they make those things' said Nuro.

In Sakarin, chocolate and cake shops were dotted all over the place – a real chocolate town where people came either to display their sweet recipes or to indulge themselves. Everything was so well organised. For instance in one street they baked cakes and you could go in and observe how they were made. Just after that, there was a Chocolate Street, then a Lollipop Street and so on.

'I wouldn't mind a lollipop' said Irian. 'Uncle Tattoo told me there's a new lollipop shop.'

'It must be that one there' said Floria, pointing to the colourful shop in the middle of Lollipop Street.

'It looks fantastic!' exclaimed Irian. 'If I worked there, there wouldn't be a single lollipop left in the shop.'

'Well, even if that did happen, you would never get fat, lucky as you are' added Grandfather.

'I guess not' replied Irian. 'I think I'm going to have papaya flavour today.'

There were all kind and sizes of lollipops in all imaginable flavours. The lollipops were put up on the shelves and each of them produced a different sound. The sound came from a little hole on the top of the lollipop, and there were many different sounds. Irian's lollipop sounded a bit like a bird.

They stayed in Sakarin the whole afternoon just wandering around and eating different sweets. There was a little girl on their return who had obviously eaten too many sweets and was sick the whole balloon journey.

'How disgusting!' said Irian. 'If she doesn't stop, I'm going to be sick myself!'

'Well, please try not to because she's already unbearable' said Nuro, wrinkling his nose in disgust.

They were all glad to be back in Destin where the Hot Air Balloon Fair was coming to an end.

'What shall we do now?' asked Floria.

'My mum said we're going to pick up my puppy' replied Irian.

'So, the big day has arrived' said Armianda. 'When your puppy grows up a bit, he'll be able to play with my dog.'

'Why not!' replied Irian. 'I'll see you all later.'

Irian left the Balloon Fair with Grandfather and joined his mother who was waiting for him at his grandparents' house.

'So, how was the fair?' she asked.

'Excellent!' replied Irian. 'It is just a shame we couldn't get on Sir Esteam's balloon.'

'I am one of the few people who was allowed to get on to it' said Grandfather proudly 'and they even took a photo of me.'

'That doesn't surprise me!' sighed his wife. 'You and your hot air balloons!'

What she didn't know was that her husband had paid a large amount of money to the director of public transport to let him onto Sir Esteam's balloon and take the photo. When it came to hot air balloons, he simply had no limits.

'So, shall we go and get the puppy?' suggested Irian's mother.

'Yes, otherwise Mrs Petsome is going to think you're not interested in him anymore' said Grandmother, joking.

They just arrived in time because Mrs Petsome was on the point of closing.

'You know, a lot of people were interested in your puppy, but I kept him for you as I'd promised' she said on seeing Irian.

'Thank you. How's he been?' asked Irian.

'Oh, fine except that he's got a little cold now but nothing serious' replied Mrs Petsome.

The puppy was actually the only animal in the shop allowed to run around, so when Irian stepped in he started jumping up at him as if to say hello.

'Hello, Ogi! I'm Irian and from now on, we're going to be friends' said Irian stroking his little puppy. Just as he said that the puppy sneezed as if to confirm their deal.

'Be careful with him!' warned Mrs Petsome. 'He's a very clever puppy and knows exactly how to get round you, but you mustn't give in all the time. Look at me, it's the only animal I've ever let out around the shop and I've run it for thirty years.'

On the way home, Irian had Ogi in a basket, but as he kept on jumping out Irian decided to carry him. Ogi obviously felt very comfortable in Irian's arms so had a wee. Irian got very annoyed about that so in the end, Irian's mother carried Ogi.

'I've obviously chosen the most spoilt puppy that exists' said Irian angrily.

'I told you that puppies need a lot of patience and attention. It is going to be up to you to teach him how to behave. You are his master now' said Irian's mother.

'Yes, but what can I do when he won't listen?' asked Irian.

'He needs to get used to you. Ogi doesn't understand you're his master yet. He must be very confused because he knows neither who we are nor where we're taking him.'

Irian felt a bit better at this, but he still didn't know how to handle his little puppy. It wasn't like with his friends where he could just get angry and they understood what was wrong.

'I suppose Ogi and I will just have to learn to live with each other' sighed Irian.

Gadious Cheater escapes from prison

It was quite early in the morning and Irian was sound asleep when he was woken up by his talkastick.

'Irian, are you still asleep?' asked Nuro on the other end of the talkastick.

'Yes, I am actually. By the way, I didn't know you had a talkastick' said Irian in a croaky voice.

'My dad bought it yesterday so I'm just borrowing it' replied Nuro. 'I've got something important to tell you.'

'So early in the morning?' asked Irian.

'You know what, Gadious Cheater has escaped from prison.'

'What?' exclaimed Irian, jumping up.

'I've just heard on the radio that he escaped from prison last night.'

When Irian heard this, he rubbed his eyes, not really sure whether he was actually awake or not.

'Listen, I'll go and get dressed, buy a newspaper and come to your place so we can talk about it' said Irian, already undoing the buttons of his striped pyjama top.

'Ok' answered Nuro. 'We can even have breakfast together.'

Irian had probably never got ready so quickly in his life, and his parents were surprised to see him leaving the house at eight o'clock in the morning. He just had time to say "going to see Nuro" and "see you later" before leaving. Mrs Horvats shrugged her shoulders and her husband just shook his head.

Nuro lived only a few houses away but Irian had to go a little bit further first to get the newspaper. The newsagent was next to the local balloon station and there was hardly anybody waiting for a balloon that morning. Walking along the street, Irian had the funny feeling that he was being followed. He turned back several times and looked around and even though there wasn't anybody, he couldn't get rid of this unpleasant sensation. At one point, he even felt as if somebody was holding him by the arm, but he rejected this idea immediately. It was a strange morning, but Irian somehow convinced himself that it was only because he had woken up unusually early that he still hadn't quite had time to pull himself together.

Nuro was so looking forward to seeing Irian that he was waiting for him in the garden.

'So, have you seen the paper?' asked Nuro, impatiently.

'Well, I've only just bought it' replied Irian. 'Let's have a look... Here we are! Of course, Mr Tappin has written it.'

"GADIOUS CHEATER ESCAPES FROM PRISON

Gadious Cheater (31), who attempted to break into the mysterious corridors of the Amphitheatre a few days ago and had been detained by the police, managed to escape from prison last night.

His method of escape has not yet been established nor the circumstances of his escape. However, we have learnt from the chief inspector working on the case that Gadious Cheater escaped without leaving any breakages behind him. The window bars remain in perfect condition as does the door, and no holes are to be seen in the walls or floor. The Prison director is said to have commented that Gadious Cheater escaped "as if by magic".

The inspector has been questioning all the prison guards in case of a possible collaboration on their part in setting Gadious free, although they all seem so extremely baffled by the event that there is very little chance of any of them having co-operated with Gadious Cheater.

Nobody actually knows very much about this man who could be very dangerous. Therefore we would appreciate your assistance should you have any information concerning this man."

Next to the text was a photo of Gadious and, for a moment,

Irian thought he had already seen him somewhere but just couldn't recall where. He had a very long thin face and small dark eyes and his lips were hidden behind a moustache. Irian was almost scared by those eyes, so he promptly closed the newspaper.

'They said on the radio that this is the first time that somebody has escaped from the prison' said Nuro. 'Apparently, they are very strict and the prison is well protected.'

'Well, obviously, not that well protected' commented Irian.

Just then, Floria came down to the garden having just woken up, so Irian and Nuro told her what had happened. Floria was so amazed that it seemed as if her big eyes were now covering the whole of her face.

'It's incredible! I dreamt about that man last night. Can I see him?' asked Floria.

She looked in the newspaper and recognised the man from her dream. When she saw his picture, she felt her legs turn to jelly.

'It's him!' she said, completely terrified.

Irian had a better look at the picture and remembered that Gadious had appeared in his dream too when he had dreamed about the book containing a description of everybody's destiny. They were all so stunned that they didn't even dare speak for a while. Irian was even thinking of telling them about his weird feeling of being followed but didn't want to scare his friends even more.

'I think we should look for this man ourselves' Nuro said finally.

'Come on Nuro! I'm not a magician, and I don't see any other way to get onto his track. He must have some kind of supernatural power to appear in our dreams' replied Irian.

'There is one thing I don't understand. I wonder why he appeared only in yours and Floria's dreams. Why didn't he show up in my dream for example?' asked Nuro.

'That's exactly what I've been trying to figure out' said Irian.

There was another pause in which each of them tried extremely hard to come up with an answer.

'Irian, there is something I haven't told you because I thought I wasn't supposed to know' said Floria suddenly, and

Irian and Nuro gave her a puzzled look.

'What is it Floria?' asked Irian.

'Well' said Floria 'remember the conversation you had with Obeese in *The Old Times*? While you were talking to him I was actually reading from his lips what he was saying and I know everything. I didn't want to tell you because I also saw you promise Obeese you wouldn't reveal it to anybody. But now, given that we're the only ones who know about it, I've begun thinking this might be the reason why Gadious is appearing in our dreams.'

Nuro couldn't understand what they were talking about so Irian explained the whole story to him. Now that he could share the secret with his friends, he also told them about Peena and his unusual dream with Obeese and Gadious. Floria and Nuro were amazed to the point of seeming hypnotised. For Floria, Irian and Nuro, any possible doubt about the existence of the Legend was wiped away for good that morning. They felt keyed up, but at the same time scared about the whole thing.

'Can we come with you and your grandfather to see Peena?' asked Nuro.

'Listen, it's not up to me. I'll have to ask Grandfather' said Irian. 'I think we should be really careful when talking about this subject' he continued.

'What was in your dream about Gadious?' Nuro asked his sister.

'I was talking to Armianda and he was observing me from a distance so I said to Armianda that we should move because there was a strange man looking at us. When she turned around she somehow recognized him and told me it was Gadious,' replied Floria.

'How can we get to know more about this Gadious Cheater? I wonder if the Local Council could help us. They have a record of everyone in Destin,' Irian thought out loud.

'If they had any unusual records about him, Mr Tappin would have known about it because he's a journalist and would already have written about it' Floria pointed out.

'Perhaps he does know more about him, but is not allowed to publish it all' said Nuro.

'Well, you know how ambitious Mr Tappin is, you know that he would risk anything to get a more exclusive article' said Irian. 'Or he might just be biding his time until he gets a more detailed picture.'

'Armianda would have told me if her father knew more about Gadious. I think he has very limited information and that's all' reasoned Floria.

By that time, Mr and Mrs Cardolito had woken up and came into the garden, so Irian, Floria and Nuro had to change the subject quickly and wait until later.

'You're up bright and early today' said Mrs Cardolito.

'We thought it would be nice to have breakfast together' lied Nuro.

'So, what did you have?' asked Mrs Cardolito.

'We haven't actually had it yet. I'm going to prepare it now' said Floria.

'Don't worry; I'll prepare it for all of us. Why not?' suggested Mr Cardolito, using his hands to explain what he meant and everybody agreed.

Irian wasn't always able to understand Mr Cardolito, so he sometimes needed help from Floria or Nuro. Therefore, he would often be fascinated to see how well Nuro and Floria could communicate with their father just by using signs.

'How is your puppy doing, Irian?' asked Mrs Cardolito.

'I think he's more obedient now but we had a difficult time with him in the beginning' replied Irian.

Ogi was so naughty the first night Irian brought him home that he thought he was going to have to take him back to Mrs Petsome. However, with the help of Irian's parents Ogi somehow got used to them all and to the house, but he refused to sleep in a basket. In the end, Irian became fed up with him whining all night and decided he could sleep in the basket at the end of his bed.

Mr Cardolito arrived with a tray carrying a beautifully decorated fruit salad and large jug of orange juice. Even Mrs Cardolito was amazed at such unexpected service coming from her husband.

'I didn't know you were so imaginative in the kitchen' said Mrs Cardolito.

'Excellent job, dad ' exclaimed Nuro.

'I think that having breakfast together was a great idea after all' said Irian.

'As it's our wedding anniversary, I thought it would be nice to have an unusual breakfast' replied Mr Cardolito in sign language.

'How sweet of you!' said Mrs Cardolito.

They had breakfast together in the garden under the big sweet-smelling cherry flower. The breakfast was truly delicious and consisted of many different fruits put together in the shape of a rose. Mr Cardolito had done this with such patience that Irian felt bad about spoiling the decoration by serving himself. He somehow forgot his sensation of being followed and was feeling better after all.

At the Creative Shop

Around midday Irian returned home because his parents had to go into town and he needed to take care of Ogi. When he arrived, Ogi was already bounding towards him to say hello. But instead of jumping at him as he usually did, he started barking aggressively and despite all Irian's efforts Ogi wouldn't stop.

'Ogi, will you stop making that noise?' said Irian angrily.

'What's happening?' asked Irian's father who had come into the garden to see what was the matter.

'I've no idea. Ask Ogi' said Irian, annoyed.

'Ogi, stop that noise immediately' shouted Irian's father.

Ogi continued barking but then after a while gradually stopped. However, he was reluctant to go to Irian at all and went off to play by himself, which was very unusual.

'Are you sure you don't want to come with us?' asked Irian's mother.

'You know I can't stand Mrs Gartika' replied Irian.

Mrs Gartika lived in the First Circle and Irian thought she looked very much like the Ugliness Creature. Her nose seemed three sizes too big and she had the biggest eye bags he had ever seen. However, that didn't bother Irian too much; what really annoyed him about her was that she was so nosey and always boasting about something or other.

'If you want, we could take you to Uncle Tattoo's, but I'm not really sure he's going to be there' said Irian's mother. 'I'll call him to see.'

She went to call her brother but there was no answer.

'He's not there' she said. 'Would you like to go to a "Creative Shop"?

A "Creative Shop" was a workshop for children where they could express their creative abilities and, if their work was well done, it could be displayed in the Amphitheatre. Once a month the Local Council organised an exhibition for children only and Irian always dreamt of having one of his works presented and the attention this would bring. However, he felt he wasn't creative enough to make something really special. Despite that, he liked going to the "Creative Shop" because there was always something interesting going on there.

'Why not!' he finally answered his mother's question. 'And what about Ogi?'

'Your father and I will take him with us.'

On the way to the First Circle, Ogi was still avoiding Irian so he decided not to pay any attention to him either.

The "Creative Shop" was on the other side of the First Circle from Uncle Tattoo's house. It was made of glass so that everybody could see inside. Irian's parents left him there and they went off to see Mrs Gartika. There were so many children in the "Creative Shop" that Irian had difficulty finding a free table to sit down at. In the end, he found a place next to a boy who seemed a bit older than him. The boy was in the middle of his drawing and he obviously had great talent. In a way, Irian regretted sitting next to him because he had no idea about what he was going to do with the blank piece of paper lying on the table in front of him nor was he that good at drawing anyway. Everybody seemed so absorbed in their work while Irian only felt like observing the others – and this is exactly what he did.

'No inspiration, eh?' the boy next to Irian noticed that Irian wasn't really sure about what he was going to do.

'I'm not very good at drawing actually' replied Irian. 'If you don't mind, I'll just watch you draw.'

'My name is Smodge' said the boy. 'Have you been here before?'

'I'm Irian. Yes, I've been here several times but when I was much younger. You seem to be a regular client. By the way, where did you learn to paint so well?'

'Both of my parents are painters' replied Smodge, whose face seemed so full of freckles that it would have been impossible to add another dot.

'Wait a minute! Are you related to Smeerius Newance, the famous painter?'

'He's my father' said the boy, his face beaming.

'That's great!' exclaimed Irian. 'I saw his latest exhibition with my Uncle Tattoo. It was very impressive I must say.'

'Thanks! I know Mr Tattoo. He used to go to school with my dad when they were very young. We saw him the other day in *The Old Times*. So, what brings you here if you're not very artistic?'

Irian felt embarrassed by this question but, as he really wasn't very talented when it came to painting, he decided to answer it without getting angry.

'I like coming to the First Circle so I thought I might just as well visit the "Creative Shop"'replied Irian.

As Irian said that, something very strange happened. While Irian and Smodge were talking, a pot of red paint that had been standing on the table next to Irian suddenly splattered across the table and then onto Irian's trousers. It was very weird because Irian had kept his hands on the chair and Smodge was at least ten inches away from the table. Both Irian and Smodge were completely baffled by the incident.

'That almost looked like some kind of nasty trick' said Smodge in amazement.

'Yeah, I really can't imagine how it happened. Oh, look at my trousers now!' said Irian annoyed.

He went to the toilet to try to clean his trousers and was terrified when he realised that the big red stain was now forming perfectly the shape of the initials G.C. He covered his eyes in disbelief, realising that his feelings of being followed weren't just the fruit of his imagination after all. That moment he understood that it was Gadious Cheater who had been following him. Irian was so shocked that he just stood there in the middle of the floor without moving. He could feel Gadious's presence very close to him, and this was making his blood run cold. Funnily enough, while he was standing there unable to move, his talkastick rang. It was Nuro.

'Nuro, you must help me!' said Irian in a panic. 'I've been followed by Gadious and I can feel him standing right next to me.

As he pronounced these words he heard laughter somewhere behind him, though when he turned round he couldn't see anybody. Irian was completely terrified – it seemed like he was in the middle of his worst nightmare.

'Turn the lights off, Irian" said Nuro. 'If he's a Creature, he won't be able to hurt you with the lights off.'

Irian did as his friend advised and, as if by magic, he got rid of the feeling of having somebody around.

'Well done, Nuro, I think that idea works' replied Irian relieved but still shaking.

Irian explained to Nuro what had happened and Nuro just listened without saying anything. It was hard for him to accept that all this wasn't just mere coincidence. However, he was happy to know that the light thing worked.

'So, Gadious definitely is one of the Creatures' said Irian

'Now I understand why he managed to escape from prison. He must have used one of the Creatures' tricks' said Nuro. 'What do you think we should do?

'I don't know' replied Irian. 'But, we must never speak about anything important when the light is on.'

'Do you think Gadious heard our conversation this morning?' asked Nuro.

'He might have' replied Irian. 'I think we'll have to be quick about going to see Peena if she's still around. She might be the only one able to help us.'

'I hope Gadious doesn't find her before we do' said Nuro.

'Well, anything is possible. I'll try to see Grandfather when I get home. We need to arrange the visit as soon as possible' said Irian.

'Are you going to be ok, Irian?'

'Oh, yes, though I look ridiculous with this strange red stain on my trousers.'

'Are you in the "Creative Shop" by yourself?'

'Yes, but I met Smodge, who is Smeerius Newance's son. Incredible, isn't it?'

'Don't tell him anything about Gadious! You never know.'

The moment he said that, Smodge came into the toilets to check if Irian was all right.

'Why don't you switch the light on?' said Smodge when he saw Irian in the dark talking on his talkastick.

'I was just about to leave, so I switched it off' Irian could hear Nuro laughing on the other end of the line.

Irian turned up his trousers so as to hide the stain. He felt completely silly.

'Have you managed to clean your trousers?' asked Smodge.

'Not really, but it doesn't matter after all' Irian answered, hoping Smodge wouldn't guess anything.

'If you want, you can come to my house and get changed there. I have a younger brother who must be about your size' proposed Smodge. 'It's only five minutes away.'

This didn't sound like such a bad idea. The Newance family lived in the First Circle in a house that was utterly hidden by flowers and a massive gate. However, the view from the gate was so stunning that Irian's lower jaw dropped in amazement. The house was built of porcelain with a big swimming pool in front of it that looked like a lake. Mr and Mrs Newance were sitting on flower shaped chairs made of glass.

'Mum, dad, this is my new friend, Irian' said Smodge pointing to Irian.

At that moment, Irian felt totally ridiculous with his trousers rolled up but Mr and Mrs Newance didn't seem to mind that.

'Nice to meet you, Irian' said Smeerius, getting up from his chair.

Smeerius was a well-known Destiner and he was famous because he painted using make-up. It was a very special technique and required particular attention as it was easy to get a drawing all smudged. Besides, Smeerius had another particularity – he used to say that every person and object had a special taste, colour and smell. As soon as he saw a person, he would get a different taste in his mouth and perceive him or her in a particular colour, which he would then use in his portraits so as to make his paintings more personal. For instance, to him, his son Smodge was a deep purple and tasted of freshly baked lemon meringue pie. Smeerius looked very ordinary, clean-shaven with distinctive greenish eyes, and instead of hair he had quite a large tattoo of the Creative Creature covering the top of his head, which had been there for many years. Apart from his tattoo, there was not really much to attract attention; he always dressed very plainly. He didn't even wear shoes as he wanted direct contact with the earth, saying that he could feel its energy.

'He's Tattoo's nephew' said Smodge.

'Oh, are you?' asked Smeerius.

'Yes' replied Irian, wondering how Smeerius perceived him. Irian only hoped he didn't taste like garlic or emanate some disgusting colour. 'How do you do?'

'You know, I think your uncle is a very talented man. I've always liked his tattoos. However, there's something I've never understood about him. We all know that Tattoo has never believed in our Legend, so I've always wondered why he only ever draws its characters.'

Irian was quite surprised at this and it was true, although this had never crossed his mind. Uncle Tattoo was so insistent about the the legend not existing that it was impossible to talk to him about it. Though, on the other hand, he spent years and years tattooing such life-like images of the Creatures and the Queen on different parts of people's bodies.

Just as Irian was about to answer, Smeerius' talkastick rang so he entered the house to take the call.

'Shall we go to my room so that you can get changed?' proposed Smodge.

'Yeah, why not!' replied Irian.

When Irian entered their house, he couldn't decide whether he was more stunned by the exterior or the interior. There was a massive hall extending towards the kitchen while on the right hand-side a spiral staircase in the shape of a piano keyboard led up to the first floor. The banister was unusual as well because it looked like a stave with a big treble clef at the bottom of the stairs. Irian was surprised to see that there weren't that many of Smeerius' paintings hanging on the walls, but he thought to himself that they might be kept in his study.

'Let's get you the trousers first. My brother's room is just over there' said Smodge pointing to the greenish door. 'Do enter, he's not here today. He's gone to south Amazeshire with our grandparents.'

'Are you sure he's not going to mind it if I borrow his trousers?' asked Irian.

'No worries. He would never ever let you touch any of his toys, but when it comes to clothes, he couldn't care less.'

'How old is your brother?' asked Irian.

'Nine. Have you got any brothers or sisters?'

'No, I haven't actually. I think I'm already enough trouble myself, so I wonder how my parents would possibly cope with a second child' replied Irian, joking.

'In my case, my father is never ever there and my mum is always busy, so I actually quite like having my brother around. We get on quite well together even though we're very different.'

'Well, thank him for the trousers anyway. I hope I meet him one day.'

'Look, why don't you go and get changed in the bathroom. It's upstairs on the right. I'll wait for you in my room on the top floor.'

Irian did exactly as Smodge suggested. The house had three floors and Irian was now climbing up to the second one where the parent's room and the bathroom were. The house had exterior walls made of porcelain whereas the interior ones were made of brick. While he was on his way to the bathroom, Irian heard Smeerius talking on his talkastick as the parent's room door was slightly ajar. At first, he didn't have any intention of eavesdropping on Smeerius' conversation, so he started walking towards the bathroom. However, just as he was about to push down the handle to enter, he heard Smeerius saying: "I can't speak to you right now, Vrag. I'll call you later. Don't forget about the meeting tonight."

Irian prayed hard that the bathroom door wouldn't make any noise. He pushed it as carefully as he could and then hid behind the door, relieved. A few seconds later, he could hear Smeerius going downstairs as his wife called to him. Irian remained there for a while without really knowing what to think. He didn't even dare put on the light because the last thing he wanted was to feel Gadious's presence. He felt his head swarming with all kinds of questions like: "Had he really spoken to Vrag, the man Nuro was telling me about? Why are they meeting?" He'd been so busy thinking that he almost forgot to get changed, so when he heard Smodge calling him he quickly put the trousers on and got out of the bathroom.

'Are you coming, Irian?' asked Smodge.

'Yes, I am. Do you have a bag for my trousers by any chance?'

'If you want to, you can leave them here and our cleaning lady will wash them for you' offered Smodge kindly.

'That's nice of you but I don't want to bother anyone' replied Irian. By no means did he want Smodge or his parents to see that stain.

Irian finally got into Smodge's room while Smodge went to the kitchen to look for a bag. Irian really liked Smodge but he found it difficult to be spontaneous particularly after the conversation he had overheard.

'I've got us a papaya juice' said Smodge, carrying a tray with two glasses filled to the brim.

'Thank you, Smodge' replied Irian. 'It's just what I need.'

'By the way, your parents called. They'll come and pick you up later.'

While Irian waited for Smodge to come back, he noticed a thick book about the Legend on one his shelves. Irian had numerous editions concerning the Sudba Creatures but he had never seen this one before.

'Do you mind if I have a look at this? I thought I had all the books about the Legend. Where did you get this one?' asked Irian.

'It was my *Imagine And Live It Day's* present' replied Smodge.

Imagine And Live It Day was every child's favourite day, held once a year. It was important to enrol for the game two months in advance, specifying what your ideal day would be like. In the meantime, the Good Will Association, which was an association for children's spiritual development, selected one participant. So, on

Imagine And Live It Day, the lucky participant would find a flying chair next to their bed, which would take them to their desired destination. Nobody ever understood how the flying chairs worked as the association never wanted to reveal this secret. However, you only had the right to take part once, so it was important to think carefully about your perfect day before enrolling.

'Really, you were selected for *Imagine And Live It Day*?' exclaimed Irian. 'I've always wondered what it would be like. So, what was your wish?'

'You see' Smodge said 'when I was quite little, I had a very unusual dream. I mean, dreams are normally bizarre and inexplicable, but when you wake up their peculiarity normally melts away in the morning sun. You know what it's like; once your dream is over you don't pay attention to it anymore. But that dream was unlike any other I had had before, and funnily enough, I still remember it perfectly. I remember visiting an amazing castle with my father and an odd-looking man in a wig, who seemed so real despite the unreality of the situation. The most remarkable thing was that the castle we went to was completely made of water. Given that I knew it was just my imagination, I couldn't ask for this when enrolling for *Imagine and Live it Day*, so I asked to visit any castle. As a treat they took me to the Summer Castle, which used to belong to Sir Esteam, and I spent a marvellous day there. Before leaving they gave me this book as a present.'

Irian felt that the papaya juice had gone down the wrong way on hearing the words 'Water Castle'. He was now desperately trying to swallow extra saliva to make the juice go down his throat properly. Was Smodge really talking about the Water Castle – the same one that Peena had seen a long time ago or was it just an extraordinary coincidence?! But is there such a thing as "coincidence"? Irian suddenly felt very hot and had difficulty breathing so he went on drinking his juice in an attempt to distract his thoughts somehow.

'What was the Water Castle like?' asked Irian when he finally plucked up the courage to continue the conversation.

'It was out of this world. The astounding thing about it was that everything was made of water; the chairs, the tables... Unfortunately, I only remember the castle – I don't remember what I did there.'

For Irian, there was no doubt in his mind that they were talking about the same place. However, he couldn't really understand how Smodge had got there. Everything was so muddled up in his head and he just couldn't see a way of putting his thoughts into order.

'What would you like to do if you were accepted to participate in *Imagine And Live It Day*?' asked Smodge.

'I would ask to visit the inner quarters of the Amphitheatre' replied Irian firmly.

He only had three more years to try his luck to participate in the game. He had applied for it from an early age, but had never been accepted. He thought that his wish was much more important than those of the other children as it could help uncover more about the Legend.

'You're ambitious!' said Smodge. 'There's the book. Apparently, it's the best book on the market on the subject, but it's quite difficult to find.'

'Have you read it all?'

'Well, not yet. Do you want to hear one of the stories?'

'Ok, go on.'

'The story is about the Hypocrisy Creature. It says:

> *"The Hypocrisy Creature was one of those natural actors who didn't need a screenplay or a stage to act on, but had a natural talent for changing personality and playing any part. However, it would never ever accept a bad role, but only the most charming and the most sought-after ones. No wonder it was the Moody Creature's best friend after all! The Sincerity Creature used to say that it would have been easier to tame a lion than to expect the Hypocrisy Creature to keep the same opinion for an entire day.*
>
> *Always innocent looking, it would dress in its white cape and interpret sincerity in an impeccable way, always pretending to be as sympathetic as possible to everybody's*

problems. Yet, its mellowing words, which it chose with the greatest precaution, had nothing to do with its real opinions. Compliments were its way of buying others, and once it had other Creatures' affection, the Hypocrisy Creature would use them as it wanted. It always spoke in superlatives to make its words as convincing as possible, though its words were only the slice of cheese on the mousetrap. If everybody was against somebody or something, of course it had to share their opinion and make sure everybody saw it in its best light. The Hypocrisy Creature had to follow the crowd unless it was talking to somebody face to face, when it would adapt its opinion to the Creature it was speaking to.

It was the Creature without principles, whose principles changed depending on situations and the interests it could draw from others."

Just as Smodge had finished reading the story, they heard Mrs Newance calling from downstairs because Irian's parents had just arrived. Irian and Smodge both ran down to meet them. Mr and Mrs Horvats seemed quite puzzled that their son was there, but they said nothing.

'Why don't you join us for dinner?' proposed Mrs Newance.

'That's very kind of you, but we really need to rush home because we have friends coming tonight' replied Mrs Horvats.

Ogi was there too and he ran up to Irian as if to say hello, but as soon as Irian stroked him he went back to Mr Horvats. "I'm sure he's doing that because of Gadious. Why would he be avoiding me otherwise?" Realising this, Irian wasn't angry with Ogi anymore and tried to be nice to him from then on.

'Are you ready, Irian?' asked his mother.

'Hope to see you soon, Smodge' said Irian.

'Me too. I'll call you on your talkastick' replied Smodge.

On their way home, something seemed to be bothering Mrs Horvats. It actually looked as if she was in quite a bad mood, which was unusual for her.

'Irian' she said firmly, giving him a withering look, 'I don't think you should see Obeese for a while.'

'But why?' asked Irian, confused.

'Because he's filling up your head with these stupid stories about the Legend' his mother replied.

'That's not true' said Irian crossly. 'And even if it were, how would you know about it?'

'Mrs Gartika told me she had heard you talking to him.'

'So, what did she say we said?'

'I don't know and I'm not even interested.'

Irian knew that when his mother was in a foul mood it was better to avoid any kind of discussions that could lead to possible restrictions on his social life like, for instance, going out to see his friends. However, right at that moment, this didn't even occur to him, but what he couldn't understand was how Gartika could possibly know about him speaking to Obeese when she hadn't been there in the tavern. It meant that somebody must have been eavesdropping on their conversation and told Gartika, though that didn't make much sense to Irian either. But Irian felt an even stronger compulsion to dislike the woman.

When they arrived at the Tenth Circle, Irian popped in to see Floria and Nuro. They had just finished their dinner, so Irian joined them for pudding after which they all went to Floria's room. As they entered, they made sure that they left the light off so that Gadious couldn't hear their conversation. The three of them sat cross-legged on the floor leaning against Floria's bed and remained like that without saying a word for the first few minutes. Then, Irian started telling them about his day; his meeting with Smodge, Smodge's house, the call from Smeerius that he had overheard and so on. Everything seemed so much like a dream that Nuro and Floria didn't even dare interrupt him.

'Are you really sure you heard Smeerius speaking to Vrag?' said Nuro after a while. 'Maybe he was talking to somebody else with a similar name.'

'Well, I could have got it wrong, but yes; I'm sure I heard the name Vrag' replied Irian. 'There was something strange about the whole thing.'

'And what about the Water Castle? He described it in exactly the same way as Peena. How can you explain that?' asked Nuro.

Nobody had the answer or even a possible idea for answering this question, which seemed like a huge mathematical problem in front of them. At least when it came to a real mathematical problem, there was always Mr Integger to help them with it. "Mr Integger" thought Irian. "Smodge had mentioned going to the Water Castle with a strange man in a wig."

'I've just thought that the strange man in a wig in Smodge's dream could be Mr Integger' remarked Irian. 'Remember the day we went to Sakarin and you two were laughing because he was in a wig? I know that it could be pure coincidence, but what if the man in the wig was Mr Integger? We know that he's been linked with the Mask Heads.'

'You're right' said Nuro. 'Maybe Smodge wasn't only dreaming. Do you mean that Smeerius belongs to the Mask Heads?

'I don't know. It's the only explanation I can think of' replied Irian. 'On the other hand, if it wasn't just a dream, why would he tell me about it? He wouldn't want to get his father into trouble.'

'Maybe his father had forbidden him to say that he had taken him to the Water Castle, and obliged him to say that it was just a dream in case he mistakenly mentioned it to anybody' thought Nuro aloud.

'Well, why would he take him there in the first place if he didn't want his son to know about it?' chipped in Floria.

'This is all so weird' said Irian. 'And what if the Queen had forced them all to go there?'

'I don't see the point in forcing them. If Smeerius and Mr Integger belong to the Mask Heads, it means that they support Ranna and the Creatures' reasoned Nuro.

'Well, I still can't understand what Smodge was doing there' commented Irian.

Irian was glad that he was on his school holiday because if he had had to go to school, he would never have been able to concentrate on his lessons. In a way, he felt he was doing the most complicated homework he had ever done before in uncovering the secret concerning the Legend. He had always wanted to do it, but at the same time he now felt as if this duty had been imposed on him in a way. Everything seemed like a game of role-play though he wasn't really sure what his own role actually was.

A Meeting with Peena

The following day, while playing in his room, Irian heard a knock on his bedroom-door. When he opened it, Grandfather was standing in front of him.

'Hello, grandpa, I thought you'd forgotten about me' said Irian.

'Oh, how could I ever forget about you' said Grandfather, laughing and showing the dimples in his cheeks in the process. 'You're the biggest Mr Trouble I've ever known.'

'So are you. That's why we're related' joked Irian. 'Is today the day?'

'Well, if you're still interested in coming.'

'Come on, grandpa – you know I've been dreaming about it since you told me about Peena. Of course I'm interested. But, what are we going to say to mum and dad? And grandma? You know what they're like.'

'Your grandma is staying with your Uncle Tattoo and Auntie Ginimma for the day, so she won't know a thing. As for your parents, they'll just think you're spending the day with me.'

'Could Floria and Nuro come too?'

'Look, you're my grandson so I can do this for you, but I can't take the responsibility for somebody else's children. It's not fair.'

'I think you're right. In any case, we should be very careful when lying to mum and dad because mum really is allergic when it comes to the Legend.'

'I wouldn't call this lying because we are spending a day together after all. I reckon it's more appropriate to say we're not telling them quite everything.'

'Yeah, that definitely sounds better' said Irian. 'So, what's the plan?'

'The plan is... Listen, why on earth don't you switch the lights on? How can you see anything in this dark?'

Irian had got so used to being in the dark that he no longer realised that what he was doing was completely abnormal to other people. However, he just couldn't stand being followed by Gadious so he preferred feeling his way around rather than being spied on. Of course, Gadious wasn't always there but he was there enough to bother him. In any case, Irian didn't want to speak to Grandfather about it and particularly not at the moment as he didn't want Grandfather to change his mind and call off their visit to Peena.

'Oh, actually I was resting a bit' lied Irian.

He lit the candle and was delighted not to feel Gadious's presence. It only took a few seconds for him to get ready before they went downstairs to say goodbye to Irian's mother who was busy with her new sculpture. The instant they were outside, Irian felt as if he had crossed the most difficult border and was now geared up for the adventure. First of all they went to get the Old Lady, Grandfather's hot air balloon.

'What do you think? Doesn't she look better this way?' asked Grandfather pointing to the balloon. 'I thought she would look even lovelier with her gondola painted yellow.'

'Oh, yeah, it's a definite improvement' replied Irian, giggling slightly.

'You know, I've had this balloon for thirty years, so I just thought I might as well give her a new look. Now she's all nice and ready for a flight.'

Irian couldn't help but laugh when hearing Grandfather talk about his balloon as if it really was a human being. He wouldn't even allow anybody to wear shoes inside it; you had to put a bag over them in order not to make the inside dirty.

'Have you got your helmet on? Ok, off we go' said Grandfather.

Once the Old Lady was aloft, Irian could feel the air getting colder, but it didn't bother him. He was so elated that he had difficulty keeping still during their flight. In his head, he didn't even want to contemplate the fact that Peena might not be there to answer all his questions.

They were flying towards the west and every so often Grandfather would take his binoculars out and look for Peena's house. The further they went, the fewer houses they could see or else they were scattered very sparsely as if hiding from each other. Irian wondered how anybody could possibly live in such a remote place, away from other people. He couldn't bear staying alone too long, as he needed to be surrounded by company. He hated solitude and would do anything to avoid it. It was also perhaps because he liked talking which, of course, he couldn't do if he was by himself. Irian's father used to say that if Irian had been locked up in a room with another person for a whole lifetime, he still wouldn't have finished everything that he had to say.

They had been flying for quite a while when Grandfather recognised the house.

'We've found it' he shouted, excitedly. 'Look, it's just there on the right!'

It wasn't difficult for Irian to see the house, as it was the only one to be seen among all the colourful fields. As soon as he put his foot on the ground, Irian suddenly felt a great commotion inside his head. For the first time he felt the sudden grip of fear and started to ask himself: "And what if Peena isn't there anymore?" Though, after all, he thought it wasn't right to think like that as it was hardly encouraging to embark on a new adventure with such negative thoughts.

When Grandfather had tied down the balloon, they started to make their way towards Peena's house. The house was in an appalling state and Irian found it difficult to believe that anybody could call it home. It was really a hovel situated in the middle of nowhere and Irian was overwhelmed with anger thinking that people could have made Peena live in such dismal conditions only on account of her unusual experience. The entrance door was so worn away that you could probably open it simply by pushing it with your finger. There were lots of holes in it, which Irian tried to peep through, but Grandfather stopped him.

'Were you sleeping on your ears when your parents were

teaching you politeness?' asked Grandfather teasingly.

Irian admitted to himself that he was being silly, but he was so impatient that he had difficulty mastering his behaviour. He gave Grandfather an apologising look and then knocked on the door. This done, Irian became so attentive to the slightest rustle that the idea even struck him that he must have looked like Ogi on the alert. Sometimes Ogi would become stiff all of a sudden listening to something that Irian couldn't hear, and this always made him laugh. He would then prick his ears up to hear better without moving any other part of his body. But no matter how hard Irian tried to hear anything, there was no answer. After a while, he knocked louder, but yet again nobody replied so all their hopes began to crumble away.

'I guess we've arrived too late' sighed Grandfather wistfully.

Irian was so disappointed that he just couldn't say anything. It seemed to him as if his world had sunk so deep that he thought nobody would ever be able to lift it up to the surface again. He was also suddenly enveloped in a gloomy spiritual blanket because he thought it had been unfair to abandon Peena and let her pass away like that. So they stayed in front of Peena's house for some time, and then as they had nobody to look for anymore, they started walking back towards the Old Lady.

However, on the way Irian heard a peculiar noise behind him. He turned around and saw a stick poking through the window, which somebody was banging against the wall.

'Look, grandpa, it's Peena! She's there!' exclaimed Irian already running back towards the house. His whole body began to tingle with excitement from head to toe.

Irian and Grandfather both heaved a sigh of relief. Not long afterwards, they saw her head out of the window.

'Who is it?' asked Peena.

Grandfather explained to her who they were, and she threw them the key to go in.

'I knew you would come back' admitted Peena to Grandfather once they got to her bedroom.

'I'm bringing you my grandson too. His name is Irian.'

Irian went to stroke Peena on her cheek and he felt so sorry for her that he brushed away two or three tears that were lingering in his eyes.

'How are you, Peena?' asked Grandfather.

'Well, I think my life is slowly extinguishing. I'm very tired. I reckon I'm not going to be breathing this air for much longer' she replied. 'There is a woman who comes in to take care of me, so she run errands for me, cooks, cleans... and she's my only visitor. I don't even know who she is; she just started coming like that many years ago.'

Grandfather knew very well about the woman because it was he who had sent her to take care of Peena, but he didn't want to mention that.

'You'll meet her later on. She's just gone out to buy some food' continued Peena. 'By the way, is the boy with you the little grandson who had just been born when you came to visit me the first time?'

'Yes, you're right' answered Grandfather. 'You've got an elephant's memory!'

'How old are you my boy?' she asked gently.

'I'm ten. I've heard your story about the Water Castle. I want to see it too' Irian could no longer hide his curiosity.

'The Water Castle' repeated Peena, laughing faintly. 'That day changed my whole life and got me into this horrible situation. But somehow, I don't regret it. It was so extraordinary!'

'Why do you think nobody believed you when you told them about it?' asked Irian.

'Because people are scared of anything that is out of the ordinary. They prefer to hide behind lies rather than face the truth. I don't blame them – it's not easy to believe in miracles' replied Peena and then continued. 'You know, the good thing about the truth is that it's very slow in comparison with lies, which are instant, but the truth always arrives at the right door. However, when it does arrive, you thank it for being slow because its effects are far more powerful than if it had been there right from the beginning of the problem. So, if you trust in your patience and allow nobody to influence your innocence, your honesty will pay off sooner or later.'

'I want to find the Water Castle and make them feel ashamed' said Irian, firmly.

'If you make somebody feel ashamed, you heap a great deal of guilt onto them. You don't want anybody to feel guilty, do you? Guilt is a terrible feeling. I prefer you to reason with them by finding the Water Castle because that will make them think properly about the whole situation. Only a clear mind can take in clear ideas.'

'How can I see the Water Castle?'

'What day is it today?

'It is the fourth day of the First Quarter week' replied Irian.

'Is it?' she commented. 'You'll have to hurry up then.'

'Hurry where?' asked Irian.

'The Water Castle is going to show up soon' replied Peena.

'But how can I find it?' asked Irian.

'Help me get off the bed, please' she asked Irian.

Irian did as she asked, so he took her arm and let himself be led by Peena. There was a chest of drawers next to the bedroom door and she opened the bottom drawer. In it, there was quite a large box. Peena took it out and then asked him to take her back to her bed.

'Take this box' she said to Irian.

'What is it?' he asked.

'You'll need it if you want to see the Water Castle.'

Irian couldn't understand what she meant.

'There is a divining rod inside and all you have to do is follow it. It reacts to underground waters in such a way that it starts moving sidewards when it senses them. This will tell you which direction you need to take. I don't know exactly the place where the Castle appears, but it must be somewhere near the village called Uklet. You need to go to the forest, which lies just behind the village. The Castle will appear on the first day of the Full Moon. Bear in mind that you should never ever look into the Creatures or the Queen's eyes if you do somehow get to see them. Look at your feet or put dark glasses on but they should never see your eyes if you don't want them to hurt you' she took a little pause before continuing. 'You must know that if they regain their powers and come back, they'll try to get their revenge by hurting everybody in the town of Destin.'

'How can anybody possibly stop them? They are so powerful!' asked Irian.

'Not as powerful as you think. But, if somebody doesn't stop them, they'll grow so strong that nobody will ever be able to oppose them.'

'What do I have to do?' asked Irian.

'Well, there is a plan of the Castle in the box that I've given you. You must know it by heart before going there. You'll need to find the library and find out as much as you can about their intentions. It is the only way to learn how to destroy them. And for goodness sake, be quick because you only have an hour.'

'But how can I avoid the Creatures and the Queen?'

'When the lake appears in front of you, you have to jump into it before two hands appear out of it and start constructing the Castle. That way, you'll avoid the guard, and be inside the Castle as it is constructed around you.'

Peena now had to rest as she really was in bad health, and couldn't speak for very long. Irian decided to open the box and see what was inside. There was a divining rod and a plan as she had said. Irian took out the divining rod and was now trying to move it.'

'How did you get this?' he asked, once Peena was able to take up the conversation again.

'That's a secret' she said and her mouth curved into an enigmatic smile. 'Anyway, you don't need to know that right now. I'll tell you about it another time' she said, licking her parched lips.

Irian had so many questions, but as she wasn't feeling well he had to let her rest and be patient. During her catnap, Irian took the opportunity to have a better look at her. Her face was so lined that it was difficult to find a smooth area of her skin at all and her lips looked practically non-existent; they were so thin and pale. She was a petite woman though she had a remarkable inner force, which Irian could feel just by holding her hand for despite her blindness and loneliness, she had never given up. It seemed as if her spirit was only hidden in that weak body which wasn't appropriate for it at all.

'Why do you want to find the Creatures when everybody else is afraid of them?' her voice surprised him because he thought she was asleep.

'I don't know. There's something inside me pushing me to do it. It's a kind of inner voice that won't leave me alone unless I obey it. '

'That's interesting' she replied. 'I wonder...'

Irian couldn't understand why she had stopped mid sentence. At one point, he even had a feeling that she had looked at him.

'No, it can't be' she said in disbelief.

'What do you mean?' asked Irian.

'Only a descendant of the couple who had saved the town from the Creatures the first time will really be able to save the town. So, you may be that descendant.'

Irian was dumbfounded.

'You see' she continued, 'if you really are their descendant, the Creatures won't be able to hurt you. They have no power over people whose destiny they couldn't decide on.'

'Yes, but the Creatures disappeared from our town a long time ago, which means that they have no power over Destiners anymore.'

'Ah yes they do because their ancestors were in the Creatures' hands, so they are too. You need to find out more about your ancestors.'

'How? They lived ages ago. '

'When you get into the Castle library, look for this information. Remember, only a descendant of the couple who saved the town from the Creatures will be able to destroy the Creatures and nobody else! '

If somebody had somehow been able to enter Irian's head at that moment; he would have seen his thoughts running up and down in all kind of directions and banging into each other like dodgem cars. The fact that he could actually be a descendant of the couple who saved the town had never ever occurred to him.

However, he did think of one thing that could be an indication.

'You know, Peena' said Irian 'I don't know if what I'm going to tell you is significant, but I once had this really odd dream. I dreamt that I found a book with a description of everybody's destiny in it apart from my own. I wonder if that could mean anything.'

'Dreams are messengers of our subconscious, don't forget that! And our subconscious is a mixture of everything we don't know about ourselves and that we ought to learn. So, when we don't understand something, our inner self sends us hints through our dreams, which can sometimes be explicit, but sometimes not. It's like a game of associations – and I think your clue was clear enough for you to understand.'

Irian was just about to tell her about Gadious, when they heard the door opening downstairs.

'That's Feenie' said Peena. 'She's back from shopping.'

A few minutes later, they heard her coming up the stairs to Peena's bedroom.

'You didn't tell me you were going to have visitors today' said Feenie when she entered the room and saw Irian and Grandfather.

'Believe me, I was just as surprised as you are' replied Peena.

'I'll go and get us a cup of bazaga' said Feenie.

Bazaga was a kind of a socializing drink made of different flower petals and people could only drink it in company. There was a special ritual about serving and drinking it. Bazaga was served in a pot with a tube extending from both sides and further split into two or more other tubes. There were pots for even a hundred people if necessary and this is because it was important to serve everybody at the same time. The brew was so strong that it was served in thimble-size cups. Once served, everybody had to drink it at the same time, holding hands.

'I haven't had bazaga for ages' said Peena. 'I even thought I would never have the chance of tasting it again.'

'My father used to make bazaga' said Grandfather. 'He even allowed me to help. I remember it as clearly as if it was yesterday...'

'Is true it contains a magic ingredient?' asked Feenie.

'I asked him that once, but he refused to answer' replied Grandfather.

Bazaga was indeed a mysterious drink because not all of its ingredients were known. Destiners said there was a magical flower in it that grew at the top of the red Oochka Mountain that could be seen from anywhere and all around. It grew at the top of the Oochka Mountain because it was said that that's where the perfect climate was. However, it wasn't easy to get to as it was situated in the North of the county right next to the Poisonous Flower Field. This particular flower's petals, apparently, had a certain influence on behaviour. If the story was to be believed, the flower had been conceived by the Good Mood Creature because the Queen was often crotchety and would punish the Creatures for the slightest mistake. The Good Mood Creature came up with the idea of creating a beverage that would improve Queen Ranna's behaviour and relax the others who were often understandably jittery. Therefore, it was believed that it put a certain dose of good mood into this flower, mixed with the other petals to obtain better taste. As a socializing drink, it stimulated a good ambience among those who partook of it.

'Actually, when I was in the Water Castle, there were a lot of pots for bazaga' said Peena.

'That doesn't surprise me. I guess it's not easy to cope with the Queen since she lost her power over the Destiners' said Grandfather and everybody chuckled.

It was getting late, so Irian and Grandfather had to leave for Destin. Just before leaving, Grandfather gave a small present to Peena. It was a talkastick.

'I thought you might need this' he said.

'Thank you so much and thank you for your visit. I'll be so happy to be able to communicate with you even through this little gadget' said Peena. 'But don't forget to come and visit me sometime too.'

Irian was so disappointed that they had to leave, but happy to know he could now speak to her whenever he wanted thanks to their talkasticks.

Back in Destin, Grandmother still wasn't at home so both Irian and Grandfather breathed a sigh of relief, her absence saving them from getting into trouble.

'Grandpa' said Irian 'will you help me find the Water Castle?

'You are a demanding little rascal, aren't you? If your parents and grandma get to know about this, they'll cut me off from the family.'

'Well, if we plan it well, they'll simply never know about it' said Irian.

'Go back home now and let me think it over. I'll come and see you when I come up with an idea.'

'Oh, thank you grandpa. I knew you wouldn't let me down!' exclaimed Irian.

'I only said I was going to give it a thought' he said, shaking his head in exasperation.

Mrs Erra Bigone's Book

When Irian arrived home, on the front door he found a message written by his mother to say she was just next-door at the neighbour's house.

Their neighbour was a delightful little woman, Mrs Erra Bigone who was in her fifties and had occasionally looked after Irian when he was little. Everybody in Destin knew Mrs Bigone because of her job. She was an archaeologist and many years ago had found out some very important historical facts in relation to the Legend. She had clarified the mystery about the master of the Creatures, Arameen, who exercised his power through the Queen. However, the Local Council and the present mayor hadn't wanted to make this official not wanting to accept the Legend as fact, so as not to frighten the people. Mrs Bigone hadn't been put off by this attitude and had continued her research. She was quite secretive, so it was difficult to say exactly what she was working on, but she was undeniably interested in the Creatures' writing. When she had been very little, she had found a book containing unusual writing and ever since she believed that the book had belonged to the Creatures. This was why she had devoted her career to finding out more about them and above all, the Creatures' writing because she believed it could explain many things about the Sudba Creatures and the Queen. Because of this, Irian and Mrs Bigone got on very well together, though she mainly kept her work private and rarely shared her discoveries with other people. It was partly because of the Local Council's response to her discovery regarding Arameen that she had decided to work on her own account. Most of her time was spent at home or in her garden and every time Irian came to visit her, she would be leafing through her Creatures' book and she never allowed anybody to touch it. Irian could only look at it if Mrs Bigone was holding it.

Her house looked very much like a library. There were books everywhere; they were even to be found in the kitchen cupboard. Her sofa was an enormous book and every day, she would turn a leaf of her book-sofa, so that whoever was sitting on it could read while she was out of the room.

That evening when Irian came to pay her a visit, his mum and Mrs Bigone were sitting on that very sofa talking.

'Irian, would you like to come to my book launch tomorrow afternoon?' said Mrs Bigone.

'Book launch?' repeated Irian, confused.

'Yes, my book is coming out tomorrow' replied Mrs Bigone.

'Really?' exclaimed Irian, grinning with delight. 'That's wonderful news! Congratulations!'

'Thank you. You know, I've been working on it for more than forty years.'

'So, we're finally going to learn what the book is about' said Irian.

'Exactly!'

Irian wanted so much to tell her about his trip to see Peena, but he wasn't really sure whether it was a good idea. At the same time he thought it would be good to speak to her about it as she could give him some useful advice. He was sure that Mrs Bigone knew much more about the Creatures than anybody else, but she would never go into the subject very deeply.

'What have you got in that box?' asked Irian's mother.

Irian had forgotten he was holding the box that Peena had given to him, which he now considered as the most precious object he possessed. However, it had to be kept secret, so he was embarrassed when his mother asked him about it.

'Oh, nothing really. Nuro left it at grandpa's so I have to give it back to him' lied Irian.

Irian had the impression that his mother had asked the question, but wasn't really listening to the answer. At the same time, it seemed to him that Mrs Bigone looked at him suspiciously. It even made him suspect that she knew exactly what was inside it.

Sometimes when talking or listening to people, Mrs Bigone seemed glued to her listener by her gaze, her irises magnetised to those of the other person. Irian felt embarrassed but tried to hide this uncomfortable feeling.

'We'd better go home' said Irian's mother. 'Your dad should be back any minute now.'

This decision definitely suited Irian, as it distracted Mrs Bigone from looking at him.

'Don't forget to come to my book launch tomorrow!' she said as he and his mother were on the point of leaving.

'Forget?' exclaimed Irian. 'I'll probably arrive there before you do!'

The moment they set foot in their garden, Irian could hear Ogi barking from inside.

'He's been barking all day today' said Irian's mother. 'I don't know what's got into him.'

Irian suddenly thought about Gadious Cheater and wondered if Ogi was behaving like that owing to Gadious.

'Your dad must be home' just as she said that, Irian's father opened the door.

'Hey, I was wondering where you two were' said Irian's father. 'What do you think about having dinner out? We haven't done that for quite a while, have we?'

'I certainly don't mind. I'm feeling peckish' replied Irian's mother. 'What do you think, Irian?'

'It sounds like a brilliant idea to me' he answered.

The three of them thought of the same place – *The Porta Aurea*. *The Porta Aurea* was the most well liked restaurant in town, situated in the Seventh Circle. The special attraction of this restaurant was that you didn't have to pay for your meal, but in return you had to do something for the town of Destin. You could order whatever meal your heart or rather stomach desired and have it on the house. The restaurant had been set up under the auspices of a Local Council's initiative with the aim of making Destiners contribute to organising their town. Some people had therefore planted new flowers or watered already existing ones; others came with a particular project and then chose to carry it out with the help of a few more dinners. There were always long queues to enter but people somehow didn't mind that and would use this time to talk to each other while uncomplainingly waiting to get in. They would sing or tell jokes in the queue. In a way going to *The Porta Aurea* was more about socialising than eating. The place was unadorned and could accept around twenty-five people who would sit around the large round table. Going to *The Porta Aurea* seemed much more like eating at friend's place than at a restaurant and it was open to the world and his wife. The moment you stepped in people would immediately start up a conversation as if you were their long-lost friend. Some people came alone, others arrived with friends or family – it was a place where your age and social class disappeared along with your hunger.

When Irian and his parents entered, the place was so steamy and dimly lit that he could only see the contours of the faces through the steam of their meals. He was searching for familiar faces, but there were only voices finding their way out through the steam in assorted odours, keeping the faces anonymous.

'I don't think he told her what happened' said one voice, obviously in the middle of describing something.

'I'm sure she knows' said another voice, blowing off a swirl of steam to reveal a well-rounded male face.

'You know what women are like' chipped in the third voice. 'If you don't tell them something, they'll read it on your forehead.'

'And she isn't just any old woman' commented the first voice. 'She knows your thoughts before they even have time to hit your own mind.'

Suddenly, there was a pause where everybody visibly reflected upon what had just been said. However, a man trying to get at the last bit of food by scraping his fork over his plate interrupted the silence. Irian waited for his parents to advance towards the table, but they seemed to be waiting for the appropriate moment to say hello.

His father was just about to tell him something, when Irian felt somebody push him aside as he was standing close to the entrance. He couldn't see the person's face properly as the man went directly to join the crowd gathered around the table. The man didn't seem to mind the steam, nor the people staring at him – he swaggered into the room, made himself comfortable and then at last said hello to the others. Irian's father used this opportunity to move on to the table while Irian and his mother followed him. A couple had just left, so Irian and his mother took their places while Irian's father went to sit on the opposite side of the table. Irian could now see the faces better, but still didn't recognise any of them. He was hunting for the face of the man who had pushed him to enter, sitting a few places further away on the left. However, there was a burly man separating them, so he just couldn't catch sight of him. For some reason he felt that the atmosphere in *The Porta Aurea* was rather tense that evening. Some people were talking but the noise level was low. Everybody appeared quiet and concentrated on their meal and they would occasionally and very timidly exchange glances with each other. Irian didn't feel terribly hungry, so he just ordered a pudding.

He was so immersed in his thoughts that he didn't even realise that the burly man next to him had left. He turned round to see whether anybody was coming to sit next to him when he finally glimpsed the man who had pushed him. At first, he couldn't put a name to the face but he eventually remembered seeing him in *The Old Times*. It was Vrag, the man Nuro was telling him about and who had spoken to Smeerius on the talkastick. Irian quickly looked at him and then even faster changed the direction of his gaze, but he could now feel Vrag staring at him. He couldn't understand why, as he didn't know the man, and Irian thought he didn't look any different than usual to be getting such attention. If his parents hadn't been there, he would simply have stood up and left, but given that he wasn't by himself, he couldn't. He didn't know how to sit or where to look and he felt uneasy. His parents were both busy talking to other people, so he pretended to be enthralled in their conversation. Despite his efforts, Vrag just wouldn't stop gawping at him.

To his relief, a group of musicians entered and everybody started dancing. People jumped up onto the table and some of them even danced on the counter. Irian went to dance with his parents and when he turned round to check what Vrag was doing, he noticed that he had left. He found it all very bewildering, but as he loved dancing, he tried not to think about it and became absorbed in the chirpy rhythm that was filling the restaurant. It looked as if the previously unpleasant atmosphere had been dispersed by the sound of music and had cheered everybody up.

* * *

The following day Irian tried hard to keep busy, impatient to go to Mrs Bigone's book launch. He went as far as to tidy up his room – something he would normally never do, but as none of his friends came round to play, he had to occupy himself somehow. At first, he couldn't be bothered, but then slowly began to enjoy it. He realised that he hadn't changed anything in his room for quite a while, and he decided to move his furniture around. He moved his bed and put it where his desk had been and placed his desk next to the window. He also replaced a few dog-eared posters on the wall with brand new ones and hung different curtains up. He filled up ten big rubbish bags and when he had done with his spring-cleaning, the room had a totally different image. He was quite pleased with its new look and he also realised that it was time to go.

The event was to take place in the Town Library, situated in the Second Circle. It was a round building located on a hill, with letter-shaped windows. The first row of letter-windows spelled out **THE TOWN LIBRARY** whereas on the top one could read **WELCOME**. The door resembled a book cover in front of which a sliding bookmarker-rug with the alphabet on led into the entrance. You just had to step on the rug, which would then transport you to the library reception. Irian found that very amusing and would sometimes re-enter several times just to be transported on the sliding rug. Inside, the books were arranged in circles, so there was an A circle, a B circle and so on, and in the middle of each circle was a machine in the shape of a hand that would take your book and then pass it over to the reception.

There was hardly anybody when Irian, Nuro, Floria, Armianda and Mr Tappin arrived. Mrs Bigone was sitting at one of the tables and was writing something down. For the first time Irian saw her hair free from her usual bun, and was surprised to see how long it was; almost touching the floor. The windows reflected the bright afternoon sunlight and she was caged up in the shadow of the letter-window B.

'Hello Mrs Bigone' said Irian. 'How do you feel?'

'To tell the truth, I wouldn't mind feeling this way every day. I've always wished I could publish this book, so I'm somewhat confused between reality and my imagination. It is hard to believe that I'm not just daydreaming' Mrs Bigone replied.

'If you want, I can pinch you to prove you that you're in the real world' joked Irian. 'I think I'm probably not going to get to sleep tonight until I finish reading it.'

'Knowing you, that wouldn't astonish me at all' she said, smiling.

Not long afterwards, the library became jam-packed with people and Irian couldn't work out when they had all came in. In the end, the place was so full that some people had to remain outside. When everybody eventually settled down, Mr Gotz Kelza, the director of the library stepped up.

'Ladies and gentlemen, I would like to thank you for being with us tonight to learn more about the book we have all been so eagerly awaiting. I consider that it is one of the most important books that Destin has ever known, which can help us gain more knowledge into our enigmatic history. I have known my dear friend Erra for more than forty years and I'm proud to say that I was with her the day she found the book I'm now presenting. I remember us both looking astounded at it, wondering what the peculiar writing was all about. I must admit I didn't imagine in my wildest dreams that we would ever learn its content. However, thanks to Erra and her tremendous will to decipher the mysterious writing, we have all gathered here today to celebrate this effort and thank her...'

Mr Kelza didn't even finish his sentence before people were already up on their feet, deafeningly applauding Mrs Bigone.

They didn't mind their hands getting sore with clapping; some people even stood on their chairs to see her better. Mrs Erra Bigone was so touched that she shed a few tears.

'And thank her for doing it' Mr Kelza continued. 'Ladies and gentlemen, Mrs Erra Bigone.'

The audience was now applauding and at the same time shouting 'Erra, Erra,' so that she had to ask them for quiet.

'My dear friends' Mrs Bigone said. 'It is with great emotion that I am here today to share this unique moment with you. This morning, as I was getting ready to come here to present my book, I was thinking a lot about the moment I found it. I knew I would discover how to decipher it and present it to others i.e. to you. The book has an almost dreamlike quality to me and even though it wasn't easy to work on it I was never ever tempted to abandon it. And I realised that in life there are three things: reality and dreams, which are separated by a gap called courage. Once you have signed your mental contract with courage, your life will be in perfect harmony. However, this book isn't only important to me – it shows that Ranna and the Sudba Creatures really existed and that their story is not only a legend, as some people would have us believe.'

There was a slight commotion in the hall as she pronounced these words. The audience became even more attentive to what she was going to say.

'The book is actually the Jealousy Creature's diary. It is very interesting because it tells us about the Sudba Creatures' life and furthermore it shows that they didn't have such an exciting existence as we may imagine. Well, I suggest I read a short paragraph from it, which I find particularly worthy of note. It says:

"I didn't sleep very well again last night. I wish there were some kind of button to switch off my thoughts, which don't allow me to sleep much. Well, the reason why I couldn't sleep is because I got really annoyed during the destiny decision meeting. Guess which number I pulled out? I pulled out number ten out of a hundred, yes; you've got it – number ten. So I had to participate in a meeting

knowing that the baby is hardly going to be jealous at all!!! It's not fair! And that stupid Confidence Creature got seventy. I don't like confident people because they have no respect for me. I can't stand that – they just don't understand that jealousy is important; I make people advance and progress in their lives. If I didn't exist, they would feel indifferent towards everything. I can spot a jealous person straight away – he or she won't let other people get in his or her way. But you see, when I try to give advice, they laugh at me. They make a fool out of me and let me be eaten away inside. What I hate most is that they always win and consider me as ridiculous. I'll make them pay and suffer one day just as much as I do.

One other thing happened. When it was time for pudding, the Greedy Creature, who was sitting next to me, received a considerably larger piece of cake than I did and I'm sure they did it on purpose. So, when it turned its back to the Love Creature, I spilt drink over its cake in order to get even. I felt much better after that, though not for long as they brought it another piece. When I saw that, I just stood up and left because the injustice was too much for me to bear. So, in the end, I didn't even finish my cake but went straight to bed. My evening was spoilt again while they continued enjoying themselves as if nothing had happened.

Nothing ever changes because the other Creatures don't want to learn their lesson and instead they blame everything on me."

While Mrs Bigone was reading the extract from the book, a petite woman standing in the middle of the audience, kept on jumping up in order to see her better. After the reading, the woman managed to elbow her way to the first row and hug Mrs Bigone.

'She's nuts!' said Irian to his friends and they all chuckled.

As he said that, he looked sideways turning towards his friends and he spotted Gartika in the corner, right next to the entrance door, though she didn't see him. She was on her own and Irian recognised that cynical look which was so typical of her. However, as he didn't want her to notice him, he quickly turned his head. He was keen to avoid any possible contact with that woman knowing how nosey and mean she was.

'Hey, the Ugliness Creature is here!' this is how Irian and his friends dubbed Gartika. 'Watch what you're saying! She's got big ears.'

'That woman really gets on my nerves ' said Armianda. 'The other day, I was in the shop with Mrs Verlic and we were talking about this and that. I didn't even realise she was there too. But later on she called my parents and repeated everything I had said.'

'I know, she did the same thing with me' said Irian. 'It's obviously her speciality. The thing is, I didn't notice her either.'

Irian suddenly remembered the scene in *The Old Times* and recalled the words that Obeese had spoken. He started wondering whether Gartika had heard the contents of their conversation. Thinking about this, he spontaneously turned his head back to see what she was doing, but she wasn't there anymore. He looked in all directions, but she was nowhere to be seen. He felt relieved not to have her there because he always had the impression that she was spying on him. He also thought about Obeese and the reason why he hadn't turned up at the book launch. Irian wanted to speak to him again, but their meetings had been very rare and brief.

'Irian, let's go and get the book' said Nuro.

'You know that the Local Council has banned it in the bookshops' announced Armianda.

'No' replied Irian in disbelief. 'You must be joking. But why?'

'Because they say there is no proof to what she's written and that she could have put anything in' answered Armianda.

'They really are stubborn. Who told you that anyway?' asked Irian.

'My dad interviewed her this morning, so he's filled me in on some of her answers.'

'So how did Mrs Bigone react to their decision?' asked Floria.

'She said that you can avoid the truth, but the truth will

refuse to avoid you. I don't think she minds so much.'

'She's right' added Irian. 'They can stop it from coming out in the bookshops, but whoever wants to read it will find a way of getting hold of it. I really don't understand their attitude. Are they trying to act like the Creatures and impose what to do on us? I can't stand that!'

Once the book presentation was over, Irian went back home with Mrs Bigone. He had never seen her in such a blissful state before and was pleased for her. She didn't speak much and Irian didn't want to disturb her thoughts, which she was probably sorting out and putting into her "memory drawer". He could feel that she was projecting the book presentation in her head over and over again and caught her smiling almost every time he looked at her. He kept on glancing at the book, which she had given him as a present, though she had asked him not to read the message she had written for him straight away. It was beyond him why she didn't want him to read it, but he humoured her.

Night fell as they were walking back home. It was somewhat cloudy, but Irian could see the moon growing to its full form. He knew that the Water Castle was going to show up very soon.

Later on, snuggled down comfortably under his duvet, he opened Mrs Bigone's book to read her dedication. She had the most beautiful handwriting, which looked more like little drawings than letters. Irian had closed and opened the book several times before looking into it, as he didn't know what to expect or think of this mysterious gesture that Mrs Bigone had reserved for him. "Why didn't she want me to read it in front of her?", he thought to himself. After flicking through it for a while, he finally went to read the first page. He found the following:

"Dear Irian,

In life, there are many CANS and CANNOTS. CAN can become CANNOT as CANNOT can become CAN. There are also two big spiritual enemies called impatience and fear. Impatience doesn't allow our thoughts to develop properly while fear squeezes the thoughts into a cramped space. Waiting is a long process, but your thoughts need time

to mature in order to become good thoughts. It is like fruit, if you pick it too early it won't taste good. Time is best for measuring the quality of any given situation. And never look at others, but allow your own intuition to tell you what is the best for you.
With lots of love,
Erra Bigone."

The message was written by hand on the left side of the book while on the right there was written:

"To my little neighbour, Irian Horvats."

Irian was completely overwhelmed by the honour of being the only person to whom Mrs Bigone had dedicated a book. He rubbed his eyes in astonishment at the idea that his name really was printed there as he considered that there were many people who were much more important than himself. He lay on the bed, his arms and legs splayed out, placing the book over his head. He needed to reflect upon everything that had happened that day, though dreams quickly overcame him. They took him to the murky world of the Creatures, a world that was becoming more and more familiar to him.

The Water Castle

As Irian constantly lived in the world of his imagination, he would often tell lies, not because he was a liar, but because his imagination was so developed that he needed to use it somehow. He thought an event wouldn't be interesting if he didn't add an extra detail to it. However, owing to the fact that he had needed to use more serious lies lately, he was starting to have a guilty conscious about it. By no means did he want to abuse his parent's confidence, yet he really needed to accomplish certain tasks, which were literally impossible without telling lies. He truly wanted to talk to his mother about the Creatures' hidden powers as well as about Peena, but as she was utterly allergic to the Legend there was no way of bringing up the subject in her presence. And now, he had to dish up another lie in order to visit the Water Castle that was due to show up that night. He didn't know exactly what to say since he would have to leave quite late that night.

He came up with the idea of saying he was going to a social club with Grandfather. There were two social clubs in the town where people could come and play all sorts of games. Grandfather was a regular member and Irian would sometimes go along with him. He liked going there, as he was usually their youngest member, which would always put him in the limelight.

All day long, Irian could feel a sort of knot in his stomach, which sent away his appetite and made him all squirmy.

'Are you ok, Irian?' asked his mother at one point. 'You don't seem well today.'

'Oh, no, I'm, I'm absolutely fine' mumbled Irian.

'We're invited to Uncle Tattoo's exhibition tonight but first, we'll have dinner all together at their place' she said. 'Isn't that wonderful?'

The exhibition had completely slipped his mind, and this clash in the timetable had now caused an additional problem. He absolutely had to find the Water Castle, as he couldn't wait another twenty years to do it. On the other hand, his parents knew very well how much he loved Uncle Tattoo, which meant that his excuse had to be a really good one. At this point he became even more restless wondering what he was going to do.

Grandfather came round in the afternoon and while his mother went to get drinks, Irian quickly whispered in Grandfather's ear the problem about the exhibition. But Grandfather only winked at him and replied softly "don't worry, I'll deal with that". Irian didn't have time to ask anything about his plan as his mother came back with drinks.

'So, where exactly is the show?' asked Irian's mother.

'One of my friends is organising it at his house' replied Grandfather. 'I've seen it once. It's absolutely amazing!'

'And what kind of show is it?' she continued.

'There's a man who can walk on walls and on ceilings' Grandfather answered.

'Really? I didn't have a clue such things existed in Destin' she commented. 'I'd like to see it myself.'

'Yes, but there are no more tickets for tonight's performance; I didn't know you'd be interested too, so I only got tickets for Irian and me.'

Irian felt himself invaded by a fit of nervous giggles; like when you're being tickled and you laugh, though the feeling is actually more painful than funny. He knew that if anything went wrong that evening, his parents would lose all trust in him and Grandfather would be in complete disgrace.

Sometime later, Grandmother arrived too, and they left after a short while for the exhibition. Irian couldn't pluck up the courage to go and say goodbye to them, so he pretended to be speaking on his talkastick, and only shouted goodbye from his room. When he heard the door shut, he discretely peeped through the curtains to make sure they had all gone. After that, he went downstairs to see Grandfather, who was sitting on the sofa reading something.

'When are we leaving?' asked Irian.

'In a minute. Listen, we have to take Ogi with us' he said.

'Oh, no, he'll spoil everything' said Irian, disappointed.

'Don't worry, he'll be all right' said Grandfather, stroking Ogi under his ears. 'Animals can feel when something is important.'

'Perhaps, but not my dog ' replied Irian.

'Hey, it's not fair of you to treat Ogi like that. He's your dog and you should be protecting him, young man. How would you feel if Ogi could speak and said the same thing about you? You would be offended, wouldn't you?'

Irian didn't want to offend his puppy, but he was so anxious about the whole thing and above all, he didn't want anybody or anything to spoil this adventure and make his plans go awry. As he looked at Ogi, the little puppy came to him and started licking his fingers.

'You have to be a good dog if you want to come with me tonight' said Irian.

He then went to get the box that Peena had given to him and checked once more that everything was inside. He had been studying the plan of the Water Castle with Floria and Nuro who had been helping him to remember everything. "I wish they could come with us", he thought to himself.

'Shall we make a move?' asked Grandfather. 'We need to find the village and that will take some time.'

'All right. Off we go' replied Irian.

It was already dark when they left the house. The Full Moon was hiding behind the clouds like a scared child searching for security behind its mother's skirt. It was one of those nights that awakens fear in you. Irian could feel the summer breeze playing against his clothes and cooling his body temperature that was so high with all the excitement.

'How are we going to find the Uklet village in dark?' asked Irian once they were in the balloon.

'I've visited it already several times to practise finding it easily' Grandfather replied. 'It's not very far. We're not looking for the Uklet village. The Water Castle actually appears in the Wild Flower Forest, which is beside the Uklet village.'

'The Wild Flower Forest?' repeated Irian. 'You mean the forest with the carnivorous flowers?'

'Yes' replied Grandfather grimly.

'But we're going to get eaten up!' said Irian in terror.

'Well, I've brought us a special cream that should put them off. Apparently, they can't stand the smell of vinegar.'

'Neither can I!'

'Well, you'll just have to grin and bear it because it is the only way to protect ourselves.'

'Oh, no! I can't believe I'm going to the Wild Flower Forest!'

'Don't be so negative! Peena didn't get eaten up and don't forget she was blind and all by herself in the forest without any cream on.'

'Yeah, I feel much better now!' replied Irian, sarcastically.

'Listen to me! You mustn't let fear get the better of you otherwise we'll get nowhere. Just concentrate on what we have to do.'

Once they were up in the air, Irian was amazed at what appeared to be Grandfather's talent of seeing in the dark. It seemed to him as if they were flying through some empty black hole. The village lights that they were flying above appeared as tiny sparkles twinkling in the distance. Every so often, the moon would come out and illuminate the abyss below.

'We're almost there' said Grandfather.

'Is that the Wild Flower Forest?' asked Irian pointing to the illuminated patch of earth as the moon had just come out.

'Yes, it is' replied Grandfather. 'We'll have to start putting the cream on. Have a look in my bag. Rub it everywhere on your skin and in your hair, too.'

'In my hair?'

'Yes, they mustn't smell our flesh at all.'

'And what about Ogi?'

'He'll be all right. When you've finished, pass it over here.'

Irian didn't dare think too deeply but did exactly as Grandfather instructed. Ogi was the only one in a good mood and couldn't wait to land probably because he had no idea about the place they were going to visit. Irian put on several layers of cream all over his body and was actually surprised that it didn't smell worse.

'Ok' said Grandfather. 'We're going to land now. Listen to me, Irian, we have a big task in front of us. If you're really afraid tell me now and we won't go. This place is the kind of a place where you can't afford to be afraid otherwise you risk your life. You have to leave fear right here behind you or we'll have to turn back.'

'I'll be ok' Irian felt so completely hypnotised by the situation that he wasn't totally in control of what he was saying.

'Good. First of all, don't talk while we're in the forest. Don't even whisper! If you've got something to say, just squeeze my hand. I'll understand.'

'But I'm sure Ogi will bark.'

'Look, Ogi is an animal and they don't care about animals. As long as they can't smell our flesh and hear our voices, we should be ok. Have you got the cream on properly?'

Irian just nodded. They landed a bit further away from the Wild Flower Forest and as they got out of the balloon, Irian could now smell the disgusting odour coming from the vinegar cream, which had been less obvious up in the balloon because of the strong air. Grandfather just put his finger over his lips to warn him that they had to be silent. Irian produced his divining rod and put the plan of the Water Castle in one of his pockets. Once Grandfather had applied the cream, they started off for the forest.

Irian had never seen such immense flowers before with such hairy petals that reached to the ground. Their stems were almost twice as large as the flowers in Destin and some of them had long roots above the surface. They had a terrible musty odour. He couldn't really tell their colours as it was dark, but he thought that such flowers could only exist in dark and ugly hues. He tried not to look too much at them but rather to pay attention to the reaction of his divining rod, which was calm for the moment. While walking through the forest, Grandfather was carrying Ogi and he stayed very close to Irian. They could feel the flowers moving but they did not move like the flowers Irian was used to seeing whose stems would bend in the wind. These flowers preyed on their victims ready to devour them in the blink of an eye. The ground was covered with old petals and they had to pay attention not to tread on one of the roots, which wasn't easy, as they couldn't see much with just a candle. Therefore, they advanced at an extremely slow pace in order not to disturb the flowers or attract their attention. It was quite cold in the forest but Irian's hands felt sweatier than ever with fear. He had the impression that they had been walking for ages yet there was no reaction from his divining rod, so he started to think that they had got the time or the place wrong – he was scared stiff. For some strange reason, Ogi hadn't barked once which was very unusual for him. He was obviously as confused and as scared as Irian.

Suddenly, Grandfather stopped and squeezed his hand. As they couldn't exchange words, Irian didn't know what he was supposed to do. Grandfather just showed him to turn in another direction and he accelerated his pace so that Irian had difficulty keeping up. At that very moment, he felt the divining rod tremble in his hands; first slowly and then almost uncontrollably, when a strong wind blew up and Irian feared that it was going to blow him away. Then the water started to appear, from a trickle into a little stream, which then turned into a huge lake radiating in dazzling light. They both had to shade their eyes when all of a sudden, Irian felt somebody grab his hand from behind.

'Grandpa!' he screamed. 'Help! The flower has got me.'

'Don't panic!' shouted Grandfather.

Grandfather pulled a big sword out to attack the flower that was now holding Irian and trying to swallow him up. Its petals were so thick that they felt like some sort of cold damp blanket. Grandfather ran right into the flower's stem, so the petal released him. But now all the flowers seemed to have been woken up and were trying to attack them.

'Irian, dive into the water, quickly!' shouted Grandfather, fighting with the other flowers.

'You have to come too!' begged Irian, totally petrified.

'I will but you go now. Hurry up! Dive in Irian! Don't worry about me. I'll meet you later.'

There was no time to hesitate, so Irian dived into the lake as Grandfather had told him. Once in, he suddenly thought about how he was going to breathe if he needed to stay in the lake for a long time, but to his surprise, he was able to breathe under the water. Everything was so blurred that he closed his eyes and when he opened them again, he was standing in the middle of a very strange room. The room was made of a red liquid that was also flowing within its extra large furniture; the chairs were as big as Irian. He didn't have time to observe things for too long before hearing somebody's feet pattering along the corridor. In panic, he ran towards the chest of drawers standing in the corner of the room and hid behind it.

'I want everybody to be extremely careful tonight!' a voice, which seemed to be neither completely male nor female, shouted.

'Oh, yes, of course' said another voice obediently.

'We don't want any incidents like the last time the Castle appeared. Is that clear?'

'Yes, my lady.'

"My lady", repeated Irian to himself, "he must be talking to Queen Ranna". Irian didn't dare move though he was standing in such an uncomfortable position. There was so little space between the wall and the chest of drawers that he could hardly breathe. Apart from that, he was pressed for time. He only had an hour and was hoping not to spend it stuck behind this chest of drawers. A few moments later, he heard them leave the room and used the opportunity to look at the sign on the door. Each room belonged to one of the Creatures and each of them had its sign to mark the Creature's residence. The room that Irian was in had a crown on the door, which meant that it belonged to the Queen. The Queen's room was exactly on the opposite side from the library where Irian had to go. He had to be very attentive while walking around as it would have been easy to get lost in the labyrinth of corridors. Besides, the Creatures could come out of anywhere and see him, given that the place was well illuminated, light being so important to them. As Irian walked around, he could hear their voices penetrating through the thin walls of the Castle, but he didn't have time to listen to what they were saying. There were no stairs, but only slopes leading to the upper regions of the Castle. The walls were changing shades just as water changes colour depending on the state of the sky. Beneath, the floor was made of a thick moving liquid and you had to step on it courageously and let it take you around. It was very strange – every time you wanted to turn left or right, you had to jump to a different stream of liquid. The lights were actually flying balls of all sizes floating in the air and Irian almost burned his hand trying to touch one of them. Apparently, they had these floating light balls for security reasons so that if anybody tried to attack the Creatures by switching off the light, the attempt would fail as each light ball functioned independently.

When he finally arrived at the library, he was amazed at its size. There were Creatures walking up and down looking for books and there was no way of getting in through the main door unnoticed. Then, Irian remembered something Peena had told him and that he could use at that moment. According to some people, the Creatures were madly greedy for food and they would run like crazy whenever somebody announced that food was ready. Given that he didn't have a choice, he decided to trick them under the pretext of an enticing meal. A little further away from the library, there was a fountain, so he came up with an idea. He cleared his voice to make it sound deeper and then shouted aloud "food everybody" before hiding behind the fountain. At once, there was an indescribable commotion among the Creatures who were thoughtlessly heading for the nearest door.

'I'm starving' said one Creature.

'Oh, I hope we're going to have that wonderful watermelon cake' said the second Creature.

'Let me pass first. I'm more important than you' said the third Creature.

'Oh, really, we'll ask the Queen and she'll tell you that I'm the most important of all' said the first Creature.

'Stop arguing, you two and hurry up! The food is going to get cold – said the second Creature.

Once they were out of his way, Irian could penetrate into the library. It was the most amazing place he had ever seen. The Creatures had a different format of books, which were in the shape of sticks with the pages of text rolled around a stick in a kind of scroll. These stick-books were arranged to create a massive flower where each petal represented one letter. Irian had no idea how to find the right book as he didn't understand the Creatures' alphabet. He recognised the form of some of the letters from Mrs Bigone's book and he wished so much that she had been there to help him. He tried to look in a few books, but they all looked the same to him. Their letters were so elaborate and each one was in a different colour. As he was looking at one of them, he felt somebody grasping his shoulder. Irian felt his heart miss a beat dreading what was going to happen to him. But when he turned round, he saw Nuro standing in front of him, holding a book under his right arm.

'Nuro, what are you doing here?'

'No time to explain. I've got the book. Let's run out of here before the Creatures get back' he whispered.

Irian's mind was a whirlpool of questions, but there wasn't a second to spare. They were running out of time before the Castle disappeared again and the Creatures could have come back at any time. If they realised they had been tricked, they could find the whole thing suspicious and send the guard to comb the place.

'We need to find the exit door' whispered Nuro.

'I know where it is' replied Irian so quietly that he could hardly hear himself.

As they were running in the direction of the exit, they heard Creatures talking.

'I'm sure I heard somebody shouting about food' said one of them.

'So am I' said another.

'You fools' they heard the Queen screaming at the Creatures. 'We have a spy in the Castle and I warned you to pay attention. Guard, quick!' the Queen yelled.

Irian and Nuro heard the alarm and footsteps of Creatures running all over. One glance told them of the danger close at hand.

'I can feel them coming' panicked Nuro. 'They're only a few steps behind. The exit door is miles away.'

'We need to hide. Let's get into that cupboard! Quick, get in Nuro!'

While they were getting into the cupboard, Irian caught a glimpse of Ranna in the distance. She was exactly as Uncle Tattoo had represented her in his drawings, but now she was there and she was real.

'What are you waiting for, Irian? Get in!' yelled Nuro seeing him standing there looking as if somebody had hypnotised him.

Irian didn't react, so Nuro grabbed and pulled him into the cupboard. Nuro tried to advance, still holding on to Irian's arm, so to make more space for Irian, when all at once they started sliding through a black corridor. They both screamed and shrieked as they tumbled headlong down a long black hole, which seemed endless and scarier than any bad dream they had ever had. They couldn't see anything and could only think of trying not to bang their heads against the wall. Then, finally, they fell to the bottom after a long and very nasty tumble. It took them a few moments to regain their breath and recover after that bumpy journey through the black hole.

'Are you ok Irian?'

'I think so, but my bottom is going to be black and blue' replied Irian still grasping for his breath with a palpitating heart.

'Where are we?'

'I haven't got the faintest idea. I can't see a thing.'

'Don't worry, I've got a torch with me' said Nuro looking for it in his pocket. 'Oh no, I think it fell out during the fall.'

'Well, it must be around somewhere, then' said Irian and they both started to look for the torch.

'There it is, I can feel it' said Nuro and he switched it on.

'This place seems like some sort of cave and it stinks.'

'I don't think it's the place that stinks. I think we stink – it's the vinegar cream.

Irian had been so absorbed in the situation, that he hadn't even noticed the smell anymore. He realised that Nuro had applied the same cream too and wondered how he had arrived at the Castle. However, there were more important things to concentrate on right then and he preferred to leave the questions for later on.

'Shhh, Nuro, I can hear voices. They're coming from over there' Irian pointed into the distance.

'Let's listen to what they're saying!' replied Nuro and they both tip-toed in that direction.

There was a large half-open door behind which was another room. As they entered this second room, they could hear the voices better. Nuro gave a sign to Irian to approach the door leading to the third room from which they could hear the conversation perfectly well. They both kneeled down near the door, one on each side, and Irian tried look through the keyhole. Irian most definitely had the beginnings of a cold and needed to sneeze so badly that it was almost unbearable.

'and I don't know how many more times I will have to repeat that' said the voice which Irian now found familiar.

'Why don't you do it then?' said a gruff voice.

'Gentlemen, if we continue this way, we won't get anywhere' a third voice chipped in.

'I think we should make a plan' Irian found this voice equally familiar but he just couldn't put a face to it.

'Why don't we simply kidnap him and drag him there?' said the gruff voice.

'It would be too dangerous' said the familiar voice.

'You should do it' said the gruff voice to the familiar voice. 'You have the closest relationship with him.'

'Why do I have to do everything?' asked the familiar voice and Irian racked his brains to identify it.

'Because it is your duty and the Mask Heads oblige you to do it otherwise you're out of here. Do you understand? We can't do anything without Cherry Taste' said the fourth voice which Irian also thought he had heard somewhere. "Cherry Taste", thought Irian to himself. "Who is Cherry Taste?"

Eavesdropping on the Mask Heads, Irian and Nuro looked at each other blankly and every so often Irian tried to peep through the keyhole. However, as they were covered by masks, he couldn't identify any of the faces, and the place was scarcely lit anyway.

'Ok, I'll do it' said the familiar voice.

'Good, the Queen will be happy to hear that. Actually I'm surprised she's not with us yet' said the fourth voice.

As he pronounced the word **QUEEN**, Irian and Nuro both had the same thought.

'We need to get out of here' Irian murmured under his breath. 'The Queen will give the alarm to them about our presence in the Castle.'

'You're right' replied Nuro, whispering. 'Look, there's the door down there.'

They tip-toed to the door and Nuro pointed the light at it. It was a massive door, probably five times bigger than either of them. Irian noticed that the handle was as big as his arm and that he could almost put his head through the keyhole. But the door was locked and there was no way of opening it.

'What shall we do?' asked Nuro.

'I don't know. This seems like the entrance door to me but there might be another one. Let's have a look.'

Just then, they heard somebody approaching the door from outside. Irian had a quick look through the keyhole and he turned as white as a sheet when he saw the Queen about to enter.

'Nuro, hide, the Queen!' said Irian as they heard the key in the door with a mingled expression of horror and fear.

'Oh, no, what's she going to do with us?' said Nuro hiding his face in his hands.

They both leaned against the wall waiting to see what would happen to them, and as they were leaning against it, something very strange occurred. The wall suddenly opened and then, as quickly as it had opened, closed again. They could see the Queen entering through the wall that was transparent from the inside and which however seemed like a normal wall from the outside. As she came in, she looked towards them for a moment and though she couldn't see them, Irian and Nuro both turned to jelly. She then walked towards the meeting room and they heaved a sigh of relief.

'That was a close shave' said Irian.

'What is this place?' asked Nuro, finally turning around.

'It's the Queen's secret room' said another voice hiding behind a mirror. Out stepped Grandfather and then Floria.

'Grandpa, Floria' said Irian in disbelief. 'How did you two get here? I'm so happy to see you.'

'No time to talk now. I'll tell you everything later' said Grandfather. 'We can't stay here because the Queen could come in at any moment. It was clever little Ogi who found the key.'

'How did he manage that?' asked Irian.

'Well, I reckon he thought it was a bone and stole it from the Queen's room' replied Floria.

'Good dog' said Irian, stroking his puppy. 'I'm sorry for treating you so badly before.'

'The door is down that way. It's probably her secret exit' said Grandfather. 'Follow me!'

The Queen's room, which Irian had seen in the Castle, was nothing like this one, which was all in dark red hues with a fluffy red carpet reaching up to Irian's knees. The window went up to the ceiling and there was a little platform next to it with a big comfortable chair. Further inside was a bed resembling an enormous cushion supported by four elegant legs in the shape of tongues. There were many candles of all shades around the room as she needed as much light as possible particularly when asleep. Apart from that, the Queen used hot wax to make her hands look firmer and softer as she was obsessed with having beautiful hands. In the corner of the room, opposite the window, was a mirror, in the exact shape of the Queen herself. Irian remembered Mrs Bigone telling him about this mirror. Apparently, the Queen was obsessed with her figure too and if she couldn't see all of her body in that mirror, it meant that she had got fatter. Next to it was a massive wardrobe where she kept her clothes. Floria wanted to see what type of clothes the Queen wore, but Grandfather made a sign for them to hurry up. After that room, there was a long corridor and then another spacious room, which she probably used as a dining room. The room was decorated with many different masks hung on the wall and a long table with only two chairs one at either end. In that room, there was something that particularly attracted Irian's attention. It was a mask on the far wall, the only mask that had been put in a frame. Irian liked it for some reason and he went up to see it properly. He discovered writing underneath it: *"Whoever betrays the Queen will lose his face"*.

'Look!' said Irian to the others. 'That must be the Kindness Creature's mask.'

'You're right' said Grandfather. 'We should take it with us.'

'But it's locked in' said Irian.

'We'll have to break the glass' said Grandfather. 'Quick, pass me that candlestick over there.'

'Why do you want the mask?' asked Nuro.

'Because it has special powers' replied Grandfather.

'What kind of powers?' asked Irian.

'I'll tell you once we're out.'

Grandfather took the candlestick and smashed it against the glass to get the mask.

'Got it' he said happily. 'Let's get out of here now!'

They managed to open the door and ran as quickly as they could towards the Old Lady. Seeing them running, Ogi thought it was a huge game and started barking.

'Quiet Ogi!' Irian tried to make him stop. 'You'll get us into trouble.'

Despite Irian's efforts, Ogi continued barking and nobody could stop him. The noise obviously alerted the members of the secret meeting and they rushed out to see who was disturbing them. They could hear the Queen screeching from inside "Somebody has been snooping around my room" before running out. "Whoever you are, you will pay for it!"

The Castle was now just a speck in the distance. However, the Queen's voice was so scary and loud that they all trembled in the balloon, which was now well out of her reach. Even Ogi stopped barking and didn't make a single sound until they had returned safe to Destin. For some reason, Grandfather didn't park the balloon in the shed as he usually did, but left it a little bit further away from his house.

'Why did you park the Old Lady here?' asked Irian.

'Because your grandma might be back and she thinks we've been to that show, remember?' replied Grandfather.

'So, you have a secret shed. You've never told me about that' joked Irian.

'You don't need to know everything, do you?' replied Grandfather.

'Grandpa, why did you suddenly speed up in the Forest?'

'Because I saw the Flower Queen, and the Flower Queen can smell people despite the vinegar cream. She was the one who attacked you.'

'Talking about vinegar cream, you even have a shower here' chimed in Nuro. 'I'm dying for a shower. I can't stand this vinegar cream any longer.'

'Ok, have you got any clean clothes?' asked Grandfather.

'No, I don't, actually ' said Nuro.

'Don't worry. I've brought some for us. I knew we'd need to get changed' replied Floria.

'Clever girl!' replied Grandfather.

They all had a shower and then huddled around the fire, but none of them spoke. They were all reliving their adventure in the Castle, hardly believing it had all really happened to them. It just wouldn't sink in.

The Letter

The next morning, Irian took longer to wake up than usual. And even when he was awake, he kept on opening and closing his eyes again, still in bed, as if he wasn't really sure that he was in the real world. He then spent some time just sitting, staring at a crack in the ceiling and thinking how he hadn't seen it before. That morning Irian seemed totally distracted – in broad daylight the events of the night before seemed like a dream. He tried to smell his skin and could still detect a slight odour of vinegar cream, which was there like a stamp to confirm everything he had been through the previous night.

'Are you awake, Irian?' his father's voice surprised him at the door.

'Yeah' replied Irian, quickly sliding back into his bed as if he had just woken up.

'So, how was the show last night?' asked his dad, opening the door.

Irian had completely forgotten that he was supposed to have seen the show and was now trying to come up with something convincing.

'The show' repeated Irian, confused. 'Yeah, it was great.'

'What was it about exactly?' continued Irian's father.

'It was about... Do you mind if I tell you later because I really do need to have a shower?' lied Irian.

'Of course, of course' replied his dad. 'I'll see you later.'

His father left the room and Irian lay down again.

'Irian' his dad knocked at the door after only a few seconds, 'I forgot to give you something. This letter arrived for you this morning.'

'Letter?' repeated Irian obviously confused.

His father gave it to him and then stood next to him as if

waiting for him to open it. Irian looked at it, but didn't recognise the writing. Apart from birthday cards, he had never really received a letter from anyone. "Who could have sent me this?" he thought to himself and then decided to be careful about it.

'Ok, I'm going for a shower' he said confidently.

'You're not going to open your letter first?' asked his father.

'No, I really need a shower.'

Irian's father stood there for a moment, surprised by his son's attitude, but he didn't say anything as it was his son's letter after all. He went downstairs to see his wife while Irian slipped it into his pyjamas and went to the bathroom.

He let the water run and then took the letter out of his pyjama top. It was ordinary paper but with unusual writing. The letters were extremely round and placed all over the envelope. It read:

Master:
Irian Horvats
9, Poola Street
51 010 Destin

He tore at the paper flap eagerly and extracted a card bearing these words:

Mr Horvats,
   I do not want to be unpleasant but you stole one of my most treasured objects from my room yesterday. I suppose you understand the gravity of the situation and you do not want me to have to pay you a visit. Therefore, I would appreciate your returning it to me and not forcing me to waste my precious time coming to look for it. Leave it at the reception of the main hotel in the village of Uklet and somebody will collect it for me.
   Queen Ranna

Irian now really did need to have a shower to freshen up his mind. "Was Queen Ranna really writing to me?" Though it was a threatening letter, the very fact that she had written to him he found thrilling and amusing. On the other hand, he knew that his parents would want an explanation, so in order to avoid this, he showered, got dressed and then ran downstairs quickly saying he was going to see Grandfather.

Before this, though, Irian decided to see Nuro and Floria. However, when he knocked at their door, nobody answered. He decided to call Nuro on his talkastick, but realised that he had left it at home trying to get out as quickly as possible. Well, he had no choice but to go back and get it and he arrived just as Floria and Nuro were knocking at his door. His mother opened it to them.

'Oh, Irian has just..' she said when she saw the two. 'Oh, he's there actually, just behind you. Didn't you say you were going to see Grandfather, Irian?'

'Yes, I did' Irian replied. 'But I forgot my talkastick.'

'So, Floria and Nuro,' she continued. 'Your parents told me you went to the same show as Irian last night. Irian hasn't told me about it yet and I'm dying to hear all the details.'

'It was marvellous' said Irian. 'Mum, I really need to speak to Floria and Nuro. See you later.'

'And that letter, Irian?' she went on. 'Who was it from?'

'Mum, can we discuss it another time? I have things to do.'

Irian didn't want to be rude to his mother, but she would never ever understand his preoccupations, as she couldn't accept the Creatures' existence. Therefore, he preferred to work things out by himself and then explain it to her when it was all over.

'What letter was she talking about?' asked Nuro once they had entered Irian's room.

'Don't speak so loud' said Irian, showing him the letter.

Nuro and Floria crouched over the letter to read it together and then Nuro read it again with his eyebrows raised so high that Irian had the impression that they would reach up to his hair-line.

'Well, I never' said Nuro, astonished. 'What are you going to do now?'

'I don't know, but I'm not going to give her the Kindness Creature's mask back. Mrs Bigone once told me that the Creatures never used to take their masks off, even when they went to sleep. So, if she had made it take off the mask, it means that she must have wanted to humiliate or punish it for some reason. Why did she want to do it? That's what I'm wondering' said Irian.

'Your grandpa said that this mask has special power' said Floria. 'What kind of power?'

'He didn't explain.'

'I don't think you should keep it here' said Nuro. 'It's too dangerous.'

'But where do you want me to keep it then?' asked Irian.

'There must be a place where she won't find it' replied Nuro.

'By the way, how did you two get to the Castle yesterday?' asked Irian. 'You scared the wits out of me when you grabbed my hand in the library.'

'Floria and I had this planned for a long time' went on Nuro 'since the first time you talked to us about the Water Castle. We really wanted to come with you and help, but you said your grandfather disagreed, which is perfectly understandable. But we couldn't imagine leaving you there without our help, so we organised it all. The most difficult thing was finding an excuse for our parents and getting to the village of Uklet. Then we got the idea of asking Mrs Bigone for help. I know you didn't want us to talk to anybody about your plans, but as she is the most knowledgeable person in town when it comes to the Creatures, we decided to spill the beans.'

'And, how did she react?' asked Irian with great interest.

'She said she knew there was something going on' explained Nuro, 'but, she had no inkling of the existence of the Water Castle. She even wanted to go there with us but then, she thought there would be too many of us in the Castle, which would only complicate matters and make the situation more dangerous. We spent the whole afternoon talking, trying to work out our plan of how to get to the Castle. So, Mrs Bigone came up with the idea of telling our parents that she was taking us to your grandfather's friend's party. The most difficult part, though, was finding the way to the village of Uklet. We thought about it over and over again and finally, Mrs Bigone decided she would take us there herself in a rented hot air balloon.'

'Mrs Bigone can fly a balloon?' asked Irian in surprise.

'Yes, she's great at it. Apparently, she flies from time to time.'

Just then, they heard the door opening slowly. In came Ogi.

'Silly-billy Ogi, you scared me' said Irian and then continued. 'And your parents, weren't they suspicious?'

'I don't think so' answered Floria. 'Nuro just kept on eating all day, you know.'

'Yep, I was so nervous. But you were more nervous in the balloon than I was' commented Nuro.

'Of course I was, I couldn't see a thing' replied Floria. 'And just as well, I couldn't stop thinking about Peena. How on earth can she move around without seeing anything?'

'You're right' answered Nuro. 'Mrs Bigone did a great job.'

'And how did you know about the vinegar cream?' asked Irian.

'Remember that article that Mr Tappin wrote about the carnivorous flowers some time ago? It says in there that these flowers can't stand the smell of vinegar because they are extremely sensitive to odours' explained Nuro.

'Mind you, I didn't think they smelt particularly good myself' said Irian.

'I didn't dare to smell them. And anyway, I must have put tonnes of that vinegar cream on' said Nuro lifting his arm to smell for any traces of the cream.

'I noticed that' replied Irian. 'So, what happened then? Did she leave you to go through the forest all alone?'

'No, she stayed with us until we had jumped into the lake.'

'I hope she had no problems getting back home' said Irian. 'Have you spoken to her today?'

'Yes, I have. Apparently, she had no trouble returning to Destin.'

'Actually, I'm surprised she let you jump into the lake alone' commented Irian.

'Well, she said she wouldn't have done it if we hadn't met your grandfather.'

'Ah, so you met grandpa?' asked Irian.

'That's right. He was just getting ready to dive in when he saw us, so we dived in altogether and Mrs Bigone left by herself.'

'Where did you come up in the Castle then?' asked Irian.

'You're going to laugh' said Floria. 'We came up in the Love

Creature's room.'

'What's so funny about that?'

'Everything in its room is heart-shaped. I've never seen anything so ridiculous in my life' said Nuro. 'Even its body cream consisted of grains in the shape of hearts.'

'Goodness me!' said Irian, laughing. 'Anyway, you were lucky because you came up close to the library. I came up on the opposite side. I still can't believe they didn't catch me while I was walking around. I mean, any of the Creatures could have crossed my path. But, why did you separate, then?'

'Because your grandfather wanted to go and check something' replied Nuro. 'What did he want to see anyway, Floria?'

'He was looking for the Queen's room' answered Floria.

'Why?' asked Irian, quite puzzled.

'I don't know. He didn't tell me' answered Floria.

'By the way, how did you two get to the Queen's secret room?' answered Irian, whose mind seemed flooded by a river of questions.

'You see, when we finally found Ranna's room we realised it couldn't be the room we were looking for. It was just too plain to be the Queen's room, knowing how fussy Ranna is. Just then, we realised we couldn't find Ogi. We looked everywhere but he was nowhere to be found, which was strange because he couldn't have got out so we searched the place thoroughly. Time was another problem. Suddenly, I caught sight of Ogi in the Queen's mirror but I couldn't actually see him anywhere in the room itself and I realised that he was in fact inside the mirror. Later on, I understood what had happened. The key to the Queen's secret room was reflected in the mirror and Ogi mistook it for a bone, so he rushed straight at it, not realising what it really was.'

'What do you mean?' asked Irian.

'You see' continued Floria, 'if you look in that mirror, you see the room reflected in it, so it seems like a normal mirror. But, when you look more closely, you can see a key, which isn't actually in the room at all. So, if you touch that key, you activate the mirror. That's the secret.'

'Activate the mirror?' repeated Irian.

'Yes, the mirror opens in the middle and leads you into the

Queen's secret room. Apart from that, this key can open all the doors in the whole of the Castle' revealed Floria, slipping her hand into one of her pockets. When she brought out her hand, she was brandishing something shiny. 'This is the key, here!'

'You've got the key!' said Irian in disbelief.

'Yes' she replied, adding somewhat quietly. 'You never know. We might need it again.'

'I'm surprised the Queen didn't ask for it in her letter.'

'She might not have realised yet' said Nuro.

'So, it means that the wall-door didn't just open to Nuro and me by itself. You were the one who opened it for us!'

'That's right. We saw you leaning against it so we opened it.'

'Yes, we were nearly caught red-handed by the Queen' said Irian. 'It gives me goose pimples just thinking about it.'

Irian suddenly remembered the very moment he saw the Queen opening the door and being struck by a total panic. Actually, the whole of the previous night seemed more like a kind of illusion to his mind. However, this morning's letter had shattered that illusion, and given him a shortcut to reality. He couldn't help thinking about the mask, which the Queen obviously wasn't going to give up so easily.

'I think we should go and see grandpa before the Queen comes to pay me a visit' said Irian.

'But didn't your grandfather say he was going to spend the day with Petalber?' asked Floria.

'Oh, yes, you're right. I'd completely forgotten. What shall we do, then?'

'Maybe we could go and see Mrs Bigone instead' suggested Nuro.

'Good idea' replied Irian. 'But please, sneak out of the house quickly otherwise mum is going to start asking us questions again.'

They managed to leave the house without being noticed by Irian's parents and went to see Mrs Bigone. She was just getting home when they arrived so they all went into her house together.

'I thought you would come and see me, so I went to get us a nice chocolate cake' said Mrs Bigone once they were all comfortably settled in her sitting room.

'Wonderful' replied Irian, pouring himself some deliciously

sweet-smelling juice. 'I didn't even have time for breakfast.'

'So, how was it then?' asked Mrs Bigone quite impatiently like a little child who just can't deal with waiting and needs an answer straight away.

They tried to sum up their adventure in the Water Castle but they ended up telling her every single detail of what had happened. However, Mrs Bigone seemed most interested in the library and her eyes flickered when Nuro got out the book from his rucksack.

'There we are' said Nuro in a normal tone just as if it were any old book.

Mrs Bigone was so overjoyed that she couldn't even speak. She just stretched her hands forward for Nuro to hand it over. She accepted it with both hands as if handling some very fragile treasure that could crumble between her fingers if she wasn't careful.

'Could you read it to us?' asked Irian, running his long spidery finger around the lip of the glass.

'Of course I can' replied Mrs Bigone, still immersed in her thoughts. 'Let's see...'

Mrs Bigone put her glasses on and cleared her voice as if preparing for a very important speech. She unrolled the first part of the book; within the text, the initials were enlarged and adorned, at times surrounded by botanical decoration. She had a quick glance over it and then started reading slowly:

"Who would ever have thought that there would be a child without a destiny necklace? Our precious necklace, indeed! But it has happened despite all our efforts to avoid such a situation. Thinking about it now, it was practically inevitable, but how can we possibly take everything into consideration or suspect everything that is going on. However, I didn't expect that one of us would ever be involved in such a thing, would betray all of us. I would never have suspected the Kindness Creature! As its name implies, the Kindness Creature is always too kind, but it shouldn't have been kind to Destiners; you see what happens when you are kind to them – they turn right against you! Apparently, the Kindness Creature insists that it was the right thing to do as Mrs Lotta

had saved its life one night. And you see, Mrs Lotta was pregnant at that time and was hiding this from us. In order to thank her for saving its powers the Kindness Creature, kind as it is, decided to help her by helping her escape from our destiny decision. It found her a place to hide during her pregnancy, a place outside the county because we Creatures have no power outside Amazeshire. Mrs Lotta bore a boy child and she called him Emo. So, Emo was lucky in a way that he didn't have a destiny, but I suppose he must have had a lonely childhood as he wasn't allowed to see anybody and particularly not us – the Creatures.

But you see, Mrs Lotta wasn't the only one who tried to avoid a destiny decision for her baby. There was a woman called Mrs Yadran who couldn't get over the loss of her baby who died – although you see, it wasn't our fault, I mean we can't give a perfect life to everybody! Therefore, when she became pregnant again, she was determined to escape from her duty of declaring the pregnancy. And she did indeed avoid it, but the Curiosity Creature managed to find her once her baby girl, Arena, had been born. The Queen was furious, of course, and decided to kidnap Arena from her mother because otherwise she was powerless over the baby. Arena knew nothing about her family or the world outside the Amphitheatre – well, as far as we were concerned. She was only allowed to go out in the presence of one of us. It's true that she was a nice girl and we all grew very fond of her. That's why I don't think she would have had the idea of destroying us... But you see she met Emo, and this thanks to the Kindness Creature who looked after her and had one day decided to take her to meet Emo because they were in the same situation as "undeclared" children. It was love at first sight – to use a favourite expression of the Love Creature. I suppose it was Emo who told her the truth and this idea must have had an impact on Arena, who just couldn't wait to go back to see Emo again. Emo had promised Arena he would set her free one day and they both worked hard on their plan. I couldn't say whether the Kindness Creature was aware of their intentions, but I did notice that Arena was getting more and more curious about the Amphitheatre towards the end of our government. However, none of us suspected anything and we patiently answered all her questions. Well, I personally never ever suspected anything.

The event took place when we least expected it, as great events are always clothed in silence. The Queen always received pregnant women in the mornings, but she would occasionally accept pregnant women later in the day if a woman was near the end of the first week of pregnancy. It was important to decide on the baby's fate before the first week was up. The Queen was told that there was a woman who had come to declare her pregnancy. Women in Destin knew they were pregnant as they had a sign in their dreams, and they had one week only to register with us. The telltale sign experienced by all women was seeing the tiny white flower "baby's breath" in some form or other every night in their dreams. Nobody ever dreamt of this unless they were pregnant and the dreams of this flower continued nightly until the mother gave birth.

Emo really was perfectly disguised; you can see the determination in his actions now. He came late in the afternoon on purpose for it was already quite dark due to a Season of Decline, which was always a hard period for us, as there was so little daylight. He played his role so well, talking to the guard just to get to the Queen's office. I don't know how nervous he was, but he definitely pulled it off. Well, I am unable to tell exactly what happened in the Queen's office, but I only remember the alarm ringing around the Amphitheatre to signal the human who had come to confirm that he had been born without a destiny. We were all so shocked and we marvelled at the same time that such a human being could exist. All of us ran to meet him and help the Queen, of course. However, what we didn't realize was that Emo was just a trap for all of us to make things easier for Arena who was supposed to turn the ventilation on in order to blow out the candles in the inner quarters. Nobody was ever allowed to turn the ventilation on while the Creatures were in *the inner quarters, as that would leave us in the dark and destroy our powers. We didn't even manage to get to Ranna's office when, all of a sudden, all the lights in the Amphitheatre went off. There was a terrible panic in the dark and we had to leave the Amphitheatre and our inner quarters while Emo and Arena became the heroes of the town. It was the end of our government and the Destiners decided to bury us under a heavy silence, as if the whole thing had never happened. Our failed government gradually became no more than a fearful whisper among the Destin townspeople and our existence only a legend in their eyes. We were like an illness to them that they wanted to get over as soon as they could."*

Irian had become so immersed in the story that he looked like a singer who has just finished an exceptionally emotional song and needed time to get back to the real world.

'What was the destiny necklace?' asked Irian.

'It was a necklace given to every child at his or her birth by the Creatures. The necklace had a little pendant on it in the shape of a hand on which the lines of the palm were engraved. And if you looked at those lines, you could tell the baby's future.'

'That's awful!' exclaimed Floria.

'I know' replied Mrs Bigone. 'That's why we should never let them rule this town again.'

'But how could they tell what these lines meant?' inquired Irian.

'Because there were Soothsayers who could read the lines and the mounts and explain their meaning.'

'How did the Soothsayers know how to read palms?' asked Nuro.

'I wouldn't be able to tell you that. They must have had a system of doing it.'

'Do you think the Creatures knew of the Soothsayers' existence?' asked Irian.

'I don't think so. I mean, I would be surprised because they didn't want anybody meddling in their business.'

Irian felt that he should tell Mrs Bigone about Gadious Cheater but he thought it would be better to do it under the cover of darkness, so he went to switch the lights off.

'Why have you turned the lanterns off?' asked Mrs Bigone, confused.

'Because I need to tell you something' replied Irian.

'What, that you are in love with me?' joked Mrs Bigone.

'No, there's something very serious you ought to know' replied Irian and then went on to tell her about Gadious Cheater, the letter he had received and the Kindness Creature's mask.

Mrs Bigone listened attentively and looked around every so often as if scouring the dark corners of the room for any intruder.

'That's no good' answered Mrs Bigone after a while. 'We have to think of something.'

'Why is this mask so important?' asked Irian.

'I don't know. You'll have to ask your grandfather. But, if the Queen is demanding it back, it must be very important. You'll have to find a good hiding place for it. Have you got any idea where to keep it?'

'Well, I'll simply carry it everywhere with me; she'll have to fight me to get it back' replied Irian.

'Be careful, she'll do anything to have it. And this Gadious Cheater? I wonder what his relationship with the Creatures is. Have you ever tried to speak to him?'

'No' it's true that Irian avoided any contact with him and would be perfectly happy for Gadious to steer well clear of him.

'I think you should try to ask him what he wants from you.'

'I don't believe he'd tell me. I mean, why would he if he's my enemy?'

'Just try and you'll see. How can you tell if you don't try?!' reasoned Mrs Bigone.

Irian suddenly needed time alone. It was very unusual for him, but too many things had happened recently and he needed to sort his thoughts out. He realised that his life wasn't the same anymore and that he was entangled in something that was mysterious as well as dangerous. Above all, he didn't know what was going to happen, nor if the end would be a happy one. He went to Mrs Bigone's garden first and then realised that he was too fidgety to stay in one place, so decided to go for a walk. "What's going to happen to my town if the Creatures come back?" he kept on asking himself. "How can I stop them? How?"

The River Irav

While Irian wandered around, he suddenly thought of Peena. He remembered that he hadn't called her to tell her about his trip to the Water Castle and it seemed important to inform her. So, he took out his talkastick to call her and she was glad to hear from him again. He briefly described all that had happened and asked her what he should do.

'Well, you'll have to find out more about their hidden powers if you don't want them to come back to Destin' replied Peena.

'But how, Peena?' enquired Irian. 'Where can I look, tell me?'

'There is a river a with liquid that reveals the Creatures' writing, but it's a long way from Amazeshire. It could help you to reveal the writings on the boards of the Amphitheatre. They might tell us more about the Creatures' hidden powers.'

'What?' exclaimed Irian, probably more confused than ever. 'How do you now about it Peena? Why didn't you tell me before?'

'Because you weren't ready to know about it. There's a time for everything in our lives.'

'So what kind of liquid is it? And where is the river?' asked Irian, impatiently.

'It's called the River Irav. However, you have to be very careful because if you ever touch this liquid, you'll lose your memory instantly.'

'Why?'

'It's a protection devised by the Creatures so that nobody can understand their writing.'

'I'll have to ask grandpa to take me there. He'll know how to find it.'

'Be careful, and remember, don't ever touch that water!'

It was early in the morning when Irian, Grandfather, Nuro and Floria set off on their balloon journey to find the River Irav. The air was fresh and sharp and the dew on the flowers was still untouched by the morning sun while the light mist coiled around the tops of the hills. There was a little iridescent bird that kept following them, curious at this early-morning party of travellers. Even when they were soaring high above the county, the bird followed them for a while and then obviously found something more important to do and left them to continue their journey alone.

'I don't think that little bird is interested in our destination' commented Grandfather. 'Never mind. At least she won't be able to reveal our secret to anybody.'

'Well, I hope we haven't got to the point of suspecting birds as spies' replied Irian.

'Hey, where's your sense of humour? Stop being so stroppy. We're all in the same boat but you're the only one complaining. I thought it was your idea to see the River.'

Irian just couldn't keep calm anymore. Everything was taking on incredible proportions and speed and it was difficult for him to handle this new strange way of life. He was restless and would snap at anyone for the slightest thing.

'I'm sorry. I'm just overwrought about this whole situation. It seems to me as if I'm the one who was meant to solve this whole enigma about the Legend' he was smiling, but his face retained a look of solemnity.

'But you are' replied Grandfather rather quietly.

'I am what?' asked Irian, distracted.

'It's up to you to free the town of the Creatures' replied Grandfather, looking straight into Irian's eyes.

'What are you talking about, grandpa?' asked Irian, completely bowled over.

'We have to talk, Irian. I didn't want to speak to you about it now, but I think I'll have to. Do you remember Peena talking about Arena and Emo's descendants?'

'Yes' said Irian, trying to work out what grandpa was getting at 'and...'

After a moment's silence, Grandpa drew a deep breath.

'Well, it's us. We are Arena and Emo's descendants.'

'How do you know that, grandpa?' Irian straightened up as if thunderstruck.

'They appeared in my dream the night after you were born and told me it was going to be up to you to protect the town from the Creatures.'

Irian was struck dumb with amazement. His face was a picture and he noticed that the news had the same astonishing impact on Nuro and Floria, who were staring at him in awe. "So, my inner voice wasn't just my imagination."

'Does that mean I'm the one the Creatures can't hurt?' asked Irian.

'That's right' replied Grandfather. 'That's your advantage and you have to use it in an intelligent way.'

'So, how do I know what to do?' asked Irian.

'You'll have to follow your inner voice as you always have. It will tell you the best thing to do.'

Irian became misty-eyed thinking about the fact that he alone had been given the honour of saving his town. However, he felt a kind of happiness mingled with fear. What had been a dream at one point now became an extraordinary reality hanging over his life.

'But, aren't I too young for such things?' asked Irian.

'There is no age for anything in our lives. There are only circumstances that we find ourselves in; like there is no age for falling in love, learning different things or even dying. Situations come and go and you have to face them whether you want to or not. Some people never have to face certain things because they've taken a different path but, on the other hand, they'll have other things to face that you won't have to. Everybody has a different road to travel, just as we all have different lessons to learn so as to bring our spirituality to a higher level. Just look at the fingers on your hand and you'll see that they're all different, never mind all the differences between people and their experiences.'

Flying, above them the sun shone hot in their faces, for up in the air there was nothing to offer any shade. The air gradually got heavy and sultry and they all began to feel impatient to land.

'We should be arriving any minute now' declared Grandfather. 'The Irav must lie somewhere behind that cone-shaped mountain.'

The area they were flying above was nothing like their own county and what their eyes were used to. There were very few flowers to embellish the landscape while the ground was of a reddish colour and was rather barren. As they approached the cone-shaped mountain, they realised that it was actually a volcano. The whole place seemed deserted, deprived of houses probably because of this imposing landform.

The volcano itself towered high, with a massive crater at its centre, which looked like the open mouth of a monster whose saliva was the boiling lava, bubbling a few feet below the lip of the crater, able to destroy anything in an instant. However, the strangest thing of all was that the River Irav could be seen penetrating through one of the vents, which meant that its source must have been inside the volcano. The Irav flowed down the volcano's surface and then twice around it like a watery bandage protecting the "big monster" that could wake up at any time.

'Hey, I thought the Irav would be more like a stream. It's huge!' said Grandfather.

'It seems like there's no end to it' added Nuro.

'What a spooky place!' exclaimed Irian. 'The Water Castle, the River Irav – why do they choose such horrible places?'

'Well, it's to keep us away' replied Grandfather. 'They don't want us to discover their horrible secret places.'

'I guess you're right' commented Irian. 'Where are you going to land?'

They landed a bit further away from the volcano as they didn't find the place very safe, seeing the streams of molten lava running down the volcano's surface. Grandfather was a bit worried as there was nothing to attach his balloon to, he just had to leave it hovering.

'So, you all know the rules' said Grandfather seriously. 'Keep your skin away from that water or else we'll be in trouble.'

'How are we going to get the water out?' inquired Irian. 'It's too far down. It's going to be difficult to reach it.'

'You're right' replied Nuro.

They approached the river flowing quietly in front of them. It wasn't transparent like normal water but was a kind of a silvery colour and appeared to be almost viscous in texture. In a way, it might have been cooled lava coming out of the volcano. You couldn't tell how deep the Irav was just by looking at it, but it definitely wasn't shallow. Irian wondered whether there were any fish in it but he rejected this idea, thinking that if he were a fish he would certainly not want to live in there. It flowed slowly, and smelled of danger and unpleasantness. What now worried Irian was how to get to it, as it was flowing some two foot below the surface. The Creatures had obviously been aware of all the risks and made it difficult for anybody to touch their precious liquid.

'So, any ideas?' asked Irian, turning to Grandfather and his friends who were all reflecting on what needed to be done.

Whenever there was a knotty situation, Nuro would lay his head on his knees, closing his eyes to concentrate better on finding a solution. He appeared so serious during such moments that Irian almost feared asking him anything. Nuro was a very logical person; he would first decide on the key factors of a situation and then contrive what was almost a mathematical formula in his head in order to work the problem out. He seemed calm, but his head was churning up inside looking for an answer. He would stay like that for a while and then all of a sudden lift up his head to express his opinion. He simply wasn't one of those people who could make up their mind just by discussing things – he needed peace and quiet to sort out his thoughts.

'I was thinking that if we attached a bucket to a rope, we might be able to get some of it out' he said at length.

'But we haven't got a rope' replied Grandfather.

'We could take it from the Old Lady' said Irian.

'We're not destroying the Old Lady, all right?' answered Grandfather who couldn't allow any changes, let alone damage, to his hot air balloon.

117

'Nuro's right, grandpa. It's the only way, you know it is' replied Irian.

'No, no and no' answered Grandfather, angrily.

'Oh, come on, grandpa. What's more important; a rope or the future of our town?' Irian knew how to get round his grandfather and he felt responsible for the whole adventure now that he knew himself to be the famous descendant.

'It's not fair' replied Grandfather, pursing his lips.

'Well, life is just not fair anyway' said Irian thinking of the Creatures because this is what they used to say to the unfortunate people coming to complain about their destinies.

Grandfather realised that it was the only way, so he started to walk towards his balloon in silence. Irian just winked at his friends in a sign of a victory and they let Grandfather do it by himself. He came back after a few minutes, with a gloomy expression on his face, carrying a long piece of rope. Irian didn't dare to ask him anything; but took the rope and tied it to the bucket.

'Ok, I think this will do it' said Irian, finishing his knot.

'Right, we'll throw it down and then pull it up to the surface very carefully.'

Irian took the bucket and slowly dropped it, holding on to the rope and letting it descend further and further until it reached the water. He observed the bucket filling up and when he felt that there was enough water he pulled it back up even more slowly than he had let it down.

'Don't stand so close to the edge' said Floria.

'Don't worry. Just move back, all of you, because I'm going to pull it out completely' replied Irian. 'It's quite heavy, actually. I need help.'

'I'll help you' said Nuro.

'Ok, can you go behind me and pull it slowly. Just follow me. We mustn't do it too quickly because the water could splash out' instructed Irian.

So, Irian and Nuro were now holding onto the rope and pulling the bucket up to the surface. It was heavy as they needed quite a lot of the liquid, so they had chosen a large bucket. They decided not to ask Grandfather for help because if anything had harmed him, it would have been impossible for Irian, Nuro or Floria to have flown the hot air balloon home. As they were pulling the bucket up, Nuro slipped over a small stone behind him and stumbled, pulling the rope with a jerk. Irian couldn't control it and a few drops of liquid spilt over his legs.

'Oh, no' exclaimed Nuro, but it was already too late. The bucket was safely standing on the riverbank, though the six pairs of eyes weren't paying it the least attention. They were looking at Irian, who had started to feel dizzy and then just fell to the ground like a discarded puppet, motionless.

'Gracious' said Floria running towards him. 'Irian, Irian, are you ok?'

Irian wasn't answering, he wasn't even moving but his eyes were wide open and were rolling up and down while his face took on an unhealthy whitish hue.

'It's all my fault' said Nuro, who felt guilty at the sight of his friend.

'No it's not' replied Grandfather. 'It was an accident.'

'He's not reacting' said Floria who had been trying to speak to Irian.

'Irian, Irian' said Grandfather worried and trying desperately to make his grandson speak. 'Say something!'

Irian looked absently at his grandfather, as if he had never seen him before in his life and was therefore suspicious towards him. His pert features suddenly turned into those of a monster.

'Who are you?' said Irian with an icy glare. 'What do you want? Leave me alone.'

'Oh, no, he's lost his memory' said Grandfather. 'Don't you remember me?'

'Go away!' screamed Irian who was now trying to escape.

'Hold him!' said Grandfather to Nuro and Floria.

'What are we going to do?' asked Floria, holding tight to Irian's arm, together with Nuro and Grandfather.

'It's my fault' Nuro kept on.

'Stop saying that! It's not your fault' replied Grandfather. 'Better try to find a solution about what we're going to do. Irian is under a spell and we have to help him.'

They had difficulty holding Irian down as he wanted to escape by any means and they were worried he would fall into the river. He just wouldn't listen and was treating his grandfather and friends as if they were his worst enemies.

'I know that what I'm going to say sounds awful, but we'll have to tie him down otherwise we won't be able to help him' said Grandfather with a sinking heart.

'You're right' said Nuro, sobbing.

'Floria, go and cut off the piece of rope that was touching the water and bring us the rest of it. And for goodness sake, don't touch the water!' said Grandfather.

'Go away. Leave me alone!' shouted Irian who was desperately trying to free himself biting at the two of them who were having such difficulty holding him down.

'Hurry up, Floria' shouted Nuro. 'He's bitten me really hard. I just can't hold him anymore.'

Floria ran towards them with the rope, which they cut into two to tie both his hands and legs. Irian was screaming his head off as if somebody was trying to kill him or torture him in some terrible way.

'I feel awful seeing him like this' said Grandfather.

'What shall we do?' asked Floria.

'I'm going to call Peena. Irian has his talkastick with him' said Nuro, going to get the talkastick from Irian's pocket. He somehow managed to get it, but in return Irian bit him hard again and Nuro's arm started to bleed.

'Ouch' said Nuro, wrapping a part of his T-shirt around his wound.

He took the talkastick and asked for Peena. Feenie answered the phone and said that Peena was sleeping, so Nuro asked her to wake her up. Once she was awake and when Nuro was finally able to speak to her, he briefly explained to her what had happened to Irian.

'How awful!' said Peena.

'What can we do, Peena?' begged Nuro. 'He's getting worse and worse.'

'Take him to the Magnesiour Field. It's quite a long way for you, but it's still daylight, so you should be ok. But you must go there now! It is the only way to help Irian.'

'Where is the Magnesiour Field?' asked Nuro.

'It's in the County of Strong Winds' replied Peena. 'It is not going to be easy because as the name suggests, there are strong winds and it's going to be difficult to fly the balloon. But it's the only way.'

'How do we get there?' inquired Grandfather.

'It's up in the North. You'll know when you arrive there; you'll feel it.'

'So, what do we have to do to help him?' demanded Nuro.

'You have to make him tea from the leaves of any of the flowers growing there. That will help him to regain his memory. Good luck!'

'Well, let's go then' said Grandfather. 'I'll carry him to the balloon and you two take care of that liquid and see that you don't splash it in the balloon. The lid is just over there; make sure you close it properly.'

Grandfather somehow succeeded in transporting Irian to the hot air balloon. He didn't even want to imagine what would happen if they didn't manage to help him and if they had to bring him back home in such a state.

'Don't run with that water' shouted Grandfather from the balloon. 'Take your time with it.'

'What shall we do with Irian?' said Floria once they were in the balloon. 'If he keeps on kicking things like that, he might kick the bucket over and spill the water.'

'Well, you'll have to hold him. I know it's tiring, but we have to get to the County of Strong Winds' replied Grandfather.

Irian just wouldn't stop kicking and being rude to them and they were all exhausted trying to keep him still.

The landscapes below were changing but they had no time to observe anything else except Irian who seemed to have become possessed by an evil spirit. Their journey seemed longer than ever and their strength was getting weaker and weaker with all this struggling. Irian, however, wasn't losing his energy and was, on the contrary, becoming even nastier.

'Keep on going a bit longer!' said Grandfather. 'We're getting there.'

'I hope so' replied Nuro. 'I just can't go on like this anymore and my arm is really painful.'

They could tell they were approaching the County of Strong Winds. Even at that distance the air was becoming stronger and colder and they could feel the wind whooshing wildly around them.

'I want you to hold on tight to the gondola or else the wind will blow you away' instructed Grandfather, whose voice was almost stolen away by the strong currents.

'And what about Irian?' asked Floria.

'I'm afraid we'll have to tie him around this block' replied Grandfather and Floria and Nuro obeyed him immediately. It definitely wasn't an easy task.

'Go away you monsters!' screamed Irian. 'I hate you! I'm going to kill you!'

'Goodness me!' said Floria. 'That liquid really has made him crazy. It's scary!'

The wind around them seemed to lose control and was bouncing them up and down so that they had to hold onto the gondola very tightly as well as keep an eye on Irian who didn't seem to care about the freak weather around him.

'I can't get to the ground' screamed Grandfather and his voice was like a tiny whisper because of the loud wind. 'It's impossible.'

'You have to!' Nuro screamed back, his scream transformed into a mere murmur. 'I'm freezing and I can't hold on to this gondola anymore.'

'I'm going to kill you. I'll have your blood!' screamed Irian who would have done anything to set himself free.

'This is not a wind' shouted Grandfather. 'It's a hurricane. Hold on, children, we'll show that wind. When we get there, I'll stay with Irian in the balloon and you two go and get the leaves. I won't be able to attach the balloon properly and we can't lug Irian around.'

'Ok' replied Nuro hunching his shoulders against the wind. He could hardly stand up once they reached the ground. 'We'll try.'

Nuro and Floria managed to get out of the balloon and were trying to advance while the icy wind nipped at their faces. It seemed to them as if they were moving against a solid wall every time they tried to go a step further. The Magnesiour Field wasn't far from where they were standing, maybe thirty yards, but they had such difficulty in advancing that it took them maybe half an hour to get there. Its flowers were not unusual in shape or size but they had an incredible perfume. Nuro and Floria later both agreed they smelled like rosemary.

'Are you ok, Floria?' shouted Nuro, but Floria just couldn't hear him, so they both used sign language.

Nuro held tight to his sister's hand and he noticed that it was freezing cold.

'I have no feeling in my fingers' Nuro said to his sister. 'Can you tear off a bit of leaf?'

'I'll try' replied Floria whose fingers were also numb.

When they finally reached the Forest, they both tried to rest by holding onto one of the flower stalks. The stalk was smooth and pleasant to the touch and it helped them to rest a bit. However, the problem was that the petals were high up out of reach. Nuro then had the idea of placing his hands like the rungs of a ladder so that his sister could climb up and get hold of the petals. But even then, Floria couldn't get to them so, in the end, she had to climb onto Nuro's shoulders and reach up to its fan-shaped petals. This way she managed to tear off a part, but only a small piece as it petals were as thick as elephants' skin.

'Excellent. Well done!' shouted Nuro, putting his thumb up.

It was a little easier to get back to the balloon as the wind was now blowing against their backs and helping them to advance.

'We won't be able to make him tea here' said Grandfather, once they got to the balloon. 'We'll have to find a calmer place.'

'You're right' replied Nuro and they all got back on the balloon and were aloft in a few seconds.

'I have no control of this balloon' shouted Grandfather, though his voice rang hollow. 'I think we'll have to let her decide where to go.'

The wind seemed heartless, not caring about them being tired and Irian unwell; it was flinging them high up in the air without mercy – they were like cocktails in a shaker. Apart from that, its whooshing was piercing their eardrums but they couldn't block the noise out as they had to hold on tight to the gondola.

Then, suddenly, the wind flung them out of its space and into the calm air, as if it had had enough of them now, like a spoilt child throwing down an old toy. Floria, Grandfather and Nuro rejoiced at leaving the County of Strong Winds far behind them and with it the many dangers they had met. They landed safely near a beautiful lake and went on to make the tea for Irian. Irian of course didn't want to drink it and spat it out, so they were obliged to force his mouth open to get at least some of it down. It took a lot of effort but they finally managed. He suddenly calmed down and stopped kicking and shouting. At one point he was no longer moving, but then he started vomiting. Seeing this, Nuro, whose stomach had also suffered from all the tumbling up and down in the balloon, found himself doing the same thing.

'Yuck, grandpa, can you get me some water, please?' said Irian, who seemed to have got back to his normal state.

'You're ok again!' Grandfather gave a great whoop of joy, throwing his arms around his grandson and forgetting he was ill.

'Ok again? What do you mean?' asked Irian, confused at the state Grandfather and two friends were in.

'Do you think he's just faking it to escape from us or do you think he's really ok?' asked Nuro. 'I just have no more energy to chase him around.'

'What are you talking about?' asked Irian, bewildered.

'You touched that water and lost your memory' explained Floria. 'We'll tell you all about it but let's have a rest first. But I have to say you were unbearable.'

Nearby there was a soapwort plant whose leaves lathered in water just like soap, so they used this to wash themselves in the lake. They had the rest they desperately needed in the dappled shade of a beautiful pink flower.

'I'm sorry, children, but we can't stay here much longer. We have to get back before dark because I haven't got a clue where we are, so it might take some time to find our way home' said Grandfather.

On the way back they told Irian what had happen and he could hardly believe it. He couldn't stop apologising for his behaviour and felt like kicking himself when he saw what he had done to Nuro's arm which was all swollen and blue. He remembered absolutely nothing of their journey although he tried really hard. He only recalled the bucket being pulled up and the rest seemed to be erased from his memory forever.

'The Creatures will pay for that' he said. 'I could have got us all into real trouble or even got us killed.'

'You see how evil they are' said Nuro.

'How come nobody in the town knows about that river?' inquired Irian.

'Don't forget, it's all just a legend in their eyes' replied Nuro.

'Well, I reckon it's because they don't want to know' replied Grandfather. 'Behind knowledge, there is responsibility and if you know something you want to get to know it better, don't you? That's why people prefer not to know things and that way they don't have to ask themselves any questions because their minds are empty. But we can't shield them from the truth forever.'

'I wonder how Peena knows about it?' Irian thought aloud.

'Well, you'll have to ask her. She knows because she wants to know and because she's not afraid of the consequences. She realises there are things that are bound to happen whether we want them to or not. She also knows that we can prevent certain things from happening if we take some preliminary measures and that's why I admire the woman. She prefers to nip danger in the bud.'

'In any case, I hope I never set eyes on that place again!' exclaimed Nuro.'

The Kindness Creature's Mask

Irian now had two things to worry about; he had to find a way to hide the liquid so that Gadious couldn't get hold of it. Apart from that, he still didn't know what to do with the mask and how to keep it away from the Queen. He wasn't sure how powerful she was and what she was capable of doing to get it back. Irian also wondered what made it so special for Ranna to care so much about it. The mask didn't seem special to him; it didn't look much different from masks that actors wear on stage. Its surface was white and exceptionally smooth, while the expression on it was pleasant, soft and welcoming. Now that he knew that he was Arena and Emo's descendant, Irian had begun to take the mask out before going to bed and he would stroke its cheeks, knowing that the Kindness Creature had helped his ancestors at its own risk. He would even put the mask on his face and look at himself in the mirror for a while, trying to imagine the Kindness Creature's movements and the way it talked. However, he spent most of his time thinking about Arena and Emo and how they had saved the town. He wished so much they could appear in his dream too so that he could talk to them and ask them for help. However, he only had Gadious appearing in his dreams to spoil his tranquillity. Gadious had become unbearable and was using any possible moment to bother Irian, who, exasperated, dearly wished he could get rid of him.

One day, when coming back home, he felt Gadious walking next to him and as there was nobody around, Irian decided to take Mrs Bigone's advice and speak to him.

'Why don't you just leave me alone?' asked Irian.

'Why don't you leave us alone?' replied Gadious, and this was actually the first time that Irian heard his voice, which sounded something like a broken whistle.

'We don't need you in this town, do you understand?' shouted Irian. 'People here want to be left in peace. They don't need anybody to decide anything for them. They know how to live their lives and make their decisions.'

'The Destiners are still in our hands and under our rule. We chose their ancestors' destinies which reflect on their descendants too because your life and your destiny also depend on your ancestors and their path. What do you think: do you think that every Destiner is independent and that his life is not connected to that of his ancestors? Of course you depend on the people who are connected to you by blood and you passively share their experiences whether you want to or not' said Gadious with a voice that was full of hatred and pride at the same time.

'How would you feel if somebody was deciding on your life?' asked Irian but Gadious didn't reply.

'Give me the mask back, or I shall make your life unbearable' ordered Gadious.

'You'll get nothing from me, all right? By the way, why did Ranna take this mask from the Kindness Creature?'

'She's not Ranna!' said Gadious. 'She's your Queen and this is how you must refer to her. Didn't you read the message under the mask: "Whoever betrays the Queen will lose his face"? It had to pay its mistake.'

'She's horrible! How could she take its mask off? What happened to the Kindness Creature?' inquired Irian.

'You don't want to know.'

'I'll make you pay for it. I'll complete the plan Arena and Emo started and you'll be gone forever' threatened Irian.

'Wait until we get our powers back and you'll be crawling at my feet.'

'Is that what you call having power; laughing at others and using cruelty? I'm not afraid of you. If you were as powerful as you think you are, you wouldn't have been defeated by Arena and Emo in the first place. If you have been defeated once, why can't you be defeated again?'

Irian could feel that Gadious had no answer to this and that his anger was ever growing, given that Irian didn't fear him at all, which was something the Creatures weren't used to. Irian was so angry that they could have tortured him and he still wouldn't have given up. There were some people in Destin who had no real opinion about the Creatures and felt indifferent towards what had happened in their town's past. They thought that they should just live their lives in one way or another, but Irian couldn't stand this way of thinking.

Later on that afternoon, Irian was lounging under a flower in his garden, not really concentrating on the book he was reading. The sun was peeping out from the clouds, appearing almost like the pupil of an eye observing the world below. Uncle Tattoo came to pay him an unexpected visit.

'I thought you would have come to my exhibition the other day' said Uncle Tattoo. 'Apparently, you had something more important to do.'

Irian winced to think that he couldn't tell his uncle the truth, but he had no choice about it until the mystery of the Creatures had been resolved. Therefore, he preferred to change the subject and nudge the conversation towards something else.

'You know, I met Smeerius Newance' said Irian. 'I didn't realise you two knew each other.'

'Smeerius Newance' repeated Uncle Tattoo somewhat pensively. 'I used to see him a lot, but he doesn't seem to socialize with his old friends anymore. Every time I go to see him, he's busy. I haven't had a proper talk with him in a long while.'

'Why?' asked Irian.

'Who knows?' sighed Uncle Tattoo. 'There's nothing more complicated than human nature. If people change, there's probably a reason for it, though I must say; their reasons are not always easy to work out. But, how come you met Smeerius?'

'Through his son Smodge.'

Irian remembered that Smodge had tried to call him when he went to the River Irav. It was while he was under the spell of that liquid, so Nuro had answered the talkastick for him and made something up. Irian thought that there was a big mystery behind that family and he was eager to find out more about it.

'So, are you interested in a tattoo today?' asked Uncle Tattoo, interrupting Irian's thoughts.

'Can I have the Kindness Creature this time?' asked Irian, trying to test his uncle's attitude towards this Creature. He suddenly thought of Smeerius' question when he had asked him why Uncle Tattoo drew the Creatures, given that he didn't believe in the Legend. Irian wondered whether his uncle knew anything about Ranna and her Creatures but just didn't want to admit it to anybody.

'The Kindness Creature?' repeated Uncle Tattoo quite suspiciously.

As Irian's mother came to join them at that moment, Irian certainly didn't want to speak about the Creatures in her presence. However, Uncle Tattoo kept his gaze fixed on Irian, waiting for an answer, and Irian had the impression that his pupils had turned into black question marks. At the same time he heard a strange noise coming from his room – like a door slamming, and the three of them turned their heads. Irian's mother didn't even have time to say hello to her brother but Irian was already running for his bedroom.

When he entered, he immediately noticed that his little rucksack containing the Kindness Creature's mask was missing. Where he had left it there was now only a note, evidently dashed off in a hurry. Irian felt like pulling his hair out at his own carelessness. He picked the note up from the floor, and read these words:

"You can't win against us. The sooner you realise, the better it will be for you! Queen Ranna"

Irian was so enraged with himself, yet there was nothing to be done. In his anger, he took the Creatures' posters down from the wall as he couldn't bear to look at them anymore. He wondered how Ranna had managed to enter his room without being noticed. She couldn't have got in through the front door nor could she have climbed in through his bedroom window, which had been closed anyway. But what troubled him the most was that he still didn't know the mask's power and in a way he preferred not to know, now that he had lost it.

With these thoughts, he heard his mother climbing the stairs and calling him, so he quickly left the room and hurried to see her.

'Is everything all right?' she inquired.

'Oh, yes' replied Irian, trying to put on his best face so as to conceal his inner state from her. 'It was just the wind I think.'

'But there is no wind' she commented.

'It might have been a draught then' said Irian, avoiding all eye contact with his mother.

'Strange' she said 'Irian...'

When she pronounced his name, he thought, "That's it! She's got me".

'I have to go and get something and when I get back we can have dinner with Uncle Tattoo. What do you think?'

Irian could just nod as words seemed beyond his grasp, suppressed by his inner feelings. He went back into the garden where Uncle Tattoo was sitting, flicking through magazines. Irian went to sit next to him, and his mother brought them some cake.

'If you want some more, it's in the kitchen' said Irian's mother before leaving.

Once she'd left, he was alone with Uncle Tattoo.

'How do you know how to draw the Creatures?' asked Irian.

'Why do you ask me that?' asked Uncle Tattoo back, putting away his magazine.

'Because I was wondering how you can draw them if you've never seen them' replied Irian quite confidently.

Uncle Tattoo was comfortably placed in his chair, his feet up on a small tool, so that when Irian asked the question, he put his feet abruptly to the ground turning his chair towards his nephew.

'Why are you suddenly so interested in that?' asked Uncle Tattoo.

'Talking about Smeerius before, it's just that he asked me the same question' replied Irian. 'I mean, you don't believe in our Legend. So, why do you give it any attention then?'

Uncle Tattoo drew in a long breath.

'When I was about your age, I used to dream about the Creatures' said Uncle Tattoo. 'They would appear in my dreams and ask me questions. I found them beautiful; they were full of colour, yet they seemed caricatures in a way. They were so different, yet so much the same and each of them thought it was the most important. So, in order not to forget them, I decided to draw them to show them to others too.'

'Why did they stop appearing in your dreams?' asked Irian.

'One day I talked to your grandma about this; I told her about my dreams with the Creatures and since that day they just stopped appearing in my dreams.'

'How strange!' commented Irian. 'And you've never wondered why they disappeared?'

'Well, I suppose it was just a phase in my life. We all go through different stages where we focus our mind on particular things and once we get our answer, we switch to something else.

'So what kind of answer did you get from that experience?' asked Irian.

'When I say you get an answer, it doesn't mean that you get a precise answer to your question, but you just develop a certain attitude towards the subject because you have thought about it for a while. Then, you either leave it or you go more deeply into the subject and spend more time on it.'

'And was that the moment you decided not to believe in the Legend?'

'I'd never believed in the Legend to start with' said Tattoo.

'But how can you not believe in it? There's so much evidence, so much proof?'

'I can't believe in something I haven't seen with my own eyes. And anyway, even if I did believe in it, what would that change?'

'I mean, you can't just ignore things. It would mean that you're just lying to yourself.'

'Irian, there is no written code in life which says what you have to believe in or not. Life is like a blank page – it depends on you what you want to do with it, doesn't it? You must act according to your feelings, not caring how other people will try to impose their opinion on you. Even if the Legend isn't just the Legend, but part of our history, if I don't want to accept it, who can force me to? It's my choice after all.'

Irian felt like shaking his uncle and telling him the truth, but he knew that Uncle Tattoo didn't want to hear it. Irian couldn't decide whether his uncle knew the truth after all but was trying to hide it from him or whether he genuinely did not believe in it. He thought that there must have been another side to the coin, but as Uncle Tattoo didn't seem very keen to go deeper into the subject, Irian decided not to go any further with their conversation that afternoon.

'So, can I have a tattoo of the Kindness Creature?' asked Irian.

'You see, I've been drawing the Creatures for many years now, but nobody has ever asked me to draw the Kindness Creature. Why do you insist on that Creature?'

'I don't know' pretended Irian. 'I suppose I just want to see how you would draw it.'

'To tell you the truth, I don't know how to draw that particular Creature. It never appeared in my dream, so I can't visualise it, but I could try to make something up if you want.'

That very moment, Irian realised that the Creatures couldn't have been only a dream to Uncle Tattoo and that he was either pretending not to know or else he really did consider them all to be simply part of his dreams. Either way, Irian thought that it was a very serious situation because it meant that the Kindness Creature was in danger and he absolutely had to find its mask again.

'It's ok' said Irian. 'Let's eat, I'm feeling slightly peckish.'

✳   ✳   ✳

In the evening, Irian tried to go and see Nuro and Floria, but they weren't at home and he recalled that they had gone away with their parents for a few days. As for Grandfather, he was helping Petalber with his new house, so he realised that there wasn't much to do. Therefore, he decided to go to bed early.

132

He kept on tossing and turning, unable to get to sleep. He couldn't stop thinking about the Kindness Creature and wondering what had happened to it. Apart from that, he had to find a way of getting hold of its mask although such a thing seemed impossible as he didn't even know where to begin searching for it. On the other hand, he felt responsible for the Kindness Creature and was ready to do anything to help it.

As he was thinking so hard, he was soon overcome by a dream. In it he suddenly found himself in a house that he knew very well, but hated so much. It was Gartika's home and she was sitting at her table, her back turned to Irian so that she couldn't see him. By no means did Irian want her to realise he was there, so he hid behind the garden wall. He recognised her laughter which to Irian sounded like the hissing of a snake and always gave him earache. He couldn't really see what she was doing, but she seemed completely immersed in it, whatever it was. From where he was standing it was difficult to see anything, but she must have been holding something because both her hands were on the table.

Then suddenly he heard her phone ringing and Gartika left the table to answer it. The phone was in the sitting room, so she had to leave the room. With the table now clearly in sight, Irian was so astonished at what he saw on it that he could hardly believe his eyes. Right there in front of him, just a few steps away, he saw the Kindness Creature's mask, the very one that had been stolen from him that afternoon. He didn't have time to look at it properly because Gartika came back to the kitchen, still talking on the phone.

'Yes, I have it' he heard her saying to the person on the other end. 'It's finally ours. I'll meet you all later on.'

"So, it's her", thought Irian to himself. "I should have thought of it before. That sleazy nasty woman. How on earth did she get into my room? Why does she need the mask? Who is she meeting later on?" Questions streamed through his mind.

And then, suddenly, Irian woke up. Lying in his bed, he wasn't sure whether he was still asleep as his dream had seemed so real. He switched on the light to see if he could feel Gadious' presence, but there was nothing. Now, the only time he had really wanted to speak to him, he wasn't there. He got dressed, and went downstairs to the sitting room. He noticed that his parents had already gone to bed, so he thought that he could perhaps go and see what Mrs Bigone had to say. He carefully opened the front door and then even more carefully closed it behind him.

He kept on looking around hoping that his parents wouldn't find him stalking around at this late hour. He noticed that Mrs Bigone's lights were still on, so he decided to knock on her door. A few moments later, he heard her footsteps approaching and the door was opened.

'Are you ok?' she said when she saw Irian standing there.

'I need to speak to you. It's important' he answered.

Mrs Bigone let him in and they sat down on the book-sofa. Irian told her what had happened with the mask and described his unusual dream to her.

'But maybe it was just a dream' she said after thinking for a while.

'I don't think so' replied Irian. 'It seemed too real to be just a dream.'

'What makes you think that it wasn't a dream? I mean, how could you possibly know that she has the mask? You would have to be there to see it.'

'It might be a kind of sign. Grandfather told me I was a descendant of Arena and Emo' said Irian seriously.

'You're what?' said Mrs Bigone in disbelief.

Irian explained the conversation he had had with Grandfather the day of the balloon ride.

'That's big news!' exclaimed Mrs Bigone. 'You know what I think we should do? I think we should go and pay Gartika a visit.'

'But she'll never let us in.'

'Well, we won't allow her to see us. If she's not there, that means your dream wasn't actually a dream.'

'Do you mean we should go and spy on her?'

'Not exactly, but we can go and try to find out what she's up to. Give me five minutes. I'll go and get ready.'

She went to get dressed, and Irian noticed that she had put on black clothes, probably to attract as little attention as possible. As they walked along in silence, the cool breeze fanned the streets, plucking at their clothes. They walked quickly, looking around, afraid of being seen. The streets were empty, abandoned by Destiners, who were snuggled comfortably in their beds, unaware of what had been happening in their town.

It took them some time to get to Mrs Gartika's house as she lived in the First Circle of the town. When they arrived, some of the lights in the house were off.

'She might be asleep' whispered Irian.

'Do you know where her bedroom is?' asked Mrs Bigone quietly.

'Yes, I do. But we have to find a way to open the gate. It always makes a creaking noise. I think we'll have to jump over it.

They somehow managed to jump over it without making too much of a clatter. Irian jumped first and Mrs Bigone followed. He had to stifle a giggle at seeing Mrs Bigone jumping over the gate, unused to seeing her in such an undignified role. They approached the bedroom window but the curtains had been drawn so they couldn't see in. The bedroom was at the rear of the house, beside the garden, and they were just about to go around to the other side of the house when they heard the gate creaking. Quickly, they hid behind the wall, waiting for her to go in. She immediately switched the lights on, so that Irian and Mrs Bigone had to be careful to avoid being seen. They sidled up to her kitchen window to see what she was doing and Irian recognised that hooked nose and humped back of hers straight away. He couldn't just keep watching as she might have spotted them, but he tried to peep in every so often. She sat down on the sofa in her sitting room, looking quite contented. Irian could see her lips moving, but unfortunately he couldn't lip-read like Floria. She remained like that for some time, and then stood up and walked to another part of the house. Irian and Mrs Bigone lost sight of her, but she came back not long afterwards.

They both noticed that she had been carrying something, but it was hard to say exactly what. When they finally caught sight of it, they realised it was the Kindness Creature's mask. Irian had to put his hand over his mouth to stop himself crying out. Mrs

Bigone looked hard at him as if trying to tell him "so your dream wasn't just a dream" with her eyes. They also realised that they couldn't do anything to get it back but would have to think of a plan first and then return to get the mask. Irian and Mrs Bigone waited for Gartika to go to sleep, as it was risky to leave the place while she was still awake. They were baffled by the fact that she had gone to bed with her lights on. It was weird as nobody else in Destin would ever have done that – the Destiners feared that light would attract the Creatures.

Luckily, they didn't have to wait long; however, jumping over the gate again seemed harder this time. Once they were safely on the other side of the gate they quickened their pace to get as far away as possible from Gartika's house.

'I don't understand anything anymore' said Irian once they were a long way from the place.

'The best way to solve a problem is to divide it into several segments and then deal with it by trying to find a solution for each segment' reasoned Mrs Bigone. 'This is exactly what we should do. There's no point in torturing yourself. We'll find the answers; it's all just a matter of time. The most important thing at the moment is that we know where to look for the mask, and that's what we wanted to know, isn't it?'

'Yes' replied Irian. 'But the Kindness Creature might be tortured by the Queen and there's nothing I can do about it.'

'Don't worry. They might be horrible to the Kindness Creature, but they still need it, so the Creature will be ok' reasoned Mrs Bigone. 'Irian, some things in life can be very frustrating, but you can't run away from them, or else you'll just make things worse. I think you should go back to sleep and let things settle in your head. Once you get a good rest, you'll be better prepared to handle the situation.'

* * *

Irian spent the following days thinking about how to get the mask back and no good ideas would come. Apart from that, the First Circle wasn't just round the corner, so he couldn't tell what

Gartika had been doing. He thought it was lucky that she hadn't taken the liquid, which would have been a real disaster, as he didn't want to go back to that horrible place. However, he looked forward to discovering the secret messages. Mrs Bigone told him that they were going to visit the Amphitheatre as soon as she had got permission from the Local Council to examine the mysterious boards.

It was the cannonball flower season, which Irian loved. They grew on the outskirts of Destin and had one particularity. When a cannonball flower's fruits were swinging in the wind and bumping into neighbouring fruits, the banging noise sounded like cannon fire. Irian would sit and wait for hours for this to happen and would then imitate the noise the flower's fruit produced. It was also a good way to distract his very busy thoughts, which kept on racing around in his head in search of solutions.

Irian wasn't the only one interested in cannonball flowers; he would often come across other children with the same intention. One day while waiting for the "explosion", he met Smodge and his father, which was a nice surprise for him. Irian somehow couldn't stop asking himself what kind of taste he evoked in Smeerius' mouth, and even felt like asking him.

'I've already seen four of them exploding today' said Smodge to Irian.

'Have you?' asked Irian. 'I've just arrived. They're amazing, aren't they?'

'You know, it was the Fun Creature who thought this flower up' said Smodge.

'Really? ' exclaimed Irian. 'How do you know?'

'It's written in that book I was given for *Imagine and Live it Day*; remember the one I showed you?'

'Yes, I do. So, what does it say?'

'It says that the Fun Creature wanted to play a joke on the Cruelty and the Arrogance Creatures, as it couldn't stand their behaviour. So, one day it invited them for a picnic in the country, making sure to find a place near the flowers. It was a windy day and at one point the fruits of the flowers started making a terrifying noise. The Cruelty and the Arrogance Creatures ran like mad, thinking that somebody was about to attack them, while the Fun Creature burst into laughter, proud of its invention. After that, the Cruelty Creature was even more cruel to the Fun Creature and the Arrogance Creature was even more arrogant.'

'How excellent, I didn't know that' commented Irian.

'I didn't see you at Tattoo's exhibition' said Smeerius, who was wearing a hat, covering the tattoo of the Creative Creature. 'I was very surprised not to see you there. Tattoo is getting better and better at his drawings. He's absolutely amazing!'

Irian had the impression that he would have to pay for the fact that he hadn't gone to Uncle Tattoo's exhibition for the rest of his life, as everybody kept on asking him why he hadn't turned up.

'I was invited elsewhere so I couldn't go' lied Irian. 'How's your work going by the way?'

'I've actually made a portrait of you' replied Smeerius.

'A portrait of me?' repeated Irian, astonished.

'Well, it was supposed to be a surprise, but as you are asking me about my job, I'm giving you the answer.'

'That's great' said Irian, somewhat confused, thinking that he might finally be able to discover the taste he created in Smeerius' mouth. 'I can't wait to see it.'

'Come whenever you want, we're all very fond of you' said Smeerius warmly. 'You'll be very welcome.'

'Thank you. That's very nice of you' Irian was quite baffled by such an invitation.

'If you like it, I'll give it to you' proposed Smeerius.

'If it's as good as your other paintings, I'll be more than happy to have it' replied Irian. 'The next time I visit the First Circle, I'll definitely pop round.'

The Boards of the Amphitheatre

Nothing happened for a few days. Irian had no news from Grandfather or from Mrs Bigone, and he was growing more and more impatient. For some strange reason, Gadious had stopped annoying him, so Irian had even begun to think he wasn't interesting to anyone anymore.

But then, one afternoon, he received a call from Mrs Bigone who asked him to come to see her.

'I've got a letter from the mayor' she said, already waving at him with it from the doorstep.

'Have you?' said Irian. 'That's good news. So what does it say?'

'Have a look!'

Irian took the letter and started to read it. It read :

"Dear Mrs Bigone,

Further to your request concerning the Amphitheatre boards, we have examined your case and we are happy to allow you access for your work. However, you will be entitled to examine the boards strictly within the limits of the Amphitheatre and not to venture beyond these limits i.e. to the inner quarters.

We hope that this opportunity will be of benefit to your new book.

Yours sincerely,

Slavio Fiume

SLAVIO FIUME"

'This is wonderful!' exclaimed Irian. 'So, when are we going?'

'Tomorrow' replied Mrs Bigone. 'Listen, what are we going

to do with that liquid?'

'What do you mean?'

'You know how dangerous it is. We'll have to transport it in some sort of special bottle with a pointed end, so that we don't have to touch the liquid when applying it to the boards.'

'My mum might have something' said Irian. 'Otherwise, I'm sure we can buy something or other.'

'Can you take care of that, and I'll organise the rest?'

'Sure' replied Irian. 'Do you think they suspect anything?'

'No, I don't think so, otherwise, they wouldn't have granted my request. But, we have to pretend to be as natural as possible.'

* * *

Irian didn't sleep all that night and neither did Mrs Bigone. Their minds shared the same thought, and their thought only differed in a few details. For Mrs Bigone, the boards were a challenge as well as revenge regarding the Local Council's negative response to her discoveries, while Irian felt a great responsibility towards saving the town. In a way, he had no personal interest in this affair at all.

They decided to visit the Amphitheatre very early, to avoid other visitors, as they didn't want anybody to find out what they were doing. At the entrance, they had to show the letter to the guards, who looked at them suspiciously. Irian wondered which faces were hiding behind those masks, as the guards never revealed them for security purposes. Mrs Bigone went through the check as if dealing with some unimportant formality, while Irian had to make fists, so that they wouldn't somehow notice how his hands were trembling. He was only hoping they wouldn't ask him to open the bag where he kept the bottle containing the magic liquid.

'What have you got in that bag?' asked one of the guards, and Irian suddenly felt his body become as stiff as a board.

'It's our packed lunch for later on' said Mrs Bigone 'Do you mind if we have a picnic in there? You know, this sun is very good for my old bones.'

The two guards just looked at her and then at Irian, and then their eyes paused on the bag.

'I want to see inside' said one of them.

Irian was already projecting a film in his head in which the guards were about to confiscate the liquid and where the mayor was calling his parents and telling them the truth about his recent activities. Mrs Bigone had obviously noticed that Irian wasn't feeling himself, so she opened the bag herself and showed its contents to the guard. Inside, there were sandwiches, napkins, a notepad and two bottles, one of which was hiding the liquid.

'You can go in, but don't stay too long' said one of them finally.

Irian had the feeling that something exceptionally heavy had just rolled down his back, and his body appeared to him to be lighter than ever. The door they were about to enter wasn't just the door of the Amphitheatre, but also a door leading to something very mysterious, something that he had so wanted to reveal. It was the border between his world and the world of the Creatures.

'Are you ok, Irian? ' asked Mrs Bigone once they were in.

'I'm still working on it' replied Irian. 'How did you manage to remain so indifferent? I felt like you must have been able to read my thoughts on my forehead.'

'Feelings are a good thing, but you have to know where and when you can show them. Being sensitive helps you to feel things in your life, but it doesn't always help you when dealing with other people, you know. If you lay everything from the kitchen out on the table, it doesn't mean that people will eat it all, just like not all of your feelings are going to be accepted by everyone' advised Mrs Bigone. 'Anyway, I think we should leave the outer boards for the end and concentrate on the ones inside the Amphitheatre.'

The sun was still floating low down on the horizon providing them with a faint light that penetrated timidly through the arched windows of the Amphitheatre. Irian had never seen the place so empty, and it now seemed huge. The boards were practically everywhere, like well-protected reminders of a secret past. Mrs Bigone was trying to work out their order, and thought they should follow them round clockwise, starting with the boards

141

next to the entrance door. The boards differed in size; some were very small, and some were as tall as Irian. They were made of stone and seemed to contain no letters. If you looked at them closely, you would never have thought there was anything written on them at all. Their surfaces were rough and unequal, like the surfaces of a broken stone.

'I think we should have a look at this one first' said Mrs Bigone after having a good look around.

'Shall I get the liquid out?' asked Irian. 'Do you think it's safe enough?'

'Yes, I don't think those two will come and bother us again.'

Irian took the bottle out. He had closed it tight and even put some sticky tape around its top to make sure the liquid wouldn't spill out.

'Good' said Mrs Bigone. 'I think we can finally proceed. Ready?'

'I'm dying to see what they say.'

Mrs Bigone took the bottle carefully and undid its top. She tried to smell the liquid, but it had no smell. She put on a pair of thick gloves and then applied a drop of it to the tips of her fingers. She did so with great precaution while Irian took a few steps back. Once she had squeezed out a small quantity, she tried to rub it into the chosen board. She did it very meticulously and with rapid movements, spreading the liquid from top to bottom. For a moment, there were no signs of any change, so Mrs Bigone started to think that she hadn't used enough of it. She was just about to pour some more liquid onto her fingers, when she noticed the letters starting to appear. She recognised the alphabet that she had spent so much time working on. The letters were large in size, and they had no colour but rather seemed engraved in the stone.

'They are disappearing' said Mrs Bigone.

'What do they say?' asked Irian astonished.

' She read:

"Dear Creature. Queen Ranna constructed this Amphitheatre by blowing the tallest dandelion clock to be found over the place where it now stands today. Its million tiny speed parachutes filled

the air and having floated for a while on the soft breeze, descended slowly to the earth. It was from these seeds that the great Amphitheatre sprang. It will never be damaged by the passing of time. The Amphitheatre is the home of the Sudba Creatures, and a forbidden place for any Destiner. The Creatures' role is to participate in creating a destiny for each inhabitant born in the town of Destin."

'Amazing!' said Irian. 'That's why the Amphitheatre still looks brand new.'

'Well, let's have a look at this big board. It's very difficult to read because the letters are disappearing so quickly. So, let's see.'

She repeated her technique and then waited for the letters to appear. When they came out, she read out:

"Before a baby is born each destiny is to be written in the Destiny Book, which is the Sudba Creatures' most precious object. The Destiny Book contains a life description of every Destiner and it may not be altered in any way or at any time during his life. Throughout his existence, the person is to follow the lines of his left hand, which represent his life path. The life path is created during the destiny decision ceremony, which preferably takes place a few days following the baby's conception.

The Creatures must remain aloof from the Destiners. The various Creatures themselves each represent individual human qualities. The Creatures bestow their powers by drawing out a number at random and this number will indicate the Creature's power i.e. the strength of the given life quality. The numbers range from one to a hundred; the higher the number is, the stronger that quality will be in the Destiner in question. Once the Creature has pulled the number out, it must cast its power in the Destiny Book. When all the Creatures have cast their powers, the Queen validates these powers by placing her hand on top of the given page. Consequently, at the baby's birth, the Queen transfers the chosen life path onto the infant's left hand by means of a diamond pen. She places the pen on infant's hand and the pen itself copies the life path from the great Destiny Book. The lines are clearly marked to represent the person's destiny.

It should be noted that not everything can be decided in this way – not everything is fated. Destiners must deal with what fate has allotted them, however, within their experience and on their path, there is always room for choice. A person might be destined to be a great singer, but if he catches a cold the night before his first performance, his voice will not be of its usual quality. However, this will not necessarily prevent him from becoming a great singer. Everything depends on how the individual deals with the obstacle on his path."

'I see' said Irian. 'You know, this might be the book I dreamt about. It contained descriptions of everybody's destiny apart from my own because I'm descended from Arena and Emo.'

'I wonder what happened to the book' said Mrs Bigone.

'So do I. Does the Jealousy Creature mention it in its diary?'

'It does speak about a precious book, but reading its diary I didn't really understand the kind of book it was talking about.'

'Do you think the Destiners knew they did have some choice in their destiny? I mean the bit about the future great singer and his cold.'

'Well, it's difficult to say, but the Soothsayers might have helped them in some way. If we could somehow get to know more about the Soothsayers, then we could probably understand things better.'

The sun had been climbing up the horizon and before Irian and Mrs Bigone had realised it, its huge shiny mass had reached the centre of the sky, as if it was trying to impose itself over the fake sun ornamenting the Amphitheatre floor. The sunrays had obviously seduced the Destiners' spirits, who were just then hurrying out to bathe in its warmth and take advantage of their beautiful town.

'I think we'll have to continue our secret investigation another time' said Mrs Bigone. 'We don't want any intruders, do we?'

'You're right' replied Irian. 'The place is starting to swarm with people.'

'But, we've done a good job, haven't we? I just hope we'll

have enough liquid to uncover all the boards.'

'Oh, yes' said Irian. 'I have plenty left at home.'

Mrs Bigone had got out a towel for them to sit down for a nice cold drink that she had prepared at home. It was cool and welcome, serving well to freshen up their minds that had been so busy thinking. After all, it was nice to spend some time in this magical site, embroidered with secrets and mysteries. If those walls could talk, thought Irian to himself, they would probably say the most amazing things.

'What is a destiny anyway?' asked Irian.

'Destiny is something that you are born with; it can be a gift or a burden. Either way, you cannot modify it. It's your path and your lesson through this existence, which is just a part of your spiritual life.'

'So, if I'd been given a horrible destiny, there would be nothing I could do about it?'

'There are no horrible or wonderful destinies, but there are only lessons. Some of them are more difficult just as some of them are easier to learn. However, I know that we all have our own special golden hot air balloon.'

'A golden hot air balloon?'

'Each of us has a golden hot air balloon that appears to us once in our life. It is often covered with dirt and awfully smelly, but everything depends on whether we're going to recognise it as our special golden air balloon and enter inside.'

Irian liked the idea of the golden hot air balloon and wondered whether the whole story with the Sudba Creatures wasn't simply hiding his own golden hot air balloon. The River Irav-experience and even the guards' questioning that morning; might not these situations simply have been "the dirt" covering his golden hot air balloon?'

When they were leaving the Amphitheatre, the two guards just looked at them in silence.

'What do you want to do now?' asked Mrs Bigone.

'I'm going to visit Smodge' answered Irian. 'His father has made a portrait of me, so I'm curious to see it.'

'Smeerius has made a portrait of you? That's something.'

'Incredible, isn't it?'

'Why did he do that?'

'No idea. I inspired him for some reason.'

'Well, enjoy your portrait, then.'

'Mrs Bigone' said Irian. 'How can we get to know more about the Destiny Book?'

'I'll go back to the Amphitheatre and try to read the rest of the boards but I'll go at night because it's impossible to do anything in the morning. There are too many people and it's too risky during the day anyway.'

'Can I come?'

'Of course, but you'll have to be careful about your parents.'

'Sure. I'll come to see you later.'

Mrs Bigone accompanied Irian to Smodge's house, which was surrounded by the most beautiful tawny-red sweet-smelling flowers that varied from trumpet-shaped to star-shaped with long, strap-like leaves climbing up the fence, spiral after spiral. They formed a natural flower barrier protecting the Newance family house. At the front door was an unusual gadget used to announce visitors; the Newance family had put up a little keyboard at the door, for the visitor to type in his name and have a personalised greeting at the same time. So, when Irian typed in his name, he heard the machine saying: "*Welcome Irian Horvats. Smodge is looking forward to seeing you.*" The door opened, allowing the magnificent view that was familiar to Irian. He saw Smodge walking towards him and waving in the distance.

'I liked the door message' said Irian once he had reached Smodge.

'I'm glad you did' replied Smodge. 'You can stay for lunch, can't you?'

Irian noticed that Smodge was wearing a beautiful necklace of reddish mineral beads, and Irian thought the colour went well with his bristly red hair.

'Nice necklace' said Irian.

'It's made of garnet, which is my birthstone and it represents constancy. What's your birthstone?'

'I don't know. I've never thought about it.'

146

'We can have a look together if you want. You know, during the Sudba Creatures' government, every baby was given a destiny necklace made of the appropriate birthstone.'

'Who told you that?' asked Irian, baffled at Smodge knowing about destiny necklaces.

'My dad. We even have somebody's necklace at home. If you want, I can show it to you.'

'How did you get it?' asked Irian, even more bewildered.

'You'll have to ask my dad, he'd probably be able to tell you.'

Irian found the Newance family the most mysterious and secretive family he had ever met. Smodge was mentioning the destiny necklace as if talking about any old necklace to be bought on the weekly market in Destin's main street. Irian wondered what else he was going to discover; what else was waiting to be unearthed behind the magnificent flower barrier of the Newance family home.

'Could I see the necklace?' asked Irian quite timidly.

'Of course' replied Smodge. 'Let's go to my room and I'll show it to you.'

'Are you by yourself?'

'No, my mum is working in her study and my brother must be around somewhere' replied Smodge. 'I'll go and get some cakes. You can go on up ahead and wait for me in my room.'

'Do you need any help?'

'Oh, I'll be ok thanks. Have a look around my room and help yourself to anything you want.'

Irian thought to himself that Smodge would probably feel claustrophobic in his own room which wasn't even a quarter of the size of Smodge's. He liked its layout and the way the things were arranged in it; he normally didn't like having too many things around, and although Smodge's room was full of objects, Irian liked the way they had been placed around. Smodge had a huge library, covering the entire left wall and it seemed like some kind of treasured collection of the most interesting books.

'Have you read any more of that book you showed me last time?' asked Irian once Smodge was back with a plate full of all sorts of cakes.

'I've finished it actually.'

'So, is it good?'

'Oh, it's brilliant. Some stories are really funny. I like the story about the Impatience Creature.'

'The Impatience Creature?' repeated Irian 'Can we read it together?'

'Sure. The book is just behind you. See it?'

Irian turned round to get the book, which was large and heavy, made of beautiful clover-shaped leaves.

'Do you want to read it for us?' asked Smodge. 'I like it when people read stories aloud. For some reason, the story doesn't sound so good when I read it by myself.'

'Well, if you want. So, let's see...'

"The Impatience Creature was so impatient that it even slept with its shoes on, so that if something happened, it could be on the spot immediately to learn all the details of what was going on. The worst punishment for the Creature was to keep it in suspense. A few moments of waiting was real mental torture, as the Impatience Creature just couldn't wait for anything and had to know everything straight away. When the Creatures were called to draw out their numbers in the ceremony that was held regularly, it was almost painful for the Impatience Creature. The ceremony was to decide on the extent to which the quality a Creature represented was to be important in a baby's life, and the Impatience Creature would hover next to each Creature to see the number they had pulled out almost before the Creature had seen it itself! Sometimes, it would even look over its shoulders, unable to wait for them to announce their numbers to the others and to the Queen of course. In any case, the Impatience Creature always had to be the first one around; the first one to see what was for breakfast, lunch or dinner – the first one to know anything happening in the walls of the Amphitheatre. Of course, this is why it got on so well with the Curiosity Creature, who also had to stick its nose in wherever possible. On one occasion the Fear Creature even found the Impatience Creature hiding in the letterbox, waiting for the letters to arrive, as it was so impatient to see their contents. This had given the Fear Creature a good old fright but the Fear

Creature would get scared for no reason anyway. Its heart had been pounding so quickly that all the Creatures were worried for its life. Following that event, the Queen ordered a smaller letterbox to make it impossible for the Impatience Creature to get up to such a silly thing again.

One day, the Queen got really angry with the Impatience Creature, as it had entered her office without permission to try to read some papers concerning the Creatures which the Queen was about to tell them of that afternoon. In order to punish the Impatience Creature, she made it wait for the whole day before letting it discover what she was going to announce. The poor Impatience Creature, it spent a sleepless night and as it simply couldn't bear to wait, it went to see the Honesty Creature because it knew that the Honesty Creature wouldn't lie to anyone. The Queen was furious at them both, so the Honesty and the Impatience Creatures weren't allowed to participate in the Creatures' meetings for a good month or so.

This was a month during which the Impatience Creature spent everything it had to bribe the other Creatures to tell it what was happening around the Amphitheatre, which of course the Queen didn't know. The Impatience Creature was always trotting around at everybody's feet getting in everyone's way, and if you weren't careful, it would make you stumble in your answers to its annoying questions."

'Well, I must say I can be very much like that Creature sometimes' said Irian. 'So, could you show me that necklace?'

'Yes, sure. And we have to see the list of birthstones too. Well, let's go down to the sitting room.'

Irian had invented a game in his mind where the stairs of the piano keyboard-shaped staircase in Smodge's house played different sounds when they were stepped on. If he went slowly, the steps produced soft, easy music in his head, whereas if he went up or down quickly, the music was hectic and loud, which amused him a lot. He would even miss his step just like you do when playing music – you don't play the keys in the right order after all.

When they arrived, the sitting room seemed endless to Irian, with its massive windows, which looked like they were trying to provide enough glass space for every single sunray to enter the room.

'Here's the destiny necklace' said Smodge, waving a very delicate object that was shining in his hand.

'Wow!' exclaimed Irian.

The necklace was made of brownish mineral beads and there was also a little pendant that attracted Irian's attention the most. The pendant was in the shape of a hand and there were lines on the palm. Nobody in Destin had lines on their palms, so Irian was surprised to see a hand with lines on. There were three principal lines covering the palm and then some smaller lines, carved into different places of the palm.

'How did they know which birthstone suited the baby?' asked Irian.

'Well, there are different birthstones and they are not the same for everyone. What the Queen did was to put a neutral mineral into the baby's hand, and then wait for the colour to appear by itself. She would then choose the right birthstone for the baby depending on the colour that had come out. I have one of these neutral minerals, so we can test your birthstone if you want.'

'But, what was the point of having a birthstone?'

'Each birthstone has a different energy which it transfers onto you. There are many different energies around us and a birthstone is a kind of personalised energy. Do you want to discover your birthstone?'

'Why not!'

Smodge went to get a transparent, neutral mineral to decide on Irian's birthstone. To Irian, Smodge's house seemed like a magician's sleeve; it hid such incredible and interesting things, and you never knew what you were going to discover.

'Right. So now you have to take it and put it in your left hand and then wait for a few moments' said Smodge, holding the mineral in a pair of tweezers.

'Why do you need tweezers?'

'Because if I touch it, I will interfere with my energy and then we won't be able to tell if the result is correct.'

Irian took the neutral mineral in his hand as Smodge had instructed him to do. The mineral was cold, but its touch was pleasant and Irian felt some kind of vibration coming out of it, and flowing through his body. The mineral itself was small and smooth, but its energy seemed strong and direct.

'Ok, let's see what it says' said Smodge.

Irian opened his hand and the mineral that had been transparent a few moments ago, was now radiating in a beautiful green colour.

'You need peridot, just like my father' exclaimed Smodge.

'What is peridot?'

'It's a mineral that provides you with married happiness' replied Smodge, giggling slightly.

'Oh, come on, Smodge!'

'It's true' replied Smodge. 'You might need it one day.'

Suddenly, they heard the front door opening and somebody whistling in the corridor. It was a lively melody filling the house.

'That's my dad' said Smodge. 'He likes whistling and I can't stand it. Sometimes he whistles just to irritate me. He says that seeing different people and objects creates sounds in his mind and this inspires him, so he whistles to represent the sound they create when he sees them.'

'Hello, Irian' said Smeerius once he had entered the sitting room. 'Finally! I thought you'd forgotten us.'

'Oh, no, I really enjoy coming here. It's just that you live quite a long way from my house.'

'I've just had a drink with Obeese. As a matter of fact, we were talking about you.'

'Really? I haven't seen Obeese for a long time. I wonder what has become of him' Irian thought to himself that he hadn't seen Obeese since their meeting on Legend Day. It now seemed to him that he had completely lost touch with him.

'He's fine, but quite busy' replied Smeerius, getting himself a drink. 'I seem to remember promising to show you the portrait.'

'I'm more than curious to see it.'

'Well, do follow me, please.'

Irian wondered what else he was going to discover about this mysterious house, which had a surprise at every corner like the pop-up books he used to have when he was younger. He had never known what was going to pop up from behind the closed windows and doors of the pages.

'You've never been to my study, have you?' asked Smeerius once they had arrived at his study.

'I think you need time to visit your house. It seems like a county all of its own; every room hides a different story.'

'Creative spirit needs space to move and explore; creativity doesn't like limits, and given that every house needs external walls, I thought I could, then, have them as large as possible so as not to sense those limits.'

'My parents are more into a cosier atmosphere and smaller surfaces, but my imagination still finds a way to break through those restrictions. It even goes well beyond the limits I'd say.'

'I'm not surprised you two share the same mineral' interrupted Smodge.

'It says that it represents married happiness' said Smeerius. 'I think that's wrong; I think it represents creativity and originality. All the people I know who are into art share this same mineral. Your Uncle Tattoo is one of them and I think he's more than original.'

'Really? I can't imagine Uncle Tattoo being involved in such business. If there were an Anti-Superstition Creature, my uncle would probably have received a hundred of its points at the Creatures' ceremony. No way can you make him believe in anything unless he sees it with his own eyes. It must also be one of my grandma's qualities. She's like that too' Irian recalled their conversation and he was still in two minds whether his uncle knew the truth about the Creatures or not.

Irian noticed that either Smodge or Smeerius' wife had signed most of the paintings in Smeerius' study. Actually, there were very few of his paintings, probably because it was his job to paint for others and sell his work. Irian's eyes searched for the portrait of himself, and he eventually recognised a familiar face, the one that he had to see every time he looked in the mirror and that sometimes annoyed him more than anything else.

'So, is that my portrait?' asked Irian.

'It isn't hard to tell, is it?' replied Smeerius. 'Do you like it?'

'I'm very impressed' Irian had a good look at it. 'There's one thing, though – I look a bit like a cherry.'

'It's because you produce a cherry taste in my mouth every time I see you.'

'That's funny. You know, I've always wondered what kind of taste I created for you, and I always hoped it wasn't something horrible.'

'Oh, no' said Smeerius, smiling. 'On the contrary, it's very pleasant. Anyway, you can have your portrait. It's a little present for you.'

'Great! I feel very honoured! Thank you, Mr Newance.'

Later on, when Irian got back home, he spent a good hour looking at the painting. He decided to hang it above his desk, which seemed like the best place and the most prominent point in his bedroom. He liked the painting, but for some strange reason, something about it definitely niggled him. The face in it had two cherries for cheeks, while the head was represented by a flower bulb. His neck was a stalk and his arms replaced by two leaves.

While he was observing the painting, he heard footsteps approaching his bedroom, and then a knock. He was nicely surprised to see Floria and Nuro.

'Did you have a good holiday?' asked Irian happy to see his friends again.

'Yes' replied Nuro. 'But we did miss you.'

'I missed you too. I have so many things to tell you. It seems like ages since we last saw each other.'

'What's that painting above your desk?' asked Floria. 'It looks like you.'

'It's a present from Smeerius.'

'You posed for Smeerius?' asked Nuro.

'No, not at all. He decided to make it himself. I didn't ask for anything.'

'He must really like you. You know that his paintings cost a fortune' said Floria.

'Well, I know. I was surprised too.'

'You look very much like a cherry flower in there' said Floria.

'Apparently, I give him a cherry taste every time he sees me' said Irian, giggling.

'Cherry taste' repeated Nuro seriously. 'Are you sure?'

'Yes, I am' replied Irian. 'Why?'

'Goodness me' said Nuro. 'It can't be.'

'What do you mean?' asked Irian confused.

'I was just thinking about something. Remember the conversation we overheard in the Water Castle. One of the voices mentioned "Cherry Taste". So, this is how they might secretly refer to you' he said, cottoning on.

'Well, that's it! I knew there was something strange about the painting and I just couldn't tell what it was. Now I understand' said Irian. 'But they were mentioning something about kidnapping "Cherry Taste". Why would they want to kidnap me? That's terrible!'

'It's true' agreed Nuro. 'What was Smeerius like with you?'

'He was very nice, I'd even say a bit too nice.'

'I don't understand. It must be something to do with this business of you being Arena and Emo's descendant' thought Nuro aloud.

'I think you should speak to your grandfather' said Floria. 'He might know what to do.'

'I know. I need to see Grandfather, but he's been busy helping Petalber, so I just never get to see him' replied Irian. 'By the way, we went to see the boards in the Amphitheatre.'

'Did you?' asked Nuro, astonished.

Irian told them about the boards and the Kindness Creature's mask and how Gartika had stolen it.

'Why would she need the mask?' asked Floria.

'Well, go and ask her' said Irian. 'She obviously has to stick her big nose in wherever she can.'

Suddenly they heard Irian's mother calling them from downstairs as Mrs Cardolito had come to collect Nuro and Floria.

'We have to go' said Nuro. 'Our grandparents have come to visit, so we're having dinner together.'

'I'll see you tomorrow then' replied Irian, 'and I'll try to see Grandfather. He always has a solution for everything.'

Soothsayers

As it began to get dark outside, Irian grew more and more impatient to go back and see the boards of the Amphitheatre. The problem was that his parents had some friends over for dinner, so he didn't know how to get out of the house. Apart from that, his mother insisted on his having dinner with them, which Irian couldn't refuse, as he couldn't tell his parents that he had to go out very late. Therefore, Mrs Bigone decided to go to the Amphitheatre by herself and then call him when she got back to let him know about her discoveries.

That evening, the time passed so slowly for Irian that he even kept asking himself if somebody hadn't stopped time all together, or whether there wasn't something wrong with the clocks in his house. He felt as if he were sitting on a hedgehog, it was difficult to keep still and participate in the conversation.

'So, Irian' said one of his parents' friends 'are you enjoying your holidays?'

'Are you still very keen on the Legend?' asked another one so that Irian hadn't even had time to answer the first question before his mother began frowning.

'Oh, he's too big for all that' said the third friend.

'I don't think so' said the first one. 'My mother's no spring chicken; yet she is a great believer in the Legend.'

'Would anybody like another helping?' asked Irian's mother and Irian knew that it was because she couldn't bear any conversation to do with the Legend.

'Some people say that the Creatures are about to return' said the first one rather quietly, not paying attention to Irian's mother's proposal.

Irian felt as if his body had come back to life – like a person who had been resuscitated. He felt his senses alive and alert again, waiting to capture and pin down any possible information just like a detective nabbing a thief and keeping him locked up, unable to escape.'

'People say all kinds of things' said Irian's mother, quite annoyed. 'It doesn't mean that we have to listen to everything they say.'

'But apparently, this time it could really happen' insisted the first one. 'People talk about a certain destiny book and they say that the Creatures are simply hiding their powers inside that book, waiting.'

'It's quite late' said Irian's mother who had obviously had enough of the Legend. 'I think it's time for bed, Irian.'

Irian couldn't believe his mother was sending him to bed now that the conversation had just started to get really interesting and also useful. However, when his mother meant something, Irian could do nothing else but obey her. He said goodnight to everybody and then as slowly as he could, went up to his room. Climbing the stairs, he tried to be very attentive to what the guests were saying, but he noticed that his mother had managed to change the subject.

His mind concentrated hard on analysing what the man had said during dinner. He couldn't understand how he had learnt about the Destiny Book and the Creatures' powers. He trusted Mrs Bigone just as much as he trusted his beloved friends Nuro and Floria who were the only people to know about the book, so how could anyone else possibly know of such a secret? However, what interested him the most was the information that the Creatures had hidden their powers in the Destiny Book. And now that he knew about it, he thought to himself that it was perfectly logical after all. It was written on the boards that this book was the Creatures' most treasured object, probably because they were indeed hiding their powers in it, and were now trying to get them back.

Time seemed to be moving at a snail's pace, not allowing the hands of the clock to turn any faster, as if they had suddenly become too lazy or too tired to show the right time as it really was. Irian didn't feel the slightest bit tired, and was getting worried about Mrs Bigone. He kept on walking to the window to check if her lights were on, but all he could see were the lights coming from the downstairs sitting room of his own house, even though the voices had lowered, probably because everyone imagined he had gone to sleep. He even had a thought for the Impatience Creature from Smodge's book, wondering what it would have done if it had been in his situation.

Waiting was becoming unbearable, so when his talkastick finally rang and he got to speak to Mrs Bigone, Irian felt the blood running through his veins again. The only obstacle to seeing Mrs Bigone was that he couldn't go out through the front door as his parents and their friends were still there. Then an idea struck him – in front of his room there was a flower, so he decided to get out this way, a way which was, in fact, one of his specialities, as he was still small enough to do it. He carefully opened the window and seized the flower to step onto it. The flower was cold and its petals humid and slippery, so he had to move very slowly to avoid slipping. Its stalk coated with soft, silvery fuzz tickled his armpits, which didn't help at all as Irian was very ticklish. Once he had reached the ground, he tried to make as little noise as possible when opening the gate. Just as he had closed it, he noticed Ogi trotting at his feet.

'What are you doing here?' whispered Irian looking at his little dog who always got so excited about things that his tail wagged at such a great speed that it amazed Irian. 'If you make a single sound, I'll be in a big trouble, you know!'

Irian had the impression that his dog was getting better at understanding him and he wasn't avoiding him anymore, perhaps because Gadious hadn't "visited" him lately or perhaps because Ogi had finally somehow understood what was happening. He took his puppy in his arms and carried him to Mrs Bigone's house. The moment he rang her bell, he heard his own front door opening and his parents saying goodbye to their friends. Irian prayed that Mrs Bigone would open the door quickly before he got caught. Mrs Bigone eventually unlocked the door, and Irian's expression told her that he had to get out of sight, so she quickly ushered him in and then even more quickly shut the door behind him without saying a word.

'How did it go?' said Irian, still whispering once they got into her sitting room.

'It was amazing' replied Mrs Bigone. 'Wait until people get to know about our discoveries.'

'I don't think we should tell them anything for the moment.'

'I know, but I can't wait to reveal the truth. We've been living a lie for too long now and I just don't approve of it.'

'You're right, but there's no point in revealing the problem if we have no solution to it. It would only create panic and would be of no help to us.'

'That's true.'

'I think people are already guessing some things' revealed Irian.

'What are you getting at?'

'One of my parents' friends was talking about the Destiny Book at dinner. I nearly choked on my dessert.'

'He mentioned the Destiny Book?' repeated Mrs Bigone 'How does he know?'

'I've no idea. It must be some kind of common secret when other Destiners know about it. What's more, he said the Creatures were hiding their powers in the book.'

'It's impossible!' exclaimed Mrs Bigone.

'Unfortunately, people do know about it somehow and I think we should let them believe it's gossip for the time being. Did you learn anything more about the book?'

'No, not really. The boards don't mention it much, but I've found out more about the Creatures and their story is just amazing.'

'Tell me then. I'm dying to hear.'

'The board that I analysed talks about the Glimmers. The Glimmers lived in the County of Coruscatia, which was a county of precious stones where everything sparkled and shone making the days seem brighter than anywhere else. Anyone who wasn't used to all that glimmering and shining would have found it difficult to live in the county, but the Glimmers were used to it. They exported their precious stones to people living in other counties, as their stones were abundant and of the best quality. The

Glimmers were great lapidaries too and particularly skilled in getting the best refraction of light to obtain the multicoloured "fire" of diamonds.'

'What is the refraction of light?' asked Irian who was absorbing every single word as much as a sponge absorbs liquid.

'The skill of the gem-cutter lies in angling the facets of the stone so that each light ray entering it is reflected many times before it emerges again' replied Mrs Bigone. 'Among others, the Glimmers differentiated from other people given that they were born with a precious stone in the place of their right eye. Apparently, one day Arameen heard of Coruscatia and the Glimmers. Being obsessed with light and anything that shone, he decided to send the Light Creatures, who served as his guard, to attack the Glimmers and confiscate all their precious stones.'

'That's horrible!' said Irian. 'How could he do something like that?'

'Well, Arameen needs to control and see everything.'

'So, what happened to the Glimmers?'

'The Glimmers then became the Sudba Creatures.'

'How could they become the Sudba Creatures?'

'You see, the Glimmers were probably in many ways like Arameen. They were used to all that shone and they couldn't survive in some dull place without much light. Arameen knew that very well, and had therefore decided to take them under his protection.'

'But how can you first attack somebody and then take him under your protection? It doesn't make sense' reasoned Irian. 'How can you serve somebody if he wanted to destroy you?'

'It's the fight for life that makes you act that way. Well, not everybody, but the great majority of people would do anything to survive under any conditions. You have to continue living whatever happens, so you accept situations as they come. It's a battle for survival. Sometimes you accept things, which you'd normally never accept, but you accept them only because you hope that you'll be able to change them and make them better one day. Hope is what leads us through life, and hope led the Glimmers to accept Arameen's protection.'

159

'So, the Sudba Creatures were Arameen's victims in a way? They didn't have the intention of controlling Destiners from the beginning?'

'Exactly. They only accepted it because they had to survive somehow. Arameen thought of a plan; he decided to send them to the town of Destin because the Destiners disliked Arameen and his Light Creatures. Destin was an independent town at the time and didn't want to be controlled by anyone. Arameen therefore gathered the Glimmers and made each of them embody a different spirit. Each spirit represented a different human quality, and this quality then became particularly developed in the Glimmer in question. Arameen ordered them to keep away from the dark, as it would diminish their powers and make them useless. He gave them masks, which showed the quality they represented – it was a way to "mark" them out I suppose. From then on they were Sudba Creatures.'

'And what about Queen Ranna?'

'Queen Ranna was Arameen's wife and she sent her to control the Sudba Creatures and the whole situation in the town of Destin.'

'Incredible!' exclaimed Irian. 'But did all of the Glimmers fall under the control of Arameen and Ranna?'

'I don't know that that much but it's a good question actually.'

'I feel sorry for the Sudba Creatures now' said Irian. 'What else did you find out?'

'The board about the Glimmers was quite long, so I used all the liquid I had on it. The letters were disappearing so quickly that I just didn't have time to read the text properly, so I had to apply the liquid several times in order to read the message.'

'So, we don't only have to save the Destiners but we also have to save the Glimmers from their spell. I wonder how we're going to manage that!' Irian scratched his head, making his hair fall out of his ponytail and look messy.

'Well, we have to find the Destiny Book and destroy the powers that are hidden inside. I think it's the only way to proceed.'

'But how do we find this book?'

'It might be hidden within the inner quarters of the Amphitheatre if the Creatures didn't take it with them. But then, if they did have it with them, why wouldn't they have used it by now?'

'That's true. You're right, the book might be somewhere in the inner quarters. But the mayor would never let us in.'

'There must be a way' thought Mrs Bigone aloud. 'Give me some time to think about it.'

'How about telling the mayor the truth?'

'I wouldn't do that. We still don't know if we can trust him or not.'

'You're right' agreed Irian. 'The Glimmers, how interesting!'

* * *

Irian was sleeping less and less as he just couldn't relax properly anymore. He decided to go and visit Grandfather first thing in the morning to see whether he had any solutions to propose. He knew that Grandfather always woke up early, so he went to pay him a visit as soon as he woke up.

'I don't think I've ever seen you come so early in the morning' said Grandmother seeing Irian at the doorway. 'What's the emergency?'

'Oh, no. It's just that Ogi woke me up and I couldn't get back to sleep' lied Irian.

'Is that the young rascal?' he heard Grandfather's voice coming from the kitchen.

'Yes, it is' answered Grandmother. 'Come in, Irian. I suppose you haven't had your breakfast yet.'

'No, not really.'

'What would you say to a slice of violet cake?' asked Grandmother.

'Good idea' replied Grandfather.

'I didn't ask you' said Grandmother. 'I was talking to Irian.'

'Well, I know what he likes' said Grandfather.

'Yes' said Irian giggling. 'I'd love some.'

Irian was trying to wink at his Grandfather to show that he needed to talk to him. Grandfather winked back to confirm he had understood.

'Oh, I've just realised I have no violet blossoms left' said Grandmother.

'Well, let's go and get some young man' said Grandfather and Irian knew that it was a good opportunity for them to speak.

The market wasn't far, but it was far enough for them to have a good talk.

'So, what's going on?' asked Grandfather.

'Many, many things' replied Irian and then went on to tell him about the Kindness Creature's mask and how Gartika had stolen it, about the boards and Smeerius' portrait as well as the Creatures' hidden powers in the Destiny Book.

'Well, you've been a busy young man' said Grandfather, astonished at all these revelations.

'What are we going to do, grandpa?'

'I'm not really sure.'

'Tell me about the mask. You said it had special powers.'

'It does indeed. We'll need it to destroy Arameen.'

'What do you mean?'

'Whoever wears one of these masks cannot be hurt by Arameen. They are designed to be worn only by the Creatures, so that nobody can hurt them.'

'Yes, but if I put the mask on, Arameen would know that it was me, so he could hurt me, couldn't he?'

'No, he couldn't. Whatever he creates is protected and he can't destroy it later because when creating something, he inserts a certain dose of his own energy into the thing. He couldn't and he wouldn't go on destroying his energy because that could destroy his own powers too.'

'But where does Arameen live?'

'I don't know, but as we might need to go and pay him a visit one day, it would be a good idea to have a mask with us.'

'It's too late. Gartika has got it now.'

'She won't have it forever. We'll get it back, you'll see' said Grandfather. 'What I find interesting is this story about the

Glimmers. I didn't know about them. And now that I think about it, something makes me feel that there is one of them living in our town.'

'What?' exclaimed Irian as if somebody has slapped him on the back making him spit the word out.

'There's a man who works in a jewellery shop in the Third Circle and he always wears a black bandage across his right eye. Who knows, he might be one of the Glimmers and is trying to hide it.'

'You know what, when I hear all these things, I have the impression that I'm just discovering my own town, as if I had never lived here before' commented Irian. 'Is he nice, that man?'

'I've never spoken to him. I've only seen him working there.'

'Can we go and see him later on?'

'If you want' replied Grandfather. 'But it could be a delicate matter asking him about the Glimmers.'

'Do you think we should tell him the truth?'

'I think we should find out first if he really is one of the Glimmers.'

When they got to the market, there were swarms of people and Irian couldn't believe that they had all woken up so early that morning.

Back at his grandparents' house, Irian was so eager to see the man in the jewellery shop that he practically finished his breakfast in an instant.

'You were hungry, my boy' said Grandmother. 'I've never seen you eat so quickly.'

'It's his age' said Grandfather. 'When I was his age, I could eat almost an entire corpse lily.'

'And you haven't changed much since, have you?' replied Grandmother as Grandfather gave an almost apologetic look.

'Do you want to go for a little walk?' suggested Grandfather to Irian. 'It'll help you digest you breakfast better.'

Irian knew of course what Grandfather meant by that, so he just nodded.

'What we could do is go to see the man and I could say something about you being my little grandson who's very interested in precious stones, and that's why we've come to his shop. So, if he's nice we'll speak to him and, if he isn't, we'll come back home and think of something else' proposed Grandfather once they got out of the house.

The shop *The Brilliant-Cut* was situated in a little street in the Third Circle, and its window was so shiny that both Grandfather and Irian had to put their hands over their eyes to see it. Irian couldn't even see inside as everything sparkled and shone so much. They had to ring a small bell before entering and then wait for a few moments.

They both heard steps approaching and then somebody unlocking the door. Even when the door had opened, Irian still couldn't see the face as he was so dazzled by all the light.

'How can I help you?' a man's deep voice almost seemed to clear Irian's vision and now that he could see properly again, the first thing he spotted was the black bandage around the man's right eye. Irian kept on staring at it, which made the man feel rather uncomfortable.

'Hello' said Grandfather trying to attract his attention and save him from Irian's stare. 'I do apologize for troubling you. This is my little grandson, Irian, and he's very keen on precious stones. He'd like to know more about his birthstone, which is peridot, so we were wondering if you would be kind enough to show it to us and teach us a little more about it.'

The man looked at them, puzzled, probably wondering who the two strange people disturbing him actually were, but as the customer is always right, he knew that he had to treat everybody with kindness and respect, as potential clients.

'Peridot' repeated the man, with a forced smile that came out more like the grimace he made in the mornings when he checked his teeth in his bathroom mirror. 'How do you know it's peridot?'

'I tested it with a neutral mineral' replied Irian, who just couldn't take his eyes off the bandage.

'Peridot is a good stone' replied the man getting more and more embarrassed. 'It's a greasy stone. I'll show it to you.'

'What do you mean by greasy?' asked Irian.

'Without light we would not be able to appreciate gemstones' explained the man. 'Light reflected off the surface of a gemstone gives the gemstone its lustre. The greater the amount of light that is reflected back towards the eye, the brighter the stone will appear. There are different types of lustre in gemstones and peridot appears greasy.'

He kept the stones piled up in pyramids and there was a pyramid for every type of stone, all of which he kept behind the glass walls. The piles looked like delicious cakes, and Irian thought that he must have extraordinary patience to place the stones so meticulously in such perfect piles. They were placed on special trays, and the man had to press a button on the side and the tray would slide out.

'There we go' said the man putting the tray with beautiful step-cut and cushion-cut greenish yellow stones in front of Irian and Grandfather.

'How much is it for one stone?' asked Grandfather.

'The small ones are about a thousand dinnies' replied the man. Dinnies were the official currency. These were coins with flower patterns engraved on them.

'Goodness me!' said Grandfather. 'Do people really buy such things?'

'Yes, they do' replied the man obviously unimpressed by such a simplistic question.

'So, I suppose the bracelet must be awfully expensive' said Grandfather.

'Peridot is too soft to be used as a gemstone in rings or bracelets, but is popular for earrings, pendants, clasps, and brooches' replied the man.

'Where do you get these stones?' asked Irian.

'We have people who provide us with the precious stones' replied the man in a quavering voice.

'Do they come from the County of Coruscatia?' asked Irian, looking straight into the man's left eye, the one that wasn't covered. He was so surprised by the question that he placed his hand over his chest.

'How do you know about Coruscatia?' he asked, flabbergasted.

'I know that you're one of the Glimmers and that's why you wear a bandage to hide your sparkling eye' replied Irian.

'What do you want from me?' asked the man and Irian could feel a great deal of fear in his voice.

'Don't worry. We're not here to blackmail you or anything like that. I'm Emo and Arena's descendant and I know that the Creatures are trying to return to the town' revealed Irian. 'I'd just like more information about the Glimmers.'

'Are you really their descendant?' asked the man, trying to get his breath back. 'So, you can save my people from their terrible slavery?'

'I'm definitely working on it' replied Irian. 'But tell me about the Glimmers, please.'

'But, where on earth did you learn about the Glimmers?' asked the man.

'Through the boards in the Amphitheatre' replied Irian and then went on to tell the man about Peena, the River Irav and all the things that had happened to him recently while the man listened, finding it hard to believe his ears.

'Let's go to my office' said the man. 'This isn't a good place to talk.'

He went to close the door of the shop and turned around a little sign on which the word "CLOSED" was written in bold black letters. His office was a large room full of different tools that Irian had never seen before, including objects whose strange names he was to learn later e.g. *"single pan balance"* or *"spectroscope"*. The man had explained to him these tools were necessary when identifying the stones in question.

'Can you take your bandage off?' asked Irian. 'I really want to see your shiny eye.'

'I have a diamond eye because I come from a diamond family' said the man taking off the bandage to reveal the most beautiful deep blue sparkling diamond. Irian and Grandfather remained breathless for a while.

'So, you don't all bear the same precious stone?' asked Irian.

'No, every family bears a different one' replied the man. 'My name is Lozendge Glintt.'

'Nice to met you Lozendge' said Grandfather. 'Are there many Glimmers like you?'

'Not as many as there used to be after Arameen sent his Light Creatures to destroy us. But yes, my people still live in the county of Coruscatia.'

'Where do you live?' asked Irian.

'I live here, just above the shop. I'll show you my house later on, if you want. You can stay for lunch' proposed Lozendge. 'My wife and daughter will be very pleased to meet you. They've gone out to do some shopping but they'll be back soon.'

'So not all of the Glimmers fell under Arameen's rule?' asked Irian with great interest.

'Luckily, some did manage to escape from the Light Creatures and preserve our culture and knowledge as well as some of our wealth.'

'How did they manage to hide from Arameen and the other Sudba Creatures for such a long time? I mean, the Sudba Creatures stayed in the town for quite a while, didn't they?' asked Irian.

'It was terrible. Arameen somehow managed to change the Glimmers' spirits and turn them into human qualities, so that our own people gradually became our worst enemies; those Creatures. The remaining Glimmers then had to hide, but it was very difficult to survive without making a living selling precious stones anymore. This is how they became Soothsayers.'

'Soothsayers?' repeated Irian, baffled.

'They then realised they had an incredible potential to tell Destiners their fortunes.'

'How could they do that?' asked Irian, realising that he was on the brink of discovering something about the Soothsayers, which was to be very important to him.

'You see, when Arameen created the Sudba Creatures, he gave them the Destiny Book, which they needed when deciding about the baby's future. He created the book and then decorated it with many precious stones from our county. The Glimmers were able to connect to the stones that decorated the book and tell what had been written inside.'

'What do you mean "connect to the stones"?' asked Irian, astonished.

'Every stone bears a different energy' said Lozendge 'and because similar energies attract, they could see through the book thanks to the energy from the stone in their right eye.'

'Even though they didn't have the book in front of them?' asked Grandfather.

'Yes. Energies don't mind distances' replied Lozendge. 'They would simply hold the person's left hand and stare at the lines on his or her palm; this is how they mentally connected to the book.'

'But how did the Destiners know about the Soothsayers?' asked Irian.

'If you want to know something, there's always a way' replied Lozendge. 'Your ancestors went to consult the Soothsayers, too. '

'Really?' said Grandfather and Irian at the same time.

'Both Arena and Emo's mothers went to consult the Soothsayers who told them they had to take a risk in order to save the town from the Creatures.'

'But when they saved the town, Arena and Emo had no idea about the Creatures' hidden powers?' asked Irian.

'No, I don't think so, otherwise they would surely have done something about it' replied Lozendge.

'And what about the Soothsayers? Did they know?' asked Irian.

'Yes, but they couldn't do anything because Sir Esteam wouldn't allow anybody to enter the inner quarters of the Amphitheatre.'

'Just like our present mayor. But why?' asked Irian.

'I don't know. This is something that puzzles us still. He was a nice man and he did a lot for this town, but he was also an incredibly secretive person. He was the mayor of the town; yet, he had very little contact with other Destiners.'

'That's strange' said Irian. 'Do you think he had any particular reason to behave like that?'

'I reckon it was because he had to change so many things in the town after Ranna's government and in a way, he wanted people to forget about the Queen and the Creatures who neverthe-less have continued to haunt the minds of every Destiner like a ghost without a grave' reasoned Lozendge. 'I mean, have you noticed how Destiners always whisper when talking about the Sudba Creatures?'

'You're right' replied Grandfather. 'That's why people call it a Legend although they know very well it used to be their past for real. They fear the truth more than anything else.'

'Truth is often bitter while lies are anything you want them to be, you know' commented Lozendge.

'What do you think we should do?' asked Irian.

'You have to find a way to destroy the Destiny Book. That way my people will be released from their terrible spell and the Destiners will finally taste real freedom.'

As he pronounced these words, they heard voices approach-ing; a child's voice and that of woman.

'This is my wife and our child' said Lozendge. 'They'll be very happy to meet you. Please don't mention anything about the Legend in front of my daughter. She's too little to understand such things.'

The door opened and a beautiful young woman came in, car-rying a small child in her arms. Everything about her seemed impeccable; she was tall and well built, and didn't have the red cheeks to be found on any Destiner's face. She was definitely one of the Glimmers as she too wore a patch over her right eye, and her left arm was full of bracelets with beautiful shiny gems from her wrist up to her elbow. She seemed puzzled to see Irian and Grandfather, and directed a questioning look at her husband who was still standing in the doorway.

'This is my wife, Turquoisin, and our little daughter, Diamantina' said Lozendge.

'Nice to meet you' said Turquoisin, obviously reassured by her husband's tone of voice.

'Daddy, daddy' said Diamantina running towards her father. 'One of the women at the market asked me why I wore a patch over my eye, and she wanted to take it off but mummy stopped her in time. I didn't like the woman.'

Lozendge gave his wife a distressed look and she gave him a sign that she would explain later.

'Well that's not very nice, is it?' replied Lozendge. 'Remember how granny and grandpa weren't careful about wearing their patches, so their eyes were damaged.'

Irian understood they had to adapt their horrible history and soften it for little Diamantina but still teach her to keep her right eye out of sight. Irian looked at the little girl, who seemed as gorgeous as if she had come out of the most beautiful portrait. She was chubby, dressed in a pretty little dress embroidered with various precious stones.

'Diamantina' said Lozendge, 'why don't you go and say hello to our new friends? The boy is called Irian and the man is his grandfather. I think they would very much like to hear your favourite story.'

'But they seem too big to like stories. Stories are for little people like me' replied Diamantina.

'Well, why don't you tell them the story and see what they say?' suggested Turquoisin.

'But we'll have to make a theatre stage, otherwise how are they going to picture my story?' said Diamantina and then quickly ran to another room and was back in a flash carrying a little box. 'Are you all ready?'

Everybody nodded and Irian waited curiously to see what this pretty creature had reserved for them. She started:

"There was once a jewellery box, which contained all kinds of the most beautiful precious stones that somebody had lost, and which lay abandoned in some remote place. Some of the stones were very little, some of them were round, the others square – they all had different shapes and colours, but they were all special in some way. However, none of them wanted to accept it was a stone, as they thought stones were too simple and ugly. They spent their time arguing, each of them thought it was the prettiest and the shiniest. "My colour is the shiniest and its light is brighter than yours. I was taken from a cave where everybody wanted me to be

theirs. They used to say there was no such beauty as me."

The jewellery box would get annoyed with them arguing all the time: "You're all precious stones. You're all beautiful". Yet the precious stones wanted to be anything else but stones. "I'm a gem. That's what one of the men who found me called me" – said one of them. "And I'm a mineral. You see, I'm not a stone" – said the other one. "Gems are more precious than minerals" – said the first one. "You only serve to decorate people's necklaces and rings. We minerals, we can help when people are sick. We can make them feel better" – replied the second one. "And I'm a crystal. Crystals are smooth and pleasant. They are so precious that they break if you don't know how to handle them". This is how they would argue the whole day long, making the box open every so often as it couldn't bear to listen to their never-ending arguments. "Wait until a human finds you, and they'll soon tell you who you are", the box would say, annoyed with the beautiful but capricious objects.

One day a man did in fact find the box. He picked it up and opened it. He was dazzled by all the light and different colours and said: "A jewellery box with precious stones. And there are so many of them."

'That's a beautiful story, Diamantina!' said Grandfather.

'My grandpa told me it's a story about people' replied Diamantina. 'People always think they're better and more special than others.'

'Well, he told you well!' replied Grandfather.

'Mummy, I think I'm a bit tired. I'll go and have a little nap. See you later' said Diamantina blowing a kiss to everybody.

'Have a good rest, Diamantina' said her mother.

This beautiful thing waved at everybody and then disappeared, carrying with her the jewellery box that she had used for the show.

'She bears her name well' said Grandfather.

'Yes, she's a real little gem' replied Turquoisin, quietly. 'But we're worried for her.'

'Why?' asked Irian.

'She attracts people's attention too much so we can't go out with her. It's dangerous' explained Turquoisin. 'Today at the market a horrible woman absolutely insisted on taking her patch off. She also looked at me suspiciously and I quickly hid my own patch with hair, so that she wouldn't notice anything.'

'Do you think the woman suspects who we are?' asked Lozendge, worried.

'I don't know' replied Turquoisin. 'But how could she know? Nobody is aware of our presence.'

'What did the woman look like?' asked Irian.

'She was ugly and had a horrible big nose,' replied Turquoisin.

'It's Gartika' said Irian angrily. 'I knew it!'

'Who's Gartika?' asked Turquoisin, and her husband quickly explained.

'What does she want?' asked Lozendge. 'Who is she? What does she do?'

'She says she does lots of things' replied Grandfather. 'She might be helping Ranna. This is what I fear; I fear she's Ranna's spy in the town.'

'That's awful' said Turquoisin, terrified.

'I think you should leave here for a while. Gartika now probably knows who you are and you don't want her to hurt you' said Grandfather quietly. 'If I were you, I would pack my stuff now that the child is asleep and leave this very afternoon. You can go to Coruscatia for some time, can't you? You'll be safer there for the time being until we find a solution. That woman is evil; who knows what she's up to.'

'I think you're right' said Lozendge. 'We could go and stay with our family for a while. What do you think my darling Turquoisin?'

Of course Turquoisin agreed with the proposal. Irian and Grandfather helped Lozendge to pack while Turquoisin stayed with Diamantina, as they thought it was important to stay with the child knowing what Gartika was capable of.

'Thank you so much for your help' said Turquoisin when Irian and Grandfather were leaving. 'We didn't even have lunch together.'

'Oh, don't worry about lunch' said Grandfather. 'Your safety is much more important. We can always visit you another time.'

'Oh, yes, please do' said Lozendge. 'Coruscatia is in the far East. Just follow the early morning sun and you'll find it.'

Before leaving, Lozendge gave a beautiful peridot pendant to Irian and a soothing blue sapphire talisman to Grandfather as it happened to be his birthstone.

'You know' said Lozendge, 'it was Shon Lustre's belief; he was one of my ancestors and also the chief of the Glimmers before Arameen attacked us, that the blue of the sky was originally caused by huge reflections from sapphire stones.'

'And some Glimmers wear sapphire stones as a protection when travelling' added Turquoisin.

'That's good to know' replied Grandfather. 'It might come in useful for the Old Lady and me.'

Irian and Grandfather were happy to have met such wonderful people and people who were so different from other Destiners.

'Coruscatia must be a great county' said Grandfather in a daydream. 'What do you think, Irian?'

'Well, I think I know what you mean. Your itchy feet want to go and visit it.'

'You know how the Old Lady likes going for a flight.'

'Well, above all, I know how you like flying that balloon' said Irian, with a big smile.

'I mean, how can you know who you are if you don't see other places? This is what I keep on saying to your cousin Petalber, who hardly ever moves from the Third Circle. If you always see the same things, your eyes don't need to open wide because you already know the things around you by heart. So, if you keep on seeing the same things, you forget that there are different things too. The worst part is that then, even when something new crosses your path, you don't see it, because your eyes are not used to seeing new things. This is when you become dull and boring if you ask me.'

'Don't worry grandpa, you could never become boring. But I think we have a few more important things to do now.'

'First I think we need to find out what Gartika is up to. She must work for the Creatures; otherwise why would she steal the mask and try to look into that child's eye?'

'Do you think we should spy on her?' asked Irian.

'How? The First Circle is miles away from us and we definitely can't spy on her during the daytime. We can't do it at night either, because we would have to find an excuse for your parents and your grandma, which would be hard work.'

'I was just thinking about something. And what if we make a false mask and then exchange it for the real one?' Irian seemed to have found a solution.

'That's an excellent idea!' exclaimed Grandfather. 'Well done my grandson! But we have to find somebody who could do it for us. Any suggestions?'

'No, not really. It has to be somebody who's very good at making things. Somebody professional.'

'Let's think' said Grandfather. 'We'll have to ask somebody we can trust, which means that we can't go around asking just anybody.'

'Uncle Tattoo is good at that sort of thing but he would never ever accept. Apart from anything, the person should at least see the mask first, otherwise how is he going to reproduce it?'

'We could take the person to see the mask with us' replied Grandfather. 'I wonder if they have such masks in the theatre.'

'They might do, but I don't think they would have the Kindness Creature's mask.'

'Why?'

'Because nobody knows what the mask looks like.'

'Oh yes they do. They copy Tattoo's drawings.'

'But he doesn't know how to draw the Kindness Creature.'

'Why wouldn't he know how to draw it? He can draw all the Creatures.'

'No, he can't. He told me that himself' replied Irian and then recounted the conversation with his uncle.

'I remember he told us once he had dreamt about the Creatures and that they had been asking him questions' recalled Grandfather 'but I thought to myself he was only a child and I didn't think they could really appear in his dreams. It's terrible, they were bothering him in his dreams. What did they want from him? I think I should speak to him.'

'Grandpa, he won't listen. He's so stubborn about the Legend.'

'I'm his father. If he loves me, he will at least try to help even if he still doesn't believe. I'll tell him the whole thing. He should understand. Let me talk to him and see.'

'Do you think he's aware of the truth?'

'I don't know. Your uncle is like your grandma; he's a hard nut. You can hammer and hammer on it, but you still won't break it. Maybe if I "hammer" him with all the facts we have, he'll crack eventually. I hope so anyway.'

'Shall we go and see him together?' asked Irian.

'I think I should go alone. I haven't had a serious talk with my son for a long time. He might have things to tell me too.'

How Irian gets the Mask back

The beautiful sunny sky suddenly turned rainy, as if somebody had pushed the sun away violently from the sky or drawn the clouds together to hide it for some reason. It also got very chilly so that some flowers even closed their petals to protect themselves from all the raindrops and the cold. It seemed as if the season had suddenly changed in the space of a very short time; like an argument, with cold winning over warmth, kicking it completely out of the game. Given that the climate in Destin was very mild, the Destiners didn't like the cold and would complain about it. As for the Sudba Creatures, when it was rainy they wouldn't even come out of the Amphitheatre for days, waiting for the sun to reappear.

It was a heavy rain, the sort of rain that somehow gets through your umbrella and finds you wherever you are hiding. The hot air balloon traffic was stopped for security reasons, and Destin seemed to calm down like a small baby, who without warning, tires of its play and falls asleep on its toys. Destiners ceded their places to the wind and the rain to stroll around their avenues, only observing the outdoor conditions through their windows. A few children tried to get out in the rain, but their mothers stopped them on any pretext, preventing them from catching cold.

The weather stayed like that for a few days, so that the little stream next to Irian's house now looked like a proper river because of all the water – you could even bathe in it! The sun re-established its position in the sky and all the extra water gradually evaporated under the sun's rays, while the flower petals re-opened to admire the sun again.

Irian spent these rainy days at home, not really doing much. Most of his time was spent reading the book that Smodge had lent him, the one that he had received for *Imagine and Live it Day*. It was a thick book but Irian had even read it several times because he had found it particularly interesting. Moreover, every time he read it, he came across a new detail that he hadn't noticed before. The book helped him realise that there was a strong hierarchy among the Creatures. There was the Charisma Creature whom all the Creatures respected, and under that Creature, there were the Anger, the Love and the Fear Creatures who were in a way responsible for all the other Creatures. Irian liked the Charisma Creature, and he read its story umpteen times. It read:

"The Charisma Creature was the one who was always surrounded by other Creatures. It was the Creature that spoke the least but received the most attention. Everybody was in its admiration and would forgive it for whatever wrong the Creature did. The Charisma Creature was almost like a magnet, making everybody come out of their rooms when it passed through the corridors of the inner quarters. Everybody had something to tell it or advice to ask and its advice was always most appreciated and never criticised even if it wasn't very good. The Charisma Creature didn't try to please or impress anybody, as it just couldn't be bothered to do such things, but there was some kind of special charm in its aura, that even the Authority Creature, who was feared by everybody, couldn't resist. The Queen herself treated the Charisma Creature differently from the other Creatures and it was the only Creature she would even have dinner with.

If any other Creature ever had a problem with the Charisma Creature, you could be sure that it would lose its battle as everybody was always on the Charisma Creature's side. It seemed as if injustice could never cross its path. The Charisma Creature did everything the way things suited it; if it wanted to go to the Destiny Decision Meeting, it would go and if it was tired, it wouldn't. The other Creatures used to say among themselves: "Lucky is the child who gets the Charisma Creature's points."

The Charisma Creature rarely expressed its points of view, but if it had something to say, nobody could disobey it because being ignored by the Charisma Creature hurt the Creatures almost more than anything else. The Creatures would have done anything to be in the Charisma Creature's good books."

As the weather got better, Irian could go out again and do all the things that he had to do. He didn't mind the rain as he didn't like to think that the weather should influence his life, but he stayed at home just to please his mother.

He went to see Grandfather as he was curious to know whether he had had the opportunity to speak to Uncle Tattoo. When he got to Grandfather's house, Grandfather was just about to lock the door and go out.

'Hello, young rascal!' said Grandfather. 'I was just coming to see you. What a coincidence!'

'You know what Mrs Bigone says?' asked Irian.

'No, what does she say?'

'She says that there are no coincidences. She believes that we create coincidences ourselves by thinking hard about something until that something really happens.'

'I guess she's right.'

'So, any news from Uncle Tattoo?'

'I've spoken to him' replied Grandfather. 'Listen, let's go for a little walk. It will do us both good to have some fresh air. Are you hungry?'

'Not particularly, but tell me, what did Uncle Tattoo say? How did he react? Tell me, tell me, tell me!'

'Well, I think he finally listened.'

'Does it mean that he's going to help us?'

'Yes, he's going to help with the mask. He said that he can easily reproduce the mask if we find a way of getting hold of the original.'

'That's brilliant!' exclaimed Irian. 'But, was he surprised? I mean, how did he treat the whole thing?'

'He knew that the Creatures were about to return and that we were Arena and Emo's descendants.'

'But why didn't he want to admit it to me when I spoke to him?'

'Because he thought you weren't aware of everything and he wanted to protect you as you're still little.'

'So, how are we going to get the mask then?'

'We have to go to see Gartika. It's the only way.'

'What do you intend to say, to knock at her door and ask her to show us the mask?'

'No, you see, Tattoo knows Gartika and Gartika knows that Tattoo doesn't believe in the Legend. Well, it's better to say that we all thought he didn't believe in the Legend. So, Tattoo is going to pay her a visit as he normally does with Maia. Maia's going to try to attract Gartika's attention by asking her to sit in her garden, while Tattoo goes to look for the mask.'

'Excellent' said Irian. 'When are they going?'

'As soon as she invites them to come' said Grandfather. 'Gartika said she'd been very busy lately.'

'Yes, she's been busy trying to destroy this town. I could flatten that big nose of hers, so that she can't stick it everywhere any more.'

'Aggression is for stupid people' replied Grandfather. 'If you really want to destroy somebody, show him that you can do things better than him. That will hurt more.'

'But that woman doesn't have feelings, so how could anything hurt her? If she could feel, why would she want to do such horrible things?'

'Everybody feels something to some extent. As long as you're alive, you feel things. But we all feel things differently. If something gives you strong feelings and emotions, it doesn't mean that everybody else is going to react the same way. We don't have the same perception of things, which is good. You wouldn't want everybody to love you; it would be too annoying and too burdensome, wouldn't it? Perception is what gives balance to this world; what you might consider right some people will consider wrong and the other way round' replied

Grandfather. 'When it comes to Gartika, we don't know exactly what her aims are, but that's what we're here to discover. And don't worry, solving the enigma about the Creatures and destroying their powers will hurt her much more than flattening her nose would.'

* * *

When Irian got back home, his mother came to meet him, and asked him if she could have a word. Irian knew very well it was time to face his mother and answer her numerous questions.

'Irian' she said in a serious tone, 'I want to know what you're up to!'

'Nothing' replied Irian looking at his feet.

'Don't lie to me! I know that you've been hiding things from me.'

'What things?' asked Irian, trying to see exactly what his mother had found out before deciding what to say next. 'Has Gartika been spying on me again by any chance?'

'Mrs Gartika has nothing to do with it. Irian, I told you I don't want to hear you involved in anything to do with that stupid Legend.'

'Why do you worry so much then if it's just a stupid Legend? I mean, legends are only stories that people invent, so where's the problem?' Irian was trying to be clever.

'Irian, that's enough!' his mother obviously couldn't find a better answer to her son's question. 'You know how I feel about it.'

'No, I don't actually' replied Irian. 'There are other people who don't believe in the Legend, but they don't have the same attitude as you.'

'Don't you speak to me like that' she said firmly. 'When I enter my son's room in the middle of the night and find that he's disappeared you can't blame me for getting worried. I want to know where you went.'

'I couldn't sleep and neither could Ogi, so we went for a little walk' lied Irian, surprised to hear that he had been found out.

'Interesting!' she commented quite sarcastically. 'Dad saw

you coming out of Mrs Bigone's house. What were you doing disturbing her at that time of night?'

'I met her on my walk' said Irian, trying to sound as convincing as he could, 'and she invited me in for a cup of tea.'

'Listen, I'm not going to try to get answers from you because I know you're not going to tell me the truth. However, from now on, I want you to ask my permission before going out' she concluded the discussion.

'But mum, you can't do that to me' said Irian disappointed at his mum's attitude. 'I haven't done anything wrong.'

'I don't want to hear any more of this' she said and then caught sight of Irian's neck. 'Who gave you that pendant?'

Irian had completely forgotten about the pendant and began desperately looking for an answer and a way to escape from her difficult questions. He so much wanted to tell her the truth; he felt so sorry for lying to his mother, but he had no choice.

'It's Nuro's' it was the first thing that he could come up with.

'It looks very expensive' replied his mother and then had a better look at it. 'It's peridot. I didn't know his parents could afford such things.'

'It's fake' lied Irian. He had to find a way to stop this conversation before she got even more curious.

Irian admired his mother, but when she talked about the Legend, she seemed to turn into a horrible monster – as if her nature suddenly changed at the sound of the word LEGEND which seemed to cast the most awful spell on her, making her suddenly unpleasant and difficult.

He also kept thinking that school would be starting again soon and that he must have things solved before going back, as studying under such conditions really would be impossible.

There were moments where Irian felt everybody was there for him, though there were also times when there was nobody to talk to and he hated the long lonely hours spent in his room. The walls of his room usually gave him an incredible do-whatever-you-want protection and sense of privacy; however, in such situations they seemed like limits separating him from the outside world. These creeping moments were rare, but Irian strongly disliked them, as they would make him think and worry about any-thing and everything. He always wondered how his father could spend such a long time reading in his study without seeing any-body. His father was somebody who travelled from his chair; somebody who didn't need to see things in reality just as long as he could picture them in his head. While Irian needed people and events, his father needed solitude as well as peace and quiet – something that Irian obviously hadn't inherited from him.

'Dad, don't you ever get bored spending long hours all by yourself?' asked Irian, who had gone to see his father one after-noon when there was nothing else to do.

'Hello, my busy little son' replied his father. 'I hardly get to see you these days.'

'Dad, what do you think about when you're alone?'

'It's good to be by yourself sometimes. It helps you put your thoughts in order.'

'Yes, but then all the thoughts that you don't want come along too.'

'Well, it means that you haven't put them in order properly and that you should sort them out before they come and bother you again.'

'You might be right' agreed Irian.

'So, what kind of thoughts don't you want in your head?'

'I think there are some thoughts that we just can't sort out because the situations that cause such thoughts don't depend just on us.'

'That's true, but then you have to find a way to accept them the way they are, so they'll become less heavy to carry along with you.'

'Well, I can't accept them because they're not right.'

'So if you know that they're not right, where's the problem? That's why you have your life to prove that your point of view is the right one. Problems are to be solved and not to be ignored. And even if you don't solve them, at least you can say you've tried. Problems should be taken as a challenge not as a burden' reasoned his father. 'Anyway, is all this something to do with the Legend?'

'In a way yes' replied Irian.

'Why is this Legend so important to you, Irian?'

'Because I know that it's not just a Legend. It's our past, I know it, dad' said Irian 'and I'm sure you all know it too but for some reason you're hiding it from me.'

'Nobody is hiding anything from you but I can't tell you something that I don't know myself or that I can't support with facts. The Sudba Creatures are pretty mighty if they really are hiding their powers. Just ask yourself why the mayor won't allow anybody to enter the inner quarters; it's because he has no solutions to the question of how to get rid of the Creatures if they ever did regain their powers. The mayor doesn't want them back, they would be his worst nightmare. So, if he hasn't done anything about it yet, it's because he's trying to find the best way to tackle the situation. You see, nobody is hiding anything, but what's the point in talking about something and spreading panic around if you don't have the relevant facts or the strategy to combat the problem?'

'I agree, but still, why call it a legend instead of admitting it's our past?'

'When you want to soothe somebody's pain, you don't go and speak to the person in a way that makes him feel even stronger pain; you tell him something to make him feel better until you do find the right medicine.'

Irian felt a bit better after this conversation, as if somebody had soothed his mental anguish.

In the evening, Uncle Tattoo and Maia came to pay them a visit, and Irian was very excited to see them. They stayed for dinner and then Irian managed to get Uncle Tattoo to his room while Maia stayed talking to Irian's parents in the dining room.

'I saw the mask' said Uncle Tattoo once they had got to Irian's room.

'Did you?' Irian was so excited that he could feel his heart pumping blood even to his toes.

'Yes' replied Uncle Tattoo. 'I've already made a copy.'

'Wonderful! So, how did it go at Gartika's?' asked Irian with great interest.

'It wasn't easy, but I managed' replied Uncle Tattoo. 'We must be very careful because I think Gartika knows we're descendants of Arena and Emo's.'

'How could she know?' asked Irian in surprise.

'She told me: "It's easy for you not to believe in the Legend because you're protected". You see, what else could she mean by that if not that we're their descendants?'

'So what did you reply?'

'Nothing, I pretended I didn't understand what she meant.'

'That woman!' said Irian angrily. 'We have to get the original mask as soon as possible.'

'We should go and get it tonight. It's the first night of the Full Moon.'

'What has the Full Moon got to do with Gartika and the mask?' asked Irian, confused.

'The only time when the Creatures' powers were protected at night was during the first night of the Full Moon, so I suppose that if they needed to have a meeting, it would be then. The mayor regularly receives letters from the Mask Heads the day after the first night of the Full Moon. So, I was thinking that the Mask Heads could be having their meeting tonight and Gartika will definitely be going, which leaves us free to get the mask.'

'Amazing' said Irian. 'It's true that when I went to see the Water Castle and when Mrs Bigone and I first went to see Gartika, it was during the night of the Full Moon. But what are we going to say to my mum? She gave me a serious telling off the other day because of the Legend.'

'We could say that you're coming to sleep at our place.'

'Excellent' said Irian. 'I'm ready.'

It was a beautiful starry night, as if somebody had sprinkled glitter over the sky, making it all wonderful and shiny. The moonlight was so intense that the streetlamps could have almost been switched off, and below, the shadows appeared as huge, banging into each other.

They went to Uncle Tattoo's house first to get the fake mask and Irian was amazed to see how authentic it looked. The expression on it was the same as that of the real mask and its surface was smooth and pleasant, which painfully reminded him of the poor Kindness Creature.

When they got to Gartika's house, they noticed that her lights were on, so they had to find a place to hide.

'She's obviously not going anywhere' said Irian, who was crouched with Uncle Tattoo behind a bench a little way from Gartika's house.

'Let's wait and see' replied Uncle Tattoo. 'It's not very late.'

Just then, they heard her gate opening and Gartika coming out. She didn't switch off all the lanterns, leaving some of them to burn. Irian remembered how she had gone to sleep with her lights on the last time he had come with Mrs Bigone. The shadow of her nose in the moonlight was so big that it covered the whole width of the avenue. Gartika carefully closed the gate and then suspiciously looked around before leaving the place.

Further in the distance, Irian and Uncle Tattoo saw two men approaching, followed by their large shadows. As they got closer to Gartika's house, Irian and Uncle Tattoo nearly screamed when they recognised Obeese and Smeerius standing there like two obedient children.

'We're ready, my lady' said Obeese to Gartika.

'Everybody is waiting for us' said Smeerius.

'Let's go then' said Gartika sharply.

Uncle Tattoo and Irian felt like somebody had poured a large jug of cold water over them.

'Obeese' said Uncle Tattoo, disappointed. 'I would never ever have believed he'd have anything to do with that nasty woman.'

'He called her 'my lady'' said Irian. 'When I was in the Water Castle, that's what the Creatures called the Queen. So Gartika really might be Ranna.'

'But how could Gartika be Ranna?' asked Uncle Tattoo.

'Who knows? You know Ranna is capable of doing all sorts of things.'

'Listen, we'll talk about that later' said Uncle Tattoo. 'We need to go and get the mask now.'

'We'll have to jump over the gate. It's the only way' said Irian.

'I'm too fat for that' said Uncle Tattoo. 'You'll have to do it while I stay here and watch.'

'Ok' said Irian 'but what shall I do if she comes back while I'm in her house?'

'Hide. Don't let her see you. I'll stay here and wait for you.'

Irian jumped over the gate and then went to see if any windows had been left open for him to climb through. However, all the windows were closed and he didn't want to break any of them to avoid making any noise, and also because that would clearly prove to Gartika that somebody had tried to break in. He had little time to find a solution and then he remembered that Gartika had a cat, so he had the idea of entering through the cat-flap. The opening was very small and Irian wished he were one of the contortionist, coming to perform in Destin, who could fit their supple bodies into all manner of small boxes – a technique he could have done with just then. So, first, he passed the fake mask carefully through the hole and then concentrated all his energy focusing it on the small opening. He managed to pass his head through, but when it came to his shoulders, he just couldn't make them narrow enough to fit. He pushed and pushed and even badly scratched his shoulder before finally managing to squeeze into Gartika's house.

The house was messy with many, many papers strewn all over, and Irian was curious to see what they were about. However, as he had a very little time, he decided to get the mask and then get out as quickly as possible. Uncle Tattoo had told him that Gartika was hiding the mask in her bedside table, so he went straight over to look for it. He was so happy to find it in there that he even kissed it. He placed it in his little rucksack and then laid the fake one in its place. Having done that, he thought to himself that he could have a quick look at the papers in her sitting room just to see exactly what Gartika was plotting next.

He put the rucksack on his back and was just about to open the bedroom door when he heard the key in the front door. Irian was gripped by a sudden panic, and his eyes darted around desperately looking for a place to hide. Gartika's bedroom was plain and there wasn't much choice, so he dived under the bed, the refuge most of the heroes in his favourite adventure books would resort to when they had some sort of monster on their tail. Irian, however, found Gartika worse than a monster, and lay waiting to see what was to become of him.

Gartika entered the house and headed straight for her bedroom and Irian could only see her ugly brownish shoes from where he was lying. He saw them moving towards the bedside table and he was so scared of being discovered that he even tried holding his breath.

'There you are' she said. 'We're going to destroy you tonight. Everybody has to learn his lesson. Now let's get back to the meeting. You always make me change things and make everything more difficult.'

Irian wondered who Gartika was talking to, as she seemed alone in the room. She stayed there for some time and then walked out. Irian heard the front door open and then close again. He remained under the bed for a little longer just in case Gartika came back. As nothing was happening he rolled out and decided to leave this horrible place as soon as possible. However, before leaving, he went to check the fake mask and realised it was no longer there. "She was talking to the mask" thought Irian to himself. "She wants to destroy the Kindness Creature's mask", Irian was terrified at the thought.

He went to the cat-flap again and proceeded to get out with the same difficulty. He pushed the mask through first and then his body until he finally reached the gate and jumped over it. Uncle Tattoo was waiting for him and they rushed home to talk, as it was too risky to hold a discussion in the silent avenues of the sleeping town. Apart from that, by no means did they want to cross Gartika's path.

'Have you got it?' asked Ginimma as soon as she saw them.

'Yes' replied Irian. 'Just in time.'

'Why? Did Gartika suspect anything?' asked Ginimma.

'No' replied Irian, 'but she wanted to destroy it.'

'But she can't destroy anything that Arameen has created. It would only be going against him' replied Grandfather, who had come round to wait for Irian and Uncle Tattoo to come back.

'Well, I don't know' said Irian and then told them what he had heard.

'Who knows' said Uncle Tattoo 'maybe Ranna is trying to get her independence from Arameen. Otherwise, why would she go and destroy his energy?'

'I think Ranna is somehow using Gartika to achieve her aims' said Irian. 'Obeese referred to her as "my lady" and that's what the Sudba Creatures call the Queen.'

'Obeese' said Grandfather, 'what has Obeese got to do with Gartika?'

Irian explained how they had seen Obeese and Smeerius come and collect Gartika.

'Why would he do something like that?' asked Grandfather. 'It's against everything his family stands for.'

'There are still things we need to find out' said Uncle Tattoo. 'Anyway, we have the mask, so Gartika is going to destroy the fake one, which gives us a little more time to think what to do next.'

'I think we need to find out what this Mask Heads organisation is all about' said Grandfather.

'Whatever it is' said Ginimma, 'it seems fishy to me.'

Imagine and Live It Day

When the mayor announced the following day that they had received another threatening letter signed by the Mask Heads, Irian didn't need any further confirmation of the fact that Obeese, Smeerius and that nasty woman, Gartika, really did belong to the organisation. Irian kept on thinking about Obeese and wondered what had made him join such a terrible group. So many things seemed to have happened since that day when Obeese had revealed the Creatures' secret to him. Given that Obeese was a Mask Head member, Irian couldn't understand why he had revealed the secret to him. Irian had the impression that his town had two different but parallel lives and its people two characters. Everybody and everything was hiding some extraordinary secret waiting to be found out.

Early that morning, Irian took Ogi to his training lesson. Thanks to these lessons, Ogi was becoming better and better trained and Irian was very impressed with the improvements in his little puppy's behaviour. Ogi could still be very capricious at times, making Irian loose his temper, however, there was a great complicity between them. Ogi followed him everywhere and was sometimes very possessive of Irian, so if Irian wanted to go out without Ogi, he had to do so very cautiously. But then, on his return, Ogi would bark at him as if telling him off for leaving him behind.

On the way back from Ogi's lesson, Irian met Armianda whom he hadn't seen for a long time. He met her in her street, so Armianda invited him in.

'You have to pick a card' said Armianda when they got into her room.

'What kind of card?' asked Irian.

'You have to pull out one of these cards and it'll tell you what your week is going to be like' explained Armianda, passing over a little silky bag to Irian.

'How can they tell what my week is going to be like?'

'Oh, it's only a game, Irian' said Armianda 'but, it's quite fun. That's why I like it.'

Irian put his hand into the bag and could feel the touch of soft plastic cards under his fingers. He found the idea quite amusing.

'There we go' said Irian, drawing out a card.

'Let's see' said Armianda. 'Do you mind if I read it? I like reading these cards.'

'Well, if you want to' replied Irian.

'So, it says: *"You're about to experience an extraordinary event that nobody else has ever experienced. Your life is going to change and you'll finally learn what you've always wanted to know. However, be careful, the changes ahead are not always easy ones"* read Armianda. 'Hey, I've never ever got this card before and I've never seen anybody else draw it out either. It's great, isn't it?'

Irian knew that it was just a game, but it still made him think. He had a look at the card that was beautifully written, the writing surrounded by botanical decoration.

'Where did you get them?' asked Irian.

'One of my mum's friends made them for me for one of my birthdays' replied Armianda. 'Have you heard about the letter?'

'You mean the letter that the Mask Heads sent to the mayor?'

'Yes' replied Armianda. 'It's terrible, isn't it?'

'Well, I don't know the exact contents of the letter, but I've heard they've threatened the Local Council again.'

'My father has got a copy of it' revealed Armianda. 'Do you want to see it?'

'Oh, yes, I'd love to' replied Irian. 'Your father allowed you to read the letter?'

'Not really' answered Armianda, enigmatically. 'Come on, let's go to his study. He's not there.'

'What's he going to say if he comes back and sees us there?'

'Don't be such a coward. Anyway, I'd be in trouble, not you!'

Mr Tappin's study was in the attic and it was a large and incredibly tidy room. Unlike Irian's father, Mr Tappin had everything meticulously arranged. Each book was catalogued in alphabetical order and there was no clutter on his desk. The desk itself was enormous, with a typewriter and a stylized book holder in the shape of a person. Above the desk was a board with an amazing amount of colourful messages, probably to remind Mr Tappin of the things he needed to do.

'I like the lamp' said Irian, pointing to the beautiful vase lamp on one of the shelves above Mr Tappin's desk.

'It used to belong to the Creatures' revealed Armianda.

'Really?' asked Irian. 'So how come your father has it now?'

'He found it abandoned in one of the north-west flower forests' replied Armianda.

'Yes, but it could have belonged to anybody. How can he be sure it really was the Creatures' property?'

'Because it has the Creatures' writings on it.'

'And does he know what it says?'

'No' said Armianda. 'That's why he's sure it belonged to the Creatures because nobody is capable of reproducing their alphabet.'

'You should ask Mrs Bigone' suggested Irian. 'She's very good at it.'

'Oh, yes. Dad probably hasn't thought about it. I'll tell him. Anyway, when the lamp is lit, the flame inside accentuates the elegant calligraphy. It's beautiful. Shall we light it?'

'Well, look' said Irian 'why don't you show me the letter first? Anyway, we wouldn't be able to understand the writings. We'd better smuggle the lamp to Mrs Bigone's house. She'll know what it says.'

'You're a coward' said Armianda.

'Stop saying I'm a coward. I was just saying what's the point in looking at the lamp if we don't understand the message. Whether the lamp is lit or not, what does that change right now?' said Irian, annoyed.

'And you're bad-tempered too' commented Armianda.

This time Irian decided not to reply to her remark. Armianda could make cutting remarks and she always had to be right.

'Can you show me the letter?' he said to change the subject.

'It's in the drawer over there. You see?' said Armianda, sitting comfortably in her father's chair.

Irian opened the drawer, and saw a leaf as Armianda had said. It had the Creatures' emblem on the top of it, which was made up of an open book, held in two white hands containing on the right page an image of a man and on the left page an image of a woman. A marker in the form of a golden key divided the two pages. It read as follows:

> *"The Sudba Creatures are about to return to the town and restore Queen Ranna to the throne. This is our last warning before coming back to the Amphitheatre. All pregnant women should be ready to come and declare their pregnancy. Whoever decides to disobey the Queen will be seriously punished. We are to return forever to rule the town of Destin."*

'It's awful!' said Irian. 'How come the mayor can't do anything against these people? He's the mayor after all.'

'His power is nothing in comparison with the Creatures. Otherwise, he would already have done something.'

'What does your dad say?' asked Irian.

'He doesn't say much. But I think he's trying to track down the members of the Mask Heads.'

'So, has he got any names?'

'I don't know' replied Armianda. 'It's so hard to get anything out of my dad. I heard him going out very late last night. Who knows where he was off to. I just heard my mum telling him to be careful.'

They suddenly heard barking in the hallway, coming from Armianda's dog and Ogi.

'That's my dad' said Armianda. 'Let's go downstairs before he catches us here.'

'Listen, I've got to go anyway' said Irian who had to hurry

home before his mother realised he'd stayed out longer than planned. She had been so strict recently whenever Irian had to go somewhere that he didn't want to take any risks.

They went downstairs and on the way down almost crashed into Mr Tappin who was rushing towards his study, carrying a large heavy bag. Irian always wondered whether there was even one single muscle on Mr Tappin, he was so thin. In his eyes even the curious pupils seemed long and thin; moreover, given the fact they were green, they looked almost like cat's eyes, seeing things that only the sharpest vision can see. Irian thought that Mr Tappin's body appeared as if somebody had taken a sausage of modelling clay and rubbed it in their palms to get his long arms and legs. Nuro used to joke that the only muscled part of Mr Tappin's body must have been his fingers as Mr Tappin always had something to type up on his machine. Whenever Irian visited Armianda, Mr Tappin would be in his study typing, the striking of the keys resounding all round the house.

'Hello, my darling' he said to Armianda. 'Hello, Irian. I haven't seen you for a long time. Excuse me, both of you, but I'm in a terrible hurry.'

'What's up, dad?' asked Armianda.

'Have to finish an article... Very little time... See you both later' replied Mr Tappin.

Irian would have loved to know what Mr Tappin was writing about, but he heard the sound of the cannon, signalling midday and that he really had to hurry home. In Destin, they had a tradition of firing a cannon ball to mark midday and although the cannon was placed well out of the town, its loud sound echoed everywhere in the town.

Irian had arrived home just in time, as his mother got back only a few moments after him. He spent the rest of the afternoon playing with Ogi, who seemed tireless whenever anybody wanted to play with him. Irian was growing fonder and fonder of his little puppy and he didn't even need to use a lead anymore to take Ogi around.

However, Irian couldn't relax – he reckoned the Creatures were almost ready to return to the town of Destin, given that they had dared to send such a letter to the mayor. He knew that the time had come to face the murky world of the Creatures – the one that everybody had been avoiding for a very, very long time.

* * *

The following morning Irian woke up very early, being thirsty, and nearly let out a scream when he noticed a chair next to his bed. It was *Imagine and Live It Day*, and this meant that he had been chosen to participate in the game! There was a letter on the chair, so he opened it and read the message:

"Dear Irian Horvats. We are happy to allow you to participate in our game. Just open your bedroom window, sit on the chair and have a good time. The Good Will Association."

Irian quickly got dressed and then opened the window before sitting down on the chair. The moment he sat down, Ogi realised something was going on, so he quickly jumped onto Irian's lap.

'Hold on tight' said Irian to his little puppy. 'Off we go!'

The chair made a sharp movement forward and then backwards again in readiness for the flight, like sportsmen do when warming up for a match. In the meantime, Irian attached the seatbelt and took Ogi in his arms. A few moments later, they were flying high up in the air. The day had just started to break, and the sunrays were straining to penetrate through the darkness. Irian had the impression that he had wings and was flying without moving from the seat. They were flying towards the First Circle and it was amazing to see how quickly they arrived there.

The chair followed Sunny Avenue, which was one of the two main avenues in the town and Irian thought it would go directly to the Amphitheatre, but the chair then suddenly turned left. Irian had no idea where the chair was taking him, and was surprised when it stopped just above Gartika's garden. It hovered there for a few moments when a little door in the middle of the garden opened, and the chair flew through. Irian didn't know whether he should panic or not, but he decided to wait and see what was going to happen. They were heading through a long corridor full of flying light balls like the ones Irian had already seen in the Water Castle. The corridor seemed endless when suddenly they passed through another door, and Irian realised it was a secret entrance to the inner quarters of the Amphitheatre. The chair took him a bit further in and then landed in the middle of a large round room.

Irian got off the chair followed by Ogi. The room was scarcely furnished and Irian was amazed at the height of the ceiling. He couldn't quite situate the room in the Amphitheatre but thought it probably served as a meeting place. Its large hematite mirrors had tarnished over time and the different coloured candles around the room were half-burned down, with wax creating various shapes on the floor. A massive door led to another long corridor with several rooms on each side. Each room was different and Irian thought they must have been the Creatures' bedrooms.

The inner quarters was such a large residence that Irian was sure the corridors spread out beneath the whole town of Destin. Walking around, he came across something very unusual. It was an enormous room with its walls covered by thousands of different clocks that had probably stopped over time and were now partly hidden beneath layers of dust. Irian went to have a closer look and saw there was a name and a flower year written under each clock. He realised that each clock actually represented the life span of a particular person. The idea that these clocks had really functioned at one time and had indicated somebody's life expectancy terrified Irian.

However, what really attracted his attention was a large book, left on the table in the middle of the room. The book was as long as one of Irian's arms, made of gold and covered with beautifully cut precious stones with their many facets sparkling by the light of Irian's candle. There was a large square stone in the middle of the book cover surrounded by other smaller round gems, each stone of a different hue.

Irian tried to lift it up, but the book was so heavy that he dropped it back on the table by accident, and as it fell, it opened up in the middle. Even Irian couldn't have imagined what was to happen next. Letters started appearing in the book and he heard a deep booming voice.

'Thank you for saving the Sudba Creatures, Irian' said the voice and then started to laugh, its laughter echoing around the Amphitheatre.

'Who are you?' asked Irian, terrified.

'I am Arameen. And you have just released the great powers of the Sudba Creatures. They will be most happy to come back to their rightful place and rule the town again now.'

'No, it can't be!' screamed Irian.

'Yes it's true! Go and tell your people that we are back and that this time we are back forever' Arameen's voice shook the room while Ogi barked in distress.

'So, this is the famous Destiny Book' said Irian desperately.

'Yes it is' replied Arameen.

Irian was trying to close the book or tear its pages out but it was impossible to destroy it or do anything with it. Its pages were made of silk and they were turning continuously, showing text that appeared and disappeared just like the messages on the boards of the Amphitheatre.

'You will not be able to close it' explained Arameen. 'Before the Sudba Creatures disappeared, the Queen ordered every Creature to hide its powers in that great book. She then cast a spell so that whoever was to open it one day, would help the Creatures to regain their powers. However, not a single Destiner would have been able to perform such a feat because the book's powers are too strong and the Destiners are still in our hands so they would have been powerless to do it. You were the only one capable of such a thing as a descendant of Arena and Emo's. You have no choice now – you will have to accept our government.'

'Never!' shouted Irian. 'I'll finish Arena and Emo's plan and you'll be gone forever.'

'It is better for you to accept us' said Arameen, 'otherwise your future looks grim.'

Irian then heard other Creatures' voices; some were laughing and some were saying: "Thank you, Irian. Thank you so much!" Irian was desperate to do something but was incapable of changing the course of events now that the Destiny Book had been opened. While he stood there, broken and angry, the flying chair came and bumped into him so that he fell back into it. Irian didn't even fasten his seatbelt before he was already flying back through that long corridor leading back to Gartika's garden, Ogi on his lap barking during the whole journey.

'Take me to Grandfather's house!' he ordered the chair and obediently the chair set him down in Grandfather's garden.

Panic hits Destin

Irian knocked at the door and Grandfather opened it. When he saw Irian all broken and in tears, Grandfather immediately understood what had happened.

'The Creatures are back, aren't they?' he said seriously.

'Yes' replied Irian. 'I opened the Destiny Book by accident.'

Irian briefly recounted what had happened while Grandfather listened carefully and walked up and down the living room nervously, unable to sit down. Irian had never seen him so serious and worried, as if he were in the presence of a person he had never met before.

'The time has come to use the powers of the mask' said Grandfather after a long moment of thinking.

'You mean that we have to go and see Arameen?' asked Irian.

'Yes' answered Grandfather seriously. 'It's the only way.'

'But how?' asked Irian. 'We don't know where he is.'

'Well, we'll have to find out.'

'And what do we tell mum?'

'The truth' replied Grandfather. 'She'll learn it anyway.'

'But she'll be furious.' Irian didn't even want to imagine his mother's reaction.

'She'll be mad at you first but then she'll understand' said Grandfather. 'Listen, I'll go and talk to your uncle and see what he says.'

'And what shall I do? Can't I come with you?'

'I think you should speak to Mrs Bigone. She might have an idea. I'll come and get you as soon as I've spoken to Tattoo.'

Irian went to see Mrs Bigone, but as she wasn't there, he left her a message to call him back urgently and then went off to see Floria and Nuro. Nuro was at home by himself so he opened the door.

'Irian!' said Nuro worried. 'You look terrible!'

'The Sudba Creatures are back in town' said Irian who was now so pale that his red cheeks had almost disappeared from his face.

'What?' Nuro could hardly breathe with shock.

'It's all my fault' said Irian and then he told Nuro about the events in the inner quarters.

'Don't say that' Nuro was trying to console his friend. 'Listen, I'm supposed to meet Floria at Armianda's place. Let's go together.'

Armianda and Floria seemed to be having a great time because Irian and Nuro could already hear them laughing from the garden gate. Irian dreaded to think that he was going to spoil the fun Floria and Armianda were having together.

'You two look like death warmed up' said Armianda when she opened the door.

Just then, they heard the gate opening and Mr Tappin rushing in. His hair, which was normally always meticulously combed flat, now looked as if he had been sticking his fingers in an electrical socket.

'Very, very bad' he kept on saying while nervously walking towards his house.

'Can somebody tell me what's happening?' asked Armianda.

'The Creatures, my darling' said Mr Tappin 'It's terrible! Absolutely terrible! What are we going to do?'

'What are you talking about, dad?' asked Armianda whose face wasn't smiley anymore.

'The Creatures are back in town' announced Irian.

Floria, who had just come down and heard Irian pronounce these words, screamed, covering her face with her hands and Nuro went to take his sister in his arms.

'So, you know' said Mr Tappin.

'How did you learn about it?' asked Irian.

'The mayor has just called me to tell me the news. The Creatures have ordered him to dismiss everybody in the Local Council and they want to use him to pass on their messages to the Destiners.'

'What are they going to do?' asked Irian.

'I think they have to obey the Creatures. There's nothing else they can do really' replied Mr Tappin. 'Let's go upstairs to my study. I think we could all do with some rather sweet tea. We shouldn't allow the Creatures to knock us down. Every problem has a solution, but the solution might not always be clear in the beginning.'

Irian was wondering whether he should tell Mr Tappin the truth about him being the famous descendant. He felt responsible for the situation and he knew he was the only one who could improve things. However, he decided to wait a bit longer before revealing anything about his secret.

'So, what did the mayor tell you exactly?' asked Irian once they had got into Mr Tappin's study.

'He told me that the Destiny Book has been opened and the Creatures' powers released' replied Mr Tappin.

'And how did they inform the mayor about it?' asked Irian. 'Who came to tell him about it?'

'Smeerius Newance. Apparently, he has been working for the Mask Heads organisation for a long time. Who would ever have imagined that somebody as respectable as Smeerius would betray his town. Wait until the Destiners get to know about it.'

'Is the mayor going to tell the Destiners the news?' asked Nuro.

'Yes' replied Mr Tappin. 'He's going to give a speech about it on the radio this afternoon.'

'And where are the Creatures now?' asked Armianda.

'The mayor doesn't know. They probably have to organise themselves before re-establishing their government in the town. Never, never, never would I have imagined such a thing' sighed Mr Tappin.

Everybody sipped tea quietly and only a little bee buzzing around the room seemed undisturbed by the new order in the town of Destin. Even Ogi didn't have the heart to chase after it, so it was left to buzz in its moment of glory amid the silence of Mr Tappin's study. After finally settling in the vase lamp on Mr Tappin's desk it began flying quickly round in circles and its buzzing became so irritating that Mr Tappin tipped it out of the vase lamp and the bee made its escape from the tense atmosphere, buzzing out through the open window. Irian looked at the vase lamp that Mr Tappin had put back on his desk and remembered that the lamp used to belong to the Creatures.

'Where did you find that vase lamp?' asked Irian.

'One day I was writing an article about carnivorous flowers, so I went to visit the Wild Flower Forest. Walking through it, I nearly stumbled over something. When I looked down, I saw this vase lamp on the floor, so I picked it up' explained Mr Tappin. 'I think it must have belonged to the Creatures because it has strange writing on.'

'Do you mind if I borrow it?' asked Irian. 'I'll ask Mrs Bigone if she can tell me what it says.'

'Of course' replied Mr Tappin. 'Take it! I'd completely forgotten that Mrs Bigone can decipher the Creatures' writing.'

'Anyway' said Irian 'I have to go. My parents will be worried sick and I've left my talkastick at home.'

When Irian arrived home, everybody was waiting for him in the living room. There was his father, his mother, Auntie Ginimma, Grandfather and Grandmother. Irian knew very well it was the moment to reveal the truth and face his mother. He felt his throat retracting, and his mouth so dry that he couldn't swallow.

'I'm sorry, mother' said Irian, not knowing what else to say.

'Don't worry, Irian' she replied. 'I knew the day would come.'

'What do you mean?' asked Irian.

'I was trying to protect you, I was trying to keep you away from reality even though I knew things would happen one day anyway' she said and then burst into tears. 'Forgive me, son!'

'I'm the one who should be apologising' said Irian, hugging his mother.

'Irian' said Grandfather, 'Uncle Tattoo has disappeared.'

'Disappeared?' repeated Irian, falling into the chair.

'The Creatures have kidnapped him' replied Auntie Ginimma, sobbing.

'Why would they kidnap Uncle Tattoo?' asked Irian, bewildered.

'I don't know' said Grandfather.

'Somebody has burned down the Birthday Cave' said Grandmother. 'Apparently, it was one of the Mask Heads.'

'Obeese, Smeerius' said Irian. 'Why would they join such an organisation? I think we should go and speak to them.'

'Obeese has disappeared too' said Grandfather. 'I tried to see him and in *The Old Times* they say they can't find him anywhere.'

'I'm going to see Smeerius then. I wonder whether they're aware of the danger' said Irian. 'I think the Queen could even have forced them to work for her. When I last spoke to Obeese, he revealed the secret about the Creatures' powers to me. Why would he tell me such a thing if he was supporting the Creatures?'

'Because he knew you were the only one who could open the Destiny Book. He already knew that you are the famous descendant of Arena and Emo's. And this is exactly what the Creatures wanted. They wanted you to release their powers' explained Grandfather.

'Actually, it makes sense now that I think about it. When Nuro and I were in the Water Castle, we overheard the Mask Heads' meeting. They were talking about Cherry Taste and this is how they secretly call me because of the taste I create in Smeerius' mouth every time he sees me. Smeerius was telling Obeese he should kidnap me because he was closest to me. They wanted to kidnap me, probably to force me to open the Destiny Book. But, given that I was chosen to participate in *Imagine and Live it Day*, I opened the book by accident and made their plan work, so they don't need to kidnap me anymore' reasoned Irian. 'I have to find a way to destroy that book.'

'We should speak to Lozendge' said Grandfather. 'He might know how to destroy it.'

'Good idea' said Irian. 'The book is covered with precious stones and he said himself they come from Coruscatia.'

'We could go and pay him a visit' suggested Grandfather.

'They'll be in danger too' said Irian. 'The Glimmers who live in Coruscatia nowadays are the same Glimmers who escaped from Arameen in the past and who became Soothsayers during the Sudba Creatures' government. You can be sure that Arameen will try and punish them just as he wants to punish the Destiners.'

'You're right' said Grandfather. 'We should inform them of the situation before Arameen gets there.'

'We have to look for Tattoo' said Ginimma.

'We'll find him' said Grandfather. 'They can't hurt him either. We're Arena and Emo's descendants. We're not in danger but the others are.'

'Oh, the mayor is about to give his speech' said mother. 'Let's hear what he's got to say.'

She went to switch the radio on and was just in time. They all gathered around the radio to hear the mayor's words:

"Dear Destiners. A terrible, terrible thing has happened today in our town. Although we all believed the story of Queen Ranna and the Sudba Creatures to be nothing more than a Legend, it has indeed proved to be an all too real part of our past. The Sudba Creatures' powers were never actually destroyed but simply waiting in the pages of the Destiny Book to be unleashed once more on our beloved town. It is with deepest regret that I must inform you all that the Sudba Creatures are back in power to rule our town once again. I am to inform you that they will be back in the Amphitheatre within a short time and that every pregnant woman is obliged under their law to declare her pregnancy to the Queen. Whoever disobeys the Sudba Creatures will be severely punished. Decisions are no longer in the hands of the Local Council; we have no more power over this town. I will do my best to try and rid the town from the Creatures, but my powers are limited. If anyone has any suggestions, any ideas to combat the Creatures, I will be most glad of their help."

Oh my goodness, Maia is pregnant!' said Grandmother referring to Petalber's wife.

'Don't worry' said Irian. 'We'll think of something.'

Just then Irian's talkastick rang and he had Smodge on the line.

'Irian. My father has disappeared' said Smodge, without even saying hello.

'When did he disappear?' asked Irian quite coldly knowing that Smeerius belonged to the Mask Heads.

'This morning. We've called everybody he knows and nobody can find him. I've just heard the mayor on the radio. I'm worried the Sudba Creatures may have kidnapped him for some reason.'

'Well, he shouldn't have been working for the Mask Heads, then' said Irian indifferently.

'My father would never work for that organisation' replied Smodge. 'He would never have accepted to be part of them.'

'I saw him, Smodge' said Irian. 'I know he does belong to the organisation.'

'But, it's impossible! He wouldn't and he couldn't do such a thing. Please, Irian, believe me! You must help me find my father!'

Smodge sounded honest and he really did seem distraught. Irian had always liked Smodge and he decided to trust him.

'Listen, Smodge, my Uncle Tattoo has disappeared too. I'll do my best, but things aren't easy.'

'Some people say that you opened the Destiny Book and released the Creatures' powers' added Smodge. 'They even say that you're the famous descendant. Is it true?'

'Who told you that?' asked Irian, surprised and worried by other people's possible reactions.

'I've heard people saying so in the street.'

'Smodge, if you're my friend, trust me as I trust you' said Irian. 'We'll find your father. Don't worry. If I can, I'll come and see you later.'

At this, Irian thought it would be a better idea not to say anything to people about him being a descendant, because everybody would blame him for the situation and it would be difficult to improve things.

'I think people somehow know that I'm Arena and Emo's descendant. I don't know how, but I think we should ignore these remarks for the moment. I'll probably have to face the Creatures and the Queen, so I would prefer to keep good relations with the Destiners. They wouldn't understand things right now anyway.'

'You're right' said Grandfather. 'Otherwise they'd blame everything on you.'

The commotion in the streets of Destin was becoming more and more evident. Everybody seemed to be out talking to their neighbours or friends about the new order in the town. Panic seemed to have set in, and the Destiners dreaded to think that the Legend had now taken the form of reality. This cheerful and pleasant town was slowly drowning in sadness and despair, and the Destiners' red cheeks appeared to have lost their brightness in exchange for a washout pallor. The Creatures hadn't yet returned, but their presence could already be felt in the town; it seemed as if no wind could blow it away, because it was so deeply absorbed in the fibres of every wall of the town.

Irian remembered he was supposed to see Mrs Bigone, so he went to talk to her about the situation.

'Irian' she said as soon as she saw him in the doorway, 'did you really open the Destiny Book?'

'How do you know?'

'Well, everybody is talking about it.'

'Yes, I did. It was an accident. I didn't mean to open it. But how do people know about it? I don't understand.'

'The Creatures might have spread the rumour around so that people in the town will blame you for the situation. If people accuse you and hate you, it will be easier for the Creatures to get rid of you. It's because they know they have no power over you.'

'That's awful' said Irian, distressed. 'I only wanted to help. Why would people accuse me or blame me? I didn't want the Creatures to come back.'

'You know what, Irian, whenever you offer help to somebody, the person will be sceptical at first because he is going to wonder why you would want to help. People generally think that if you want to help it is because there's something in it for you' explained Mrs Bigone 'I know that you genuinely want to help and finish Arena and Emo's task, but it is going to be your duty to prove it to the Destiners. People are accusing you because they're scared; it was easier for them to accept lies than the truth. You see, every time I found out something to do with the Creatures, they would ban my books or accuse me of spreading panic. Whenever you introduce something, you have to fight to make people understand that your idea is the right one.'

'Apparently, I'm the only one who can do something about the situation, but I have no idea what to do.'

'Ranna and the Sudba Creatures are only Arameen's puppets. If you really want to change things, I'm afraid you'll have to go and pay Arameen a visit.'

'That's fine with me, but where am I going to find him?'

'You should speak to the Glimmers. They might be able to help you.'

'By the way, I've got something for you' Irian suddenly remembered that he had brought the vase lamp that bore the Creatures' writing that Mr Tappin had found in the Wild Flower Forest.'

'What is it?'

'It's something that you only can understand. See what is says please.'

'It's the Creatures' writing' said Mrs Bigone almost enchanted. 'Can you pass me the matches, please? They're there on the table.'

Irian passed the matches and Mrs Bigone lit the lamp to see better what was written on it. The lamp seemed to have changed its colour under the candle light, and from green it turned into a bright orange while the letters appeared clearer and easier to read.

"The Sudba Creatures are here to obey their master. Arameen is the master of all and the ultimate leader. The first ray of the morning sun will point to Kinoont Temple, which is Arameen's residence; just follow it and it will show you where your master lives"

'The first sunray' repeated Irian. 'But there isn't only one sunray that appears in the morning.'

'I don't know, I've never tried to look, but I think we should definitely look for it. We have nothing to lose anyway.'

'It's amazing' said Irian. 'Mr Tappin has had this lamp for such a long time and we only got to discover its meaning now.'

'The Creatures must have lost it in the forest.'

'Yes, they were hiding in the Wild Flower Forest. It makes sense that Mr Tappin found the lamp there.'

'Have you spoken to Peena? Have you told her the news?' asked Mrs Bigone.

'No, I haven't. We could call her now, what do you think?' said Irian.

'Yes, I think she should know what's happening. She might be able to tell you what to do.'

Irian took his talkastick out and asked to be connected with Peena. He realised he hadn't spoken to her for quite a while and he felt bad about it. However, time hadn't been much on his side and he had also been waiting to be able to give her some good news. He so much hoped that she would have some kind of solution to help him send away this nightmare that had enveloped the town of Destin.

'If the book has been opened' said Peena after Irian had told her everything 'there is no other way but to destroy Arameen. That will break the spell he cast on the Glimmers, and Ranna will be useless once she finds herself without the Sudba Creatures and Arameen. She will have to leave the town.'

'But Arameen will never let me set foot in his temple' said Irian.

'You said you have the mask' said Peena. 'Arameen is blind and he only feels things through energies and it's the same thing for the Light Creatures. With the mask he'll simply think that you're one of the Creatures or Ranna who has come to ask for advice. The only place where he can see who you really are is in the Mirror Room. You should never let him take you to that room. That's why you have to feel very confident when you go, otherwise he'll sense through your energies that there is something wrong and might want to take you to the Mirror Room to make sure that you're one of the Creatures. The good thing is that the Creatures will not even imagine that you'd be going to face Arameen because they'll think that the real mask has been destroyed. That will make things easier for you. That's why they were desperate to get the mask back.'

'How do you know all this, Peena?' asked Irian.

'When Ranna blinded me, she also transferred some of her powers onto me, even though she might not be aware of it. I can't see with my eyes, but when I sense things that belong or used to belong to the Creatures, they help me penetrate their world and get to know more about them.'

'So, let's imagine that I manage to get to the Kinoont Temple and meet Arameen. What do I do then?'

'Arameen controls everything by the power in his stick. Without that stick, he would be nothing. So your duty is to destroy the stick but I wouldn't know how to do it because its powers are enormously strong. I think you should speak to your Glimmer friends. They might be able to tell you how to do it. The stick is covered in precious stones, which I don't know much about. Speak to them and see.'

'What do I do if Ranna comes for me? I'm sure she'll try to take revenge on me.'

'She can't do anything to you, but she can try to find ways to blackmail you. Don't fall into her traps. You can't go against her will, but you mustn't allow her to persuade you to take the destiny necklace or accept her government. You must know that you have more power than she does, so whatever she says she's going to do, you must ignore her. She'll be tough, but that should only motivate you to find the way to destroy her. You have very little time, so call the Glimmers now and go and see them as soon as you can.'

'But if I leave the town now, people will think that I'm trying to escape because it's all my fault' said Irian.

'Never mind what they say. They are powerless. On the contrary, you have the power to change things and they'll be thankful to you one day. When people are scared, they can think anything' explained Peena 'but don't worry, you know the truth and truth will clear their eyes and their minds one day. If the Destiners had known about Arena and Emo, they would probably have gone to denounce them to Ranna but only because they were scared of being severely punished. However, when Arena and Emo saved the town, the people were so grateful to them that they became the most honoured people in the town. Don't let anybody influence you. Fight for what you think is right.'

Past Secrets now revealed

The mayor had received the order from the Creatures to disband the Local Council and to remove his guard from the Amphitheatre. Arameen had sent the Light Creatures to survey the town temporarily until the Sudba Creatures and the Queen returned. Irian thought that it was a good thing in a way, because that would mean fewer Light Creatures to face when visiting the Kinoont temple. The mayor had forbidden all the women to get pregnant until the Local Council had found a solution, and he was secretly trying to send already pregnant women out of the town for a while to save their babies from the destiny decision.

The next day Nuro and Floria came to Irian crying and he could hardly understand what they were saying when he opened the door. They seemed in such a state of shock that Irian had to let them calm down first before they could actually say anything.

'We've got lines' said Floria.

'What lines?' asked Irian confused.

'Look at my left hand!' said Nuro. 'It has lines on it. It means that my destiny is already in the Creatures' hands.'

'No, it can't be' said Irian, looking at his friend's hand and then at his own hand which looked just the same as usual.

'The Creatures have distributed leaflets to tell us they'll be back very soon' said Nuro.

'Have you got a leaflet?' asked Irian.

'Yes, here you are' said Nuro, still sobbing.

'Who gave you this?' asked Irian.

'They threw the leaflets out from hot air balloons so that everybody can read them' replied Floria.

'You're so lucky' said Nuro. 'At least they can't do anything to you.'

'Oh, don't say that' replied Irian. 'I'm at the top of their revenge list. Remember, it was my ancestors who sent them away from the town in the first place. And seeing that Arena and Emo are not here anymore, they'll try to make **ME** pay. Apart from that, the Destiners now hate me too because they think it's my fault that the Creatures are back. So, you see, I wouldn't call that being lucky. And also, if anybody has to go and face them, then it is up to me to do it, isn't it?'

'Sorry I shouldn't have said that' said Nuro. 'I feel so strange. I don't feel responsible for what I'm saying.'

'Don't worry' said Irian. 'Every cloud has a silver lining. Can I see the leaflet, please?'

'Yes. Here' said Nuro, passing a yellowish leaflet to Irian. Irian opened it and then read out:

"We would like to inform you that we, the Sudba Creatures, are back to the town of Destin. We shall be returning to the Amphitheatre very soon. Whoever tries to escape the town will be severely punished. All pregnant women are obliged to come and report their pregnancy. We invite them to come and enrol on our list, which you can find at the entrance to the Amphitheatre for an appointment with the Queen."

'I hope there are not many pregnant women in the town' said Irian.

'Isn't Petalber's wife, Maia, pregnant?' asked Floria.

'Yes, she is unfortunately' replied Irian.

'And have you had any news from Uncle Tattoo?' asked Nuro.

'Apparently, the mayor said that the Creatures have kidnapped him because Ranna wants him to draw them all'.

'What do you mean?' asked Nuro.

'The Sudba Creatures only remained alive in spirit form when they had to hide their powers. So, Uncle Tattoo is going to draw them all, as he is the only one capable of doing it and then, they are going to embody their images and so return to the Amphitheatre. They can only return once Uncle Tattoo has drawn them all.'

'He's going to have an amazing job' said Floria.

'I know' said Irian. 'Poor Uncle Tattoo.'

'Who would ever have thought that the Sudba Creatures would come back!' sighed Nuro.

Things had begun to change rapidly in the town and every day there was a new law to respect. Irian received a call from Smodge who told him that his father had returned home and that he would like to speak to him.

'I'm so glad to see you' said Smeerius once Irian had arrived 'I apologise, I'm so so sorry.'

'Why would you need to apologise?' asked Irian.

'I nearly caused you so much trouble. It's terrible, Irian. I'm so sorry' said Smeerius.

'I don't understand, Mr Newance. What are you saying?' asked Irian, completely confused.

'I used to belong to the Mask Heads, not because I wanted to, but because Ranna used her powers to manipulate me for such a long, long time. She needed the most influential people in the town; people nobody would suspect to be involved in such a horrible organisation' revealed Smeerius.

'I knew there was something going on' said Irian. 'But why didn't you tell me that before?'

'I couldn't. I was under her spell. She put us in a state of hypnosis, so when she wasn't around we were just normal people and we would forget about our secret life. But, as soon as she was around, she could do anything with us.'

'"WE"'said Irian 'Who do you mean by "WE"?'

'Obeese, Mr Integger too.'

'But how did she manage to cast a spell on you?' asked Irian.

'Well, Ranna was hiding in Gartika's body for a long time...'

'Oh, I knew it. I knew it' said Irian. 'I knew that Gartika had some connection with Ranna. It was so obvious. How could she hide in Gartika's body, though?'

'It's a long story but I'll tell you if you really want to know and I suppose you do' said Smeerius and then took a deep breath before continuing. 'When Arena and Emo saved the town from the Sudba Creatures, Ranna ordered everybody to hide their powers in the Destiny Book, hoping that somebody would open it one day. The Sudba Creatures then had to leave the town, but of course Ranna didn't want to abandon the Amphitheatre and her position. She was desperate to get her powers back and rule the town again. Arameen gave her one chance to change things and he helped her possess the body of a baby who was to be born the day following their fall. However, the baby was so ugly, that the mother abandoned it outside the town, so her plan didn't work. Arameen was furious at her for allowing Arena and Emo to defeat the Sudba Creatures, though on the other hand, he still wanted to keep control over them. Therefore, he gave them the Water Castle, and Ranna managed to reunite the Creatures who had been hiding, powerless, all over the place. The Water Castle became their secret residence, but it appeared only every twenty years, as the Creatures were still too weak to show up in their full form the rest of the time, apart from Ranna who could still appear for a short time during the first night of the Full Moon.'

'And what happened to the Kindness Creature?' asked Irian. 'Ranna must have realised that he had been helping Arena and Emo.'

'The Kindness Creature became no other than Sir Esteam' revealed Smeerius.

'But how?' asked Irian, bewildered.

'The Kindness Creature grew very fond of Arena and Emo and on no account did it want to abandon them. After the fall of the Sudba Creatures, Emo was asked to rule the town' replied Smeerius 'and I think it was an arrangement between Emo and the Kindness Creature for the Kindness Creature to rule the town itself. I think their arrangement will remain an enigma forever; nobody knows how the Kindness Creature became Sir Esteam, not even the Creatures themselves. The Kindness Creature might have chosen to become a mortal so as to become a Destiner. It could have been an arrangement with Arameen.'

'Why? Because the Creatures can't die?'

'No, you have to destroy their powers if you want them to disappear.'

'That's incredible!' commented Irian. 'But why didn't the

Kindness Creature allow anybody to enter the inner quarters of the Amphitheatre, then?'

'Because it knew about the Creatures' secret and the powers hidden in the Destiny Book. It knew that opening the book would have helped the Creatures to regain their powers and it obviously had no solution about how to destroy it. It was a way to protect the Destiners from Ranna and her government.'

'Do you think the Kindness Creature was aware that it was once a Glimmer?' asked Irian.

'I don't know' replied Smeerius. 'It might have been. It's difficult to say.'

'So how did Ranna become Gartika?'

'As I told you before, Ranna and the other Creatures lived in their secret residence, which was the Water Castle, situated in the Wild Flower Forest. So, one day when walking around the Castle, Ranna met a man who was neither scared of her nor of the carnivorous flowers. He started to speak to Ranna and he told her he was hiding after playing a nasty trick on his boss. The man used to work as a magician and his name was Gadious Cheater.'

'Gadious Cheater' repeated Irian. 'I wondered what his relation with the Queen was. He's been following me around, threatened me...'

'I know' said Smeerius. 'You see, Gadious was very good at disguising himself and he was also very good at hypnosis and becoming invisible. Moreover, he could also accept people entering his body.'

'What do you mean?' asked Irian.

'He could "lend" his body to other people, which means that different spirits could embody him. Given that Ranna was desperate to get back to the town of Destin, Gadious was just what she needed because thanks to him, she could settle down in Destin and eventually find a way to unleash the powers of the Destiny Book. He taught her the skills of hypnosis and she was becoming very good at it. Once she was ready, she entered Gadious' body and moved into the town. She disguised herself well and she called herself Gartika.'

'I thought Gartika looked more like a man than a woman. I

knew there was something going on with that woman. But how could Gadious Cheater become invisible when visiting me?'

'It wasn't Gadious visiting you. It was Ranna, her spirit actually, because she was too weak to appear in her full form.'

'But why did she say she was Gadious then?'

'Because it was too dangerous to tell the truth. She couldn't reveal the truth before finding a solution for unleashing her powers. The time she tried to enter the Amphitheatre, she appeared as Gadious, because nobody knew Gadious in Destin anyway. And using Gadious' tricks, she escaped from the prison.'

'So how did you get to meet Ranna and become a Mask Heads' member?'

'You see, in order to fulfil her ambition, Ranna needed people. Tricks and hypnosis were not enough to do what she needed to do. And don't forget, she needed you to open the Destiny Book, as you were the only one capable of doing it. Nobody else in the town would have been able to do it because the book's powers were too strong and Ranna was worried they would have had the wrong effect if somebody else had opened the book' explained Smeerius. 'She needed the influential people of the town, who have credibility in the eyes of the other Destiners and whom nobody would ever suspect.'

'And this is how she came to you?'

'Exactly' replied Smeerius. 'She made me become one of the Mask Heads' members.'

'How did she do it?'

'I remember that I was at home with Smodge and she came to pay us a visit.'

'How could you tell it was her if she couldn't appear in her full form?'

'She could only appear during the first night of the Full Moon, because the Full Moon has an influence on the Creatures and it gives them energy just like the sun.'

'During the whole night?'

'No, they can only use this energy for a certain period of time, so she came during that time. She told us to follow her and I didn't dare to disobey her. Now I think it was because she had used her hypnosis skills. She led us to the Water Castle.'

'That's why you were talking about visiting a castle that was made completely of water, Smodge. Because she actually took you to the Water Castle.'

'That's right' replied Smodge.

'Do you remember how you finally became a Mask Heads member?'

'What Ranna did was very clever because she made sure that we wouldn't remember anything once we got out of the meeting. So, I led a normal life where I was completely myself, but as soon as she appeared, and it was always during the first night of the Full Moon, she would transform us into her slaves and we would have done anything for her.'

'So, how did you get rid of her spell?'

'First of all, she doesn't know that I'm not under her spell anymore, so I have to pretend that I am. It could help save the town from the Creatures' replied Smeerius. 'One of the Glimmers helped rid me of the spell. He put two malachite stones on my eyes and then pronounced some special words to release me.'

'Do you know his name?'

'Yes, his name is Lozendge.'

'Really?' said Irian. 'Lozendge saved you?'

'Do you know the man?' asked Smeerius.

'Yes' replied Irian and then he told him how he had met Lozendge and his family. 'That's so nice of him. There's one other thing I don't understand. Why did Ranna want to destroy the Kindness Creature mask? This would have affected Arameen's energy as well.'

'Unfortunately, she destroyed the mask during our last meeting' replied Smeerius.

'No, she didn't. I've got it' revealed Irian, telling Smeerius how they had stolen it from Gartika and then showing the mask that he carried everywhere with him. He always kept a little torch switched on in the bag together with the mask to give it enough light, as it was important for the Kindness Creature to maintain its powers.'

'You have the mask? That's wonderful! But be very careful

when carrying it around because the Light Creatures could sense its energy and confiscate it from you' replied Smeerius. 'Ranna wanted to destroy the mask because she wanted to get rid of the Kindness Creature before the Creatures got their powers back. She realised that the powers would help the Kindness Creature to come back too and she would have to accept its presence in the Amphitheatre because Arameen wanted all his Creatures back. And, I think she also wanted revenge on Arameen for all those years during which he had abandoned her.'

'Even if doing that would have diminished Arameen's powers?'

'Yes' replied Smeerius. 'I think Ranna is somewhat fed up of always being in Arameen's shadow.'

'Does that mean the Kindness Creature has regained its powers then?'

'Yes, it has, just like all the others.'

'So, where is the Kindness Creature now?'

'I don't know' replied Smeerius. 'I haven't even thought about it.'

'I'd like to meet the Kindness Creature' said Irian.

'Well, you never know. The way things are going, anything is possible.'

'Who else belongs to the Mask Heads?'

'Obeese, Mr Integger, Vrag and Zlob.'

'Were they hypnotised too?'

'Obeese and Mr Integger yes, but not Vrag or Zlob.'

'Apparently, Zlob and Vrag used to be Obeese's friends' said Irian.

'They weren't really his friends, but as they used to go to his tavern quite regularly, they formed a sort of friendship. They were strange people and nobody really liked them. But, you know what Obeese is like; he loves talking and meeting people and he has no prejudice about anybody. So, one day he drank a bit more than he should have and he told them the secret about the Creatures. He somehow remembered it even though Ranna wasn't there to control him. Ranna really panicked when she found out, so she persuaded them to join the Mask Heads. She also promised them a good position in her government once she had regained her powers just to keep them quiet, so the two fools agreed to join the organisation. The worst was that both of them really wanted the Creatures to come back.'

'I thought they had something to do with the Creatures, because once when I went to *The Porta Aurea*, Vrag kept on staring at me and at that time I didn't understand why' said Irian. 'But, there's one thing that seems illogical to me. Gartika, I mean Ranna sent Obeese to tell me about the Creatures' secret powers to make me open the Destiny Book and then went to tell my mother that I'd been talking to Obeese about the Legend. Why would she go to my mother if she wanted me to release their powers? It doesn't make sense!'

'You see, Ranna likes complicating things. She did want you to come and release their powers, but she also didn't want you to have good relationships with your family. Don't forget, she's evil and she takes pleasure when other people are in pain.'

'Do you think Obeese and Mr Integger have been released from their spell?' asked Irian.

'I hope so' replied Irian. 'We're supposed to be having a meeting tonight. Your Uncle Tattoo has finished drawing them.'

'When are the Creatures going to be back then?'

'I think tomorrow or at the latest by the end of the week' replied Smeerius. 'There is one thing, though. You have to come to the meeting too.'

'Me? Why?'

'Ranna told me to order you to come too' revealed Smeerius. 'We'll have to pretend I'm still under her spell.'

'What does she want from me?'

'She wants you to obey her.'

'Obey her? How can I obey her?'

'She wants you to reject Arena and Emo and accept her government.'

'I would never ever do that even if she decided to torture me to death. No way!'

'I know, and your reaction is the right one. She has no powers over you but she can give you a hard time.'

'I don't care. I'll give her a hard time too.'

'Have you got any idea of how to rid the town of the Creatures?'

Irian had a plan for freeing the town but he preferred to keep it to himself for the time being. He trusted Smeerius, but knew him to be just another Destiner, a pawn in Ranna's hands, so he thought it wise not to take the risk of saying anything to anybody.

'No, I haven't' lied Irian. 'I need time to think of something.'

'Are you coming to the meeting tonight, then?' asked Smeerius.

'I wouldn't want to cause any trouble for you and also, I suppose she can't hurt me so I'll come.'

'I'm sorry if I might appear cold or horrible to you, but remember, we have to play our game till the end if we want to free our town.'

'Don't worry. Just act as you need to and I'll be ok.'

* * *

Irian couldn't believe that he was having a meeting with the Queen and that he could represent a threat to her. When he announced to his mother that he was going to meet Ranna, she nearly had a heart attack and went through several pots of camomile tea in an attempt to calm down. It was like sending her son to a war where he would be fighting all alone against thousands of mighty monsters.

When he got out late in the evening, the fresh air almost made him think it wasn't a warm season, but one of those uninviting cold season nights that only make you want stay in your cosy house. Grandfather came to take him to Smeerius and they walked through the avenues of the town in silence, each of them imagining the conversation with the Queen. Irian felt as if the buildings and things around him had disappeared, and he was walking through an empty space that was full of voices all talking in a jumble. The voices were extracts from various conversations he'd had with different people about the Legend, and they were echoing around within his brain, each of them louder than the other. Irian could hardly hear what they were saying and he so wished there were some kind of window in his head to toss them all out of. He didn't want to think, he wanted to have an empty mind, but his mind was packed with thoughts that he just couldn't get rid of.

Smeerius was expecting them and he said they should leave straight away. He seemed very tense and kept on cracking his perfectly shaped fingers while talking to Irian and Grandfather.

'Where's the meeting?' asked Irian.

'In the Amphitheatre' replied Smeerius. 'Let's go, otherwise we'll be late and Ranna can't stand anybody being late.'

Smeerius' wife threw water in front of them, which was an old tradition in Destin to clear a person's path. Destiners believed that this would help the person in question go through a difficult situation more smoothly.

'Don't mention anything about the Kindness Creature's mask' warned Smeerius. 'Ranna mustn't know you have it.'

'Of course' replied Irian.

'She'll definitely try to blackmail you, but you mustn't fall into her trap' instructed Smeerius. 'She'll try anything, but don't forget that she has no power over you or your family. You must be strong and resist her threats. Whatever she says or whatever she tries to make you do it's only her attempt to destabilise you. If you're not sure about something, just look at me and I'll try to make a sign so that you'll understand.'

When they got to the Amphitheatre, Irian noticed that the site was better illuminated than usual. There were many burning sticks attached to its walls, symbolising the Sudba Creatures' return to glory. The two fat guards dressed in black clothes and white gloves and boots had been replaced by the Light Creatures, which Irian now saw for the first time. The Light Creatures were of medium size and had a sturdy muscular body, but its smooth curves gave it a supple appearance. They had a heart-shaped face with a large flat forehead and large, upright ears, which sat high on their head ending in rounded tips. Their large, yellow eyes were set far apart and opened wide and were too large for their faces. They looked like feline dragons blowing fire through their nose at whomever they disliked. Irian dreaded to think that he had to pass near them, but it was the only way to enter the Amphitheatre. Smeerius explained to him that everybody had to put his left hand through a special little gadget, and by the lines on the person's hand, the Creatures could identify the individual, which was their new protection system.

'But I have no hand-lines' said Irian in an undertone.

'That doesn't matter' replied Smeerius. 'You still have to put your hand in the identifying gadget.'

There were two Light Creatures protecting the entrance who were looking vaguely into the distance and Irian remembered how Peena had told him they were blind and only reacted through energies.

'What do you want?' said one of them, whose voice sounded like a horse trying to speak.

'We have an appointment with the Queen' replied Smeerius and Irian noticed his voice tremble.

'You have to identify first' said the other one and its voice was identical to the first guard.

Smeerius identified himself and then it was Irian's turn. The identifying gadget looked like a big white glove that you had to fit over your left hand for a few moments. The glove was kept on a small table near the door and Irian put his left hand into it as Smeerius had instructed him. The glove seemed to take a longer time with him than it had done for Smeerius and Irian wondered if he had placed his hand properly inside. Then suddenly, the glove started to shake, turned red and went on to produce a terrible piercing noise just like the sirens on the emergency hot air balloons in Destin for when there was a problem.

'Who are you?' screamed one of the Light Creatures.

'He doesn't have a destiny' said the other Light Creature.

'Attack him! Everybody has to have a destiny' yelled the first one.

They were starting to spew fire towards Irian while Smeerius tried to explain the situation but the Light Creatures wouldn't listen and were bolting towards Irian like wild animals after their prey.

'Stop!' Irian heard a loud voice shouting, which seemed somehow familiar to him. 'He is here at my invitation. Before you is the famous descendant, Irian Horvats. He's our special guest tonight.'

Through the heat of the flames coming out of the Light Creatures' noses, Irian recognised Queen Ranna standing only a few yards away from him. This time it wasn't one of her drawings nor her weak spirit. She was there in her full form, as powerful as ever, waiting to lead him into the Amphitheatre.

'Nice to meet you, Irian Horvats' she said as her eyes sparkled under the light of the burning sticks. 'I've waited a long time for such a pleasure. I heard you were a great fan of mine before you realised I actually existed. Why is that? Aren't you more pleased to see a real me rather than just a drawing on your bedroom wall?'

'You know what they say; we appreciate the things we don't have and despise the things we have' replied Irian.

'You have a good sense of irony. Does that mean that you despise me? I can't believe that' replied the Queen. 'Come this way, I think we have many things to say to each other. Let's have a little talk. Follow me, please.'

The Amphitheatre was so illuminated inside that it seemed like daytime. There were many Creatures going up and down, but when they saw Irian, they all stopped and stared at him. Irian was impressed to see all these Creatures gathered together in one place. Not that long ago, Irian used to look at the starry sky and wait for shooting stars; there were many of them but his wish was always the same – to meet the Sudba Creatures. And now they were there and they were real, though this time he would have done anything to send them away.

'What are you all staring at?' asked the Queen, glaring at the Creatures. 'Back to work! Don't you have enough to do?'

The Queen led them to the entrance door to the inner quarters, which was set in the floor of the Amphitheatre. Access to the inner quarters was by means of a steep spiral staircase, which was also rather narrow, so that Irian had to concentrate very hard not to miss his step. There were bare walls all around, decorated only by burning sticks. It looked like an empty hall, which smelt of humidity and appeared endless. Finally, on reaching the bottom of the stairs, there was a huge solid iron door and Irian had to tip his head back almost horizontally to see the top of it.

The Queen opened the door and on the other side there seemed to be another world, one of luxury and extravagance. It consisted of highly ornate rooms and corridors connecting to different parts of the inner quarters with elaborate plaster decoration adorning the ceilings and walls.

They passed through numerous corridors until they finally reached the meeting room. The first thing that Irian noticed in this large circular room was that its ceiling was covered in very small red roses, such as he had never seen before. Smeerius later explained to him that red roses symbolised secrecy for the Creatures.

Irian was surprised to see that the Mask Head members weren't wearing masks at all, but he supposed that this was because there was no need to hide their identity any longer. There was Obeese, Mr Integger, Zlob and Vrag as he had expected. Obeese and Mr Integger seemed extremely embarrassed to find themselves in such place together with Irian, which made Irian think that it was possible that they were not under the Queen's spell anymore. Quite different were Vrag and Zlob, who seemed perfectly comfortable and were now staring at Irian in the way wild beasts stare at their prey before devouring it.

'So, Irian. Welcome to our humble party' said the Queen once they had all gathered around a long table, the size of which made Irian wonder how they could possibly communicate at such a distance. Each of them was seated at least two yards away from the other. 'We thought you would like to join us and discuss our return. I suppose you have many things to tell us.'

'What do you want from me?' asked Irian who simply couldn't stand such hypocrisy.

'We're trying to be kind to you despite your ancestors' despicable act, and you can't even make an effort to appreciate our respect for you' replied Ranna.

'Your false kindness will not help you make me renounce Arena and Emo. I've always been and I always will remain proud of their act' replied Irian firmly.

'Arena and Emo wanted rid of us to rule this town themselves. So, you see, it wasn't in the interest of the Destiners. They only wanted power for themselves.'

'Well, if they did free the town just for the power to rule it, why didn't they do that then? Why did they let Sir Esteam become mayor? It doesn't make sense.'

Ranna didn't seem to have an answer to Irian's question; instead she served herself a drink that one of the Light Creatures had brought in. Irian looked at Smeerius from the corner of his eye just to see what his reaction was, and Smeerius winked at him.

'We are back in town tomorrow whether you like it or not' the Queen's voice changed into a more serious one. 'You know, people are not accusing us, they are accusing you apparently. They seem unhappy with you and I also heard some unpleasant comments concerning Arena and Emo.'

'The Destiners say such things not because they like you or because they hate me, but only because they are scared of their future. My mother thinks that you should never judge a first reaction, because it's just an impulse. Real thoughts need time to develop, and the Destiners haven't had enough time to think properly about the new situation in the town' replied Irian, who by no means wanted to show Ranna that he was scared of her, though his body kept turning hot and then cold every few seconds. However, he was adamant not to show it to the Queen.

'You're very much like Emo' said Ranna. 'You don't only resemble him psychologically, but physically too. It's incredible, after all these years and generations... He had the same aquamarine coloured eyes and long hair too, and you share the same attitude. But you see, his plan didn't work either. We are the proof that he wasn't intelligent enough to win over us.'

'The reason why you're here tonight is because of me and not because of Emo' reasoned Irian, enchanted to hear that he resembled Emo, who had become his major hero and role model. 'I opened the Destiny Book because I wasn't careful enough. My act has nothing to do with Emo.'

'If Emo really did want to get rid of us, he should have destroyed the Destiny Book too.'

'How could he if he didn't known about it?'

'Well, if you start something, you should finish it. Otherwise, what's the point?'

'Haven't you heard of the word TRY? People have lives to try and change things in order to improve them. They are here to learn. Emo and Arena escaped your destiny decision and they were free to do whatever they liked, which other Destiners weren't able to do because they were in your hands. You can't understand the word freedom because you're not free yourself either, because you yourself depend on Arameen. As far as the Sudba Creatures are concerned, they only obey you because they're under Arameen's spell. I know that the Glimmers would do anything to have their freedom back' said Irian, and he knew that such a statement would infuriate Ranna, but for some reason he couldn't care less.

'That's enough' said the Queen. Irian couldn't see her facial expressions because of the mask she was wearing, but he could feel that she was having great difficulty stifling her anger. 'I give you three days to accept our government and submit to our rules, otherwise I shall be forced to take special measures against you.'

'Such as?'

'I know that you have some dear friends whose lives are in our hands. There's also the question of Maia's child. I have plenty of choices' Ranna seemed to feel better when remembering her power to decide about people's destinies again.

'If you want revenge, then take it out on me. My friends have nothing to do with the situation. Don't you dare hurt them' replied Irian, immediately thinking of his dear friends Floria and Nuro as well as Maia and Petalber, who so much wanted to have a child.

'I'll do whatever I feel important. I give you three days to submit to us as everybody else does and if you do there will be no trouble. It is not a good idea to be different from other people you know.'

'I prefer to be different, but to stick to my principles and remain myself' replied Irian.

'As you say, it's your choice, but every choice has its consequence' said the Queen and then shouted. 'Guard, show him out.'

The two Light Creatures appeared and they kept on sniffing Irian strangely, just as Ogi sniffed people he didn't like.

'I look forward to seeing you again in three days, Irian' said the Queen as Irian was leaving followed by the Light Creatures. 'Have a good think about the opportunity I am giving you, and think about your family and friends. You know how Maia and Petalber have dreamed of having a baby.'

'Don't count your chickens before they are hatched' replied Irian.

The Queen laughed loudly and the cruel tones of her laughter kept on echoing in Irian's ears even when he was back home again and lying safely in his own bed. The Queen was back and she was all powerful, while he had only three days to find an answer. Time, which sometimes seemed to pass at a snail's pace, now appeared to be flying faster than ever.

The Destiny Decision Ceremony

Irian woke up late but had the impression that he hadn't slept at all, as he kept on waking up during the night, and every time he had been woken up by a nightmare, he hoped that it was only a dream that would disappear the moment he opened his eyes. He dreamt about Maia going to declare her pregnancy to Ranna, and Ranna telling her how her baby would not develop properly. Or else he dreamed about Floria and Nuro, and how Ranna was planning to harm them. They were only bad dreams, but Irian knew that they could come true if he didn't think of something very quickly.

Once fully awake, he got dressed and went downstairs to see his parents. His mother was on the phone with Petalber, and as she didn't hear Irian come down, she continued her conversation.

'He's not too young, Petalber!' she was saying. 'He knows what he needs to do. We have to trust him. It's a very difficult time for him and what's worse, we can't help him much. Maia will be fine. When does she have an appointment with the Queen? Tomorrow. Dear, oh dear! Listen, everything will be all right. We'll try to come and see you later.'

Irian didn't want his mother to know that he had overheard her conversation, so he crept quietly up the stairs and then came back down again, but this time making a lot of noise to let her know that he was coming.

'Oh, hello Irian' she said, somewhat confused. 'Your eyes are red. Are you ok?'

'Well, I didn't sleep much, but I'm ok' replied Irian.

'What are we going to do, son? Maia is obliged to go and see the Queen tomorrow. I don't think she can postpone it or change the date.'

'No, she can't. I had a call from Smeerius last night.'

'And?'

'He's arranged for me to meet the Kindness Creature. He thinks the Kindness Creature could help me fight Arameen.'

'Really?' exclaimed his mother, and Irian had the impression that her eyes had brightened at this. 'So, when are you meeting the Kindness Creature?'

'Tomorrow.'

'But, isn't it dangerous for the Kindness Creature to go out at night? What about its powers? And how is it going to avoid the Queen?'

'I don't know' replied Irian. 'I hope the Kindness Creature has some good advice to give me.'

'When are you going to meet Arameen, then?'

'In two days, but I'm going with Grandfather and not with Mrs Bigone.'

'Why?'

'Because again, she's in the Creatures' hands too, so it could be risky.'

'Have you spoken to Lozendge?'

'Yes, yesterday, just before I went to see the Queen.'

'What did he say?'

'He's very worried too. Apparently, Arameen is going to send the Light Creatures to control them.'

'That's awful. What are they going to do?'

'They are going to help me fight Arameen. It's the only way. Grandfather and I are going to pay them a visit before going to Kinoont Temple to see Arameen. Anyway, Coruscatia is not very far from Arameen's land' replied Irian.

* * *

Maia and Petalber had to go and declare Maia's pregnancy very early the next morning, as the Creatures were to decide on the baby's future the following evening. Maia had had her first vision that she was pregnant just the night after Irian had opened the Destiny Book.

When Maia and Petalber arrived at the Amphitheatre, some women were already waiting to register with the Queen. Their expressions were serious and their faces worried as they stood quietly waiting in the queue. Some women were sobbing and some were just absently staring into space until the Queen arrived.

The Queen appeared followed by the Light Creatures that had been staying in the town until Ranna reorganised her government.

'Oh, how nice to see you all here!' said the Queen, sarcastically. 'Let's see! Who's first?'

'Me' said a small woman, thoughtfully stroking her tummy.

'Follow me, please' said the Queen.

The Queen and the woman then disappeared into the Amphitheatre, while the others continued to queue, dreading their own turn.

It was Maia's turn at last and she felt sharp pains in her stomach as if it was the scene of a battle where her nerves were to fight exterior enemies. She couldn't even look up at the Queen when the latter appeared to call for her next victim.

'I've been expecting you' said the Queen, recognising Maia. 'Irian and I had a nice little talk the other day. I suppose he must have informed you about it.'

'What are you going to do with our baby?' asked Petalber, angrily.

'That doesn't depend on me. Anyway, come, let's go into my office' replied the Queen.

Her office was to be found behind the place where the ticket office used to be, which now served as a guardroom. The room was pretty large, divided in two by four large columns covered in reddish wallpaper, which appeared as thick as velvet.

'When exactly did you have your vision?' asked the Queen, once they had all sat down.

'I want to know what you are planning to do with our baby' said Maia, who was having difficulty holding back her tears.

'If Irian accepts our government, your child will be treated like everybody else' replied the Queen.

'And if he doesn't?' asked Petalber.

'Well, I can't answer that now. I haven't had time to think about it yet' replied the Queen.

Apparently, when the Queen didn't like one of the mothers or the family of the future baby, she would manipulate the destiny decision ceremony. In such cases, the Creatures were allowed to cheat while pulling out the numbers and choose the ones they wanted, and the Queen could proceed with her part, as she liked too.

The Queen wrote down Maia and Petalber's names in the large register, and announced the time when the baby's destiny was going to be decided. Maia and Petalber left the place heartbroken, also because they couldn't tell what the Creatures were going to decide, as the baby's sort was never revealed to anyone.

* * *

Smeerius had arranged for Irian to meet the Kindness Creature in the Town Library, as he had the keys to it, having often worked there as a good friend of Gotz Kelza, who was its owner. The Kindness Creature wanted Irian to come by himself, and Irian even arrived a little early. It was unusual for him to enter the library at such a late hour, and Smeerius instructed him not to light the torches.

Irian went in and sat down at one of the tables. It was dark and he could only see things by the moonlight that was penetrating through the letter-shaped windows, and helping him to feel his way around.

'Thank you for coming' Irian heard a deep voice coming from behind him.

'Kindness Creature!' said Irian, impressed. 'I'm so grateful to you for all that you've done for my ancestors. If only I could express my gratitude to you...'

'Don't mention it, please' said the Kindness Creature and then went to sit at the opposite side of the table. Irian couldn't really see it properly because the light was scarce and the Creature was enveloped in a dark coat, probably to hide its identity in the street. 'I have very little time to stay with you.'

'Why did you help my ancestors? Why do you want to help me? We only cause you trouble' asked Irian, who didn't know which question to ask first as there were so many of them in his head.

'It's not your fault and it wasn't their fault either.'

'But because of them you lost your mask and the Queen's respect!'

'I would rather say that I lost my independence the day Arameen came to attack us and turned us into Sudba Creatures.'

'So, you're aware that you used to be a Glimmer?'

'I've always been aware of it because I used diamond powder to protect myself from the spell.'

'What do you mean?'

'You see, before Arameen came to attack us, I used to be the chief of all the Glimmers, just as my father and my grandfather before me. I felt guilty for not being able to protect my people, and when Arameen took us over and stole all our precious stones, my people started to suffer terribly and I had to find a way to protect them. That's why I accepted "Arameen's protection", if it can be called that, just to let my people live to see another day' explained the Kindness Creature and then continued. 'Before my father died, he told me that the Glimmers have a secret weapon, which nobody apart from the chief should know about, which is a special diamond powder. My father told me to use it only in an emergency and only to protect my people.'

'But what is this diamond powder?'

'Our legend says that in the county of Coruscatia there used to be a huge volcano that erupted several times a day, which made it impossible for anybody to live there. Apparently, there was a man who didn't know about it, and as he was passing through Coruscatia one day he stopped to have a rest. He fell asleep and woke up in the middle of a volcano eruption that was striking the area. While trying to run away, a drop of molten lava entered his right eye. For some strange and inexplicable reason, he felt no pain when it happened. The lava dried up after a short while, and the man's eye turned into the most beautiful diamond, whereas his eyesight remained unaltered. The man was a healer and in his bag were many healing plants that he had collected around Coruscatia. When he got home, he had a good look at them and realised that their pollen actually consisted of a diamond powder. The man extracted some of the diamond powder from the plants and realised that a deep injury he had in his hand had suddenly disappeared when he had touched the powder. He realised that the powder had special powers and decided to keep it safe in case he needed it again. Not long afterwards, he and his family settled down in the volcano area, and for some strange reason, the volcano never ever erupted again. After a while, they invited their friends who came to settle in the area and they all became the first Glimmers. However, the man decided to keep the diamond powder a secret. Indeed, he passed on the secret to his son before he died, asking him to keep it hidden and use it only in an emergency.'

'This is amazing!' said Irian. 'But how did the diamond powder help you with the Creatures?'

'Arameen gave us a potion we had to swallow in order to embody the human quality that we were to possess, and before I swallowed it, I put some of that diamond powder over my tongue hoping it would send the spell away. That's exactly what it did.'

'But why didn't you give it to the other Glimmers?'

'I had so little of the powder that it would have been impossible to give it to everybody.'

'Did you know that the Glimmers who got away became Soothsayers for the Destiners?'

'Of course, I told them of this extraordinary power they had of being able to predict the future and told them how to do it.'

'There is one thing I don't understand. Why am I the only descendant who can rid the town of the Creatures?' asked Irian.

'When the Queen cast a spell on the Destiny Book saying that whoever opened it would help the Creatures come back, letters appeared in the book, letters that read: "**one day a male child** called Irian will be born. He will resemble Emo and think like Arena, and he will open the Destiny Book and release its powers." You look very much like Emo and you do sound like Arena, I must say.'

'It's crazy! Does that mean that I'm also controlled by the powers of the Destiny Book?'

'No, you are not, but if you don't find a way to destroy it, you eventually will have to accept it, because its powers are too strong to resist.'

'That's awful! So, what shall I do?'

'Smeerius told me that you still have my mask.'

'Yes, I do. Do you need it back?'

'No, keep it. You will need it. You must go and see Arameen tomorrow' said the Kindness Creature and then put a little silk bag on the table. 'Here take this!'

'What is it?'

'It's diamond powder. Please take care of it. It's all I have left.'

'Wow! But what shall I do with it?'

'You might have an idea when you get to Arameen's temple. I'm sure that if you use it properly, you can find a way to get rid of his spell. I once overheard the Queen in conversation with Arameen and she was saying she feared diamond powder more than anything else.'

'And if I don't find a way to use it?'

'You will, you're intelligent enough – I know you have the lamp with the instructions concerning Arameen's temple on it.'

'How do you know?'

'Well, I learnt that from Smeerius too.'

'Yes, Mr Tappin found the lamp. Did you throw the lamp away?'

'Yes, I made the lamp a long time ago and I wanted to pass it on to you somehow. One day, I saw a man walking in the Wild Flower Forest that turned out to be Mr Tappin and I left it on the ground so that he would pick it up. It was a way for me to pass you the message about Arameen, because I didn't know that you already knew about him.'

'Yes, it's thanks to Mrs Bigone. She found out about Arameen.'

'I have to go now, otherwise the Queen will notice my absence.'

'What is your real name, I mean your Glimmer name?'

'Shon Lustre. Good luck, Irian. I have trust in you!'

* * *

The following evening, Petalber and Maia went to sit on the bench outside the Amphitheatre to observe the site while the Creatures were deciding on their baby's destiny. The Amphitheatre seemed deserted; there were no Light Creatures to guard the place because the building was protected by a magnetism that allowed no entry. Besides, the Sudba Creatures had covered the Amphitheatre with a thick sheet of iron, which made it completely inaccessible. The only thing that penetrated through its lower walls was an abundance of light coming from the inside of the building, which was so intense that it could be spotted from far away in the distance. No Destiner was ever allowed to see the ceremony behind the heavy stonewalls or participate in the destiny creation.

Inside, the Creatures were getting ready for the destiny decision ceremony. They seemed excited, as they hadn't performed it for such a long time, and when the Queen announced that it was time for everybody to gather in the Amphitheatre, there was a great commotion in the inner quarters as all the Creatures scrambled to get first place in the queue. Each Creature had to draw out its number before the meeting and this number was used to decide on the exact degree of the human quality the baby was to possess. The numbers, ranging from one to a hundred, were engraved on small equally sized precious stones, from which the Creatures had to choose one without looking. The stones were placed in a large glass ball that each Creature had to turn and then wait for one to emerge through a small hole in the ball. The spinning ball was placed next to the Queen's desk, in the middle of the Amphitheatre. Once the Creatures had drawn their numbers, they went to take their places in the Amphitheatre.

'Quiet!' demanded the Queen, annoyed that everyone was talking. Everybody was seated except for the Impatience and the Curiosity Creatures who were walking around, eagerly trying to see everybody else's numbers. 'Has everybody got his number?'

'Yes, yes!' shouted the Creatures all at the same time.

'Good!' said the Queen. 'Well, I must say, it is nice to see you all back in the Amphitheatre after so long. I think it was a good lesson, but one that should never be repeated. This time the Sudba Creatures are back forever!'

The Queen's voice was so loud that it echoed around the whole Amphitheatre. She sounded invincible and extremely confident in her words, so that her voice was enough to make anybody tremble. The Creatures got to their feet and shouted in unison with the Queen: "We are back! We are back!"

'Let's proceed then' said the Queen. She looked through the list of babies that were to be born and then opened the Destiny Book that was lying on her desk. 'Who have we got tonight? We've got Maia and Petalber's baby. That's very interesting, isn't it? Let's see what we have for this baby. We haven't heard from Irian as we asked, so it's time to teach them a lesson. I want everybody to lower their numbers, as this baby is not to enjoy our blessings.'

'Are you ready, Charisma Creature?' asked the Queen.

'Yes, I am, my lady' said the Charisma Creature, and all the other Creatures turned their heads in admiration to see what this Creature was going to say. The Charisma Creature was one of those Creatures that gave its points away unwillingly, and whenever it was possible to take some points off, it would do so with a great pleasure.

'What is your word?' asked the Queen.

'I am wonderful and marvellous, as you all know, I cannot be generous with everybody, though. I say that two points are better than none, which is the dose of charisma this baby has won!' having said that, the Charisma Creature placed its chosen stone with its right hand in the middle of its forehead. It pressed it hard and then repeated its message twice more. The yellowish stone suddenly became bright and a large ray appeared from it and darted towards the Destiny Book. The words the Creature had spoken reappeared in the silky pages of the book and then disappeared again.

'Thank you, Charisma Creature' said the Queen. 'Now, Love Creature. What have you got for us?'

'My words are a mellow song to your ear, and my blessings what everyone wants to hear. Your life can become a sweet fairy tale, if you have my points you just can't fail. Ten points I give you from my heart, to use them well, you must be smart'. announced the Love Creature and then proceeded in the same way as the Charisma Creature, except that its stone was pressed to its heart.

'Very well!' said the Queen. 'Fear Creature, can we hear your decision?'

'If a lion roars at you, there's not much you can do. You really mustn't pause as you'll end up in its claws. Risk is a two-edged sword, you truly can't afford. I prefer you to avoid it at all costs my dear, here are seventy points to help you steer clear' said the Fear Creature and then placed the stone to its head and performed the same gesture as the previous Creatures.

'Thank you, Fear Creature' said the Queen. 'Are you ready Anger Creature?'

'A wild beast I am not, but my temper can be hot. From a sparkle to a blaze, my enemies I amaze. For the baby here tonight, sixty points should be all right' said the Angry Creature in an angry voice, as if disturbed at having to participate in the meeting at all. It then placed the precious stone on its palm and closed it in a tight fist before casting its spell.

'I see you are all very eager to participate tonight' said the Queen. 'Very well. I must admit I'm enjoying this meeting a lot. Who do we have next?

The Queen went to call the other Creatures and every Creature proceeded in the same way by transferring its powers into the Destiny Book. When all the Creatures had expressed themselves, it was the Queen's turn to add her own words to the destiny decision. The Queen was responsible for deciding the baby's lifespan, luck and gender. In order to do that, she needed three cards. The lifespan card bore the image of a bobbin of thread, the luck card a four-leafed clover, whereas the gender card was a picture of a little boy looking at a little girl in front of him. The cards were put face downwards and the Queen turned them over one by one.

Once she had turned over the lifespan card, she had to spin the roulette wheel, which was the device used to determine the extent of the baby's lifetime. The golden wheel was the central and movable part of an enamel bowl, and was divided into different segments. A spin of the destiny wheel would give a reading of the year, month, day and exact time when the child's life would start and end.

The next card was the four-leafed clover card, which was to show the degree of luck of the child. For this card, the Queen had a diamond dice with a hundred facets where each facet contained a different number ranging from one to hundred. The Queen would roll the dice over the Amphitheatre floor and then impatiently wait to see the number that would come up.

'Eighty-two' said the Queen. 'It can't be. No, no, no! We can't allow this baby to have such a high level of luck. It is not fair after all.'

She threw the dice several times but the number never fell below seventy, which enraged the Queen excessively. She might have tried the baby's luck ten times and afterwards decided to drop the diamond dice softly enough to make sure it fell on the number she desired.

'Eight' said the Queen. 'That's much better!'

Now it was time to decide on the baby's gender, which was the Queen's favourite part. In order to decide whether the baby was going to be a boy or a girl, the Queen would have at her disposition a hair from the head of each of the parents. She would then put the hairs one next to the other and ask one of the Creatures to help her with the task. She would put a hair in one of her hands and the Creature had to do the same. They would both have to pull the hair, the Queen towards her, and the Creature towards itself, and the hair that split in two first was the winning one. If the father's hair split first, the baby was to be a boy.

'Who is going to assist me?' ask the Queen and the Clumsy Creature came forward.

'Tell me what to do, my lady' said the Clumsy Creature, looking rather silly with its cloak turned inside out.

'I'm going to hold one end of the hairs and you have to hold the other. When I say now, you have to pull the other end. Do you understand?' asked the Queen.

'Yes, yes, I do' said the Clumsy Creature. It took the left hair in its right hand and the right hair in its left hand.

'You won't be able to do it properly that way' said the Queen. 'Why can't you simply take them with the appropriate hand?'

'I don't know' said the Clumsy Creature.

'Well, you aren't called clumsy for nothing' said the Queen. 'Are you ready? Now!'

The Clumsy Creature simply held the hairs without pulling them, so the Queen had to explain everything again. She actually had had to explain the procedure several times before the Clumsy Creature understood what it was supposed to do. It then pulled the hairs with such gusto that it even fell on the floor.

'You are useless' said the Queen. 'Concentrate, do you understand?'

They tried again and this time the Clumsy Creature finally pulled the hairs properly. The first hair to split was the one that had belonged to the mother.

'The baby will be a girl' announced the Queen and there were different opinions among the Creatures.

Now that all the baby's characteristics had been decided on, the Queen had to confirm them in the Destiny Book.

The Kinoont Temple

Earlier that day Irian had woken up very early to see the first sunray that was to indicate the whereabouts of Arameen's temple. He knew that he mustn't fail in his mission, because he had to express himself in front of the Queen before the Destiny Decision ceremony that was to take place that evening and where the Queen and the Creatures were to decide on the destiny of Maia and Petalber's baby.

He went to sit in the garden with Grandfather well before the sun was about to rise, as he didn't want to miss the first sunray. The air was cold but Irian's mind was steaming hot under the pressure of his busy thoughts and nothing was cold enough to cool it down. It was like a machine, whose switch is broken so that it's impossible to stop it from going full steam ahead.

'I spoke to Lozendge' said Irian. 'We won't be able to go and see them.'

'Why?' asked Grandfather.

'The Light Creatures have come to control them' replied Irian.

'Oh, no!' said Grandfather. 'But what are they going to do now? They can't escape them, can they?'

'Well, the only thing they can do now is hope that I destroy Arameen's powers' replied Irian. 'It's the only solution, for us and for the Glimmers.'

'I wonder if Arameen suspects that we're thinking of visiting him.'

'I don't think so' replied Irian. 'Remember, he doesn't know that we have the mask. It's the only weapon I have against him apart from the diamond powder. The only thing is that I still don't know how to use the diamond power. The Kindness

Creature, I mean Shon Lustre only hopes it can destroy Arameen's powers, but it's not sure. So, we'll see. Everything seems to be hanging in the air for the moment.'

'Listen, even if you fail, it doesn't matter. The worst thing is not to try to change things at all and to content yourself with the situation instead of trying to improve it. Luck follows the brave, that's what I believe' said Grandfather.

They sat in the dark, both looking eastwards trying to catch sight of the first sunray. The sky was a lapis lazuli blue with some darker patches in places when, all of a sudden, a strong light, just like the light of the human quality colours in the Birthday Cave, appeared in the sky. It was a yellowish ray that stretched through the middle of the horizon and created a kind of arrow pointing to a precise spot in the distance.

'Wow, can you see that?' said Irian, astonished. 'That must be the first sunray. What do you think, grandpa?'

'I think you're right!' Grandfather replied as amazed as Irian. 'Well, I reckon it's time to go. Let me consult my compass.'

He took his compass out and examined it by candle light. He followed the direction of the first sunray and the points of the compass stopped right on the spot representing the east, not a fraction to the right nor to the left of it.

'Okay, I understand. We have to go to the point furthest east. His temple must be at the sun's rising point. We will need some time to get there. I must say I've never been such a long way from home' said Grandfather, somewhat worried. 'Let's move now! We must hurry!'

They went to get their things and then Irian got on the Old Lady. Grandfather went to look for the talisman that Lozendge had given him before joining his grandson on the balloon.

'I think we'll both need it' he said and then got his balloon ready for the flight. 'Wish us good luck, sleepy Destin!'

They had a long journey in front of them, so they had prepared some food and enough fuel for the balloon. At one point, it got so hot that Grandfather put up a parasol to protect them from getting sunburnt. There were times where the heat was absolutely unbearable, obliging them to pour water over their heads.

'We have to be careful with the water as we haven't got much of it and we'll need it on the way back' warned Grandfather.

'I suppose we could stop and have a little bath in a lake if we see one' suggested Irian. 'I'm sweating like a pig!'

'Why not!' replied Grandfather. 'If you spot one, we'll land.'

The land below was dry with hardly any vegetation to make it look habitable. Even the rare flowers that grew there seemed strange and of unusual shape in dull and unattractive colours. At times, the land was either flat with hardly any hills, or irregular in shape, but then, they also flew above a high chain of mountains covered with snow, where they had to wrap up well so as not to catch cold.

Flying above the mountains, they saw a lake, which seemed very appealing, with amazing flowers that embellished the landscape.

'This place looks good to me' said Grandfather. 'What do you think?'

As he looked into it, the lake reflected Irian's weary and somewhat filthy face, which was also sunburnt in places despite all their efforts to protect themselves from the violent sunrays. He gently washed it and then spent some time looking at his reflection in the water.

'If the Birthday Cave still existed, I wonder how I would have changed for my next birthday after all these recent experiences' said Irian. 'I would probably look two or three years older when leaving the place.'

'I suppose you're right.'

'What do you think; how are we going to embody the knowledge we have gained throughout the year once we've defeated Arameen, now that the Birthday Cave has been destroyed?'

'That's a good question' replied Grandfather. 'I reckon we'll embody our experiences naturally as it should be. There won't be anyone or anything to decide on our lives and our destinies.'

'It would be great to taste real full freedom. I get goose pimples just thinking about it.'

The air was cold despite the sunny sky, but the soaring

snowy mountains imposed their own temperature over that of the sunrays that were struggling to defeat the chill air of the high altitudes. Despite the cold, Irian managed to doze off and Grandfather unfastened his cloak, putting it around his grandson's shoulders. He only let him rest for a short while because they had to continue their journey.

Back on the balloon, Grandfather kept on checking his compass to make sure they were heading in the right direction, with his mind set on Arameen's temple. The journey seemed endless, as if they were trying to reach the bottom of eternity.

'I think we should be spotting Arameen's temple very soon' announced Grandfather. 'Peena said it was set among a circle of mountains, which appear as gold in colour due to the strong sun. If my eyes are to be trusted, those mountains there seem to fit her description. Can you pass me the binoculars, please?'

'I'm not surprised to hear that Arameen and his Light Creatures are blind with all this light. You need at least ten pairs of sunglasses to protect your eyes from all the shining rays. How are we going to manage?' asked Irian, getting his eye on the place.

'I can't come with you anyway as you know, so I'll be okay. But you can always put sunglasses on under the mask. They won't know, as they're all blind, remember?'

'I feel like I'm off to put my head straight in the lion's mouth' said Irian.

'Oh, don't say that' replied Grandfather. 'You hold all the winning cards; the mask, the diamond powder and your destiny isn't in their hands. When you enter the game, you must enter like a winner, not a loser. Otherwise, what's the point in trying if you convince yourself from the beginning that you're going to lose? It doesn't make sense, does it?'

They decided to fly very low though they knew that being blind, the Light Creatures couldn't see them. However, Grandfather didn't want to take any risks, so he piloted the Old Lady scarcely a yard above the sandy surface. He decided that he should not park the balloon too close to the mountain ring, so he stopped behind a nearby hill that was some two hundred yards away from their destination. The hill was high enough to offer him protection from being seen and close enough to spot any trouble or see Irian coming out.

'I think you should put your mask on now' instructed Grandfather. 'Have you got the diamond powder?'

'Yes, I have' replied Irian. 'But I can't control my legs. They're trembling.'

'That's a good sign. It means that you feel the responsibility, that's what it means!' replied Grandfather, though he was trying hard to keep his tears back in front of his grandson. 'Go now, you have a long way to walk!'

'And if ever they catch me?' asked Irian.

'They won't catch you. Your destiny depends only on yourself while their destiny is in your hands. Don't forget that!' reasoned Grandfather, before hugging his grandson and letting him go. If he could have cried all the tears he had in his eyes, he would probably have sunk the whole universe when he saw the grandson he so doted on leaving to face what lay ahead.

On his way to the Kinoont Temple, Irian kept on falling into the sand as it was very deep in places and he had to be careful not to hurt himself. The sandy surface spread out for some hundred yards, then the ground was harder and easier to walk on. He rested for a while in the shade of the mountains that enclosed Arameen's temple. The mountains seemed as if they had been planted there because they were arranged in such a perfect circle and were all exactly the same height.

When he got closer, he was surprised to see that there was no Light Creature protecting the entrance, and he found this rather bewildering. He had to find the hole to place the key that Ogi had found in the Water Castle as Peena had told him to do. It was the only way to create the passage in the mountains and penetrate the Kinoont Temple. It seemed to him that there was only one passage, as the other mountains seemed attached, not leaving any space in between. He expected some spectacular door and a guard, but there was absolutely nobody and nothing. The passage was rather long, and Irian couldn't see or guess what was hiding at the other end.

And then, all of a sudden, he reached the end of the path.

Standing upon the rim of the mountain circle offered the most amazing view he had ever seen or imagined. He was standing above an amazing temple, which looked like a huge cushion-cut diamond temple that shone and sparkled as if fire was kept inside. The temple was situated in the valley below and Irian nearly fainted when he saw the number of steps he needed to descend in order to reach the site. He had a sudden thought that whoever managed all these stairs could easily have won the annual muscle competition that was held in his town. Apart from that, he could hardly see as he was dazzled by such strong light, so he had to be extremely careful not to miss his step. Whenever he thought about having to climb back up all these steps again, he started reciting poetry he had learned to stop his mind thinking about the ordeal. He didn't even dare to count them as there were simply too many and he preferred to concentrate on his mission instead. He was descending and descending, and with every step, his legs were becoming heavier and his body more unbearable to carry on the tiny sticks that happened to be his legs. Besides, there was nothing to hold on to and only narrow stairs, so Irian concentrated on the next step only, refusing to let his gaze wander sideways.

When he finally got to the bottom, he could have kissed the last step in relief at reaching the ground again. He had to rest as his legs couldn't take any further effort and he was breathless and exhausted. It was a perfect place to have a closer look at the temple that was now standing not very far off in the distance. The Kinoont Temple was in the central point of the valley, and there were four other sites around it, where the Light Creatures probably lived.

However, he spent the longest time observing Arameen's temple, so as to find the best way to approach it. There was a massive stone entrance that was reached by high steps. Irian imagined the Light Creatures and Arameen to be incredibly fit to have to deal with all these steps every day. He could also see the Light Creatures prowling around like beasts looking for a chance to attack. He realised that there was no alternative way to enter the temple but by the main entrance where the Light Creatures stood.

'Why me?' thought Irian to himself. 'Why do I need to perform such a task? Why did the Destiny Book choose me? It could have chosen anybody else in the town. Everybody says I'm the smallest, the tiniest. So why? Why?'

Irian was trying to find an answer in vain, but he knew very well that an answer wouldn't help him anyway, because he had to go and meet Arameen. He drew a few deep breaths, then finally plucked up the courage to walk to Arameen's temple.

There was a story concerning Arameen, about a certain sun family, a Mother, a Father and a Baby Sun that lived happily in the sky. However, with Arameen being so obsessed with light, he kidnapped the Baby Sun so as to have it all for himself and he wouldn't let the baby stop shining, not even at night. Therefore, the Father Sun transformed himself into the Moon, so as not to leave his son alone to control the sky and Arameen's land at night, whereas the Mother Sun remained there in the daytime to share its sunrays with her baby.

Everything around Irian seemed enormous and he felt like a tiny moving spot on the vast landscape that anybody could remove with the slightest effort. He was treading on red hot clay, but for some strange reason, the temperature was pleasant and mild despite the abundance of sunlight. He noticed that there were only baby flowers around and he found them particularly cute. It seemed to him as if nobody had really noticed his presence, so he continued walking as if he had been invited to come and visit. He was heading towards the temple, when one of the Light Creatures finally stopped him.

'What are you doing here, Sudba Creature?' it said in its horsy voice.

'I need to speak to our master' replied Irian, as calmly as he could.

'Why do you need to speak to the master?' the Light Creature asked again.

'It's personal!' replied Irian, looking at the Light Creature who had steam coming out of its nose.

'Follow me' said the Light Creature.

The Light Creature led Irian to one of the buildings next to the temple, where Irian was asked to wait to see whether Arameen would accept him. He was left in the room with some other Creatures that didn't mind his presence and were talking to each other, completely ignoring Irian.

'The Glimmers' said one of them. 'They're really stupid! They didn't even try to run away and they knew we were on our way.'

'So, what is the master going to do with them?' asked the other one, although Irian could hardly tell them apart because all the Light Creatures looked exactly the same, as if somebody had put one of them in a photocopying machine and then simply copied all the others.

'He wants to confiscate all their diamond powder' said the first Creature.

'Why would he want the diamond powder?'

'Whoever possesses diamond powder is invincible' revealed the Creature. 'If you have it, nobody can do anything to you if you use it in a proper way.'

'Why don't the Glimmers use it then?'

'Because they're thick, they don't know how to do it. They don't even know they have it.'

'What do you mean?'

'There are plants that grow near the extinguished volcano that contain diamond powder instead of pollen. And there are plenty of these plants, but they aren't aware of it.'

'How can these plants help the master?'

'Oh, you are stupid! You're as thick as they are!' replied the first Creature. 'He could then control everybody and not only the town of Destin. Apart from that, he still hasn't decided on the fate of that nuisance of a child who is giving him such a hard time.'

'Who do you mean?'

'The one whose ancestors had avoided the destiny decision.'

'What is he going to do with him?'

Irian realised they were actually talking about himself and he was annoyed when the Light Creature returned with Arameen's answer, so he couldn't listen to more of their conversation about him.

'The master is waiting for you. Hurry up! He doesn't like to be kept waiting, as you know' said the Light Creature. 'Don't bother the master too much because he already has many things to think about.'

"Yes, he needs to find the best way to destroy me", thought Irian to himself. "What are they going to do with the Glimmers once they have taken these diamond flowers away from them?", wondered Irian.

'Be careful what you're thinking!' warned the Light Creature that was guiding Irian around.

'Why?' asked Irian.

'Oh, come on!' replied the Creature. 'You know that the master can read our thoughts and he hates silly thoughts. You see, you've just been silly to ask me such a stupid question. Don't do such things with the master!'

"He can read thoughts? But what am I going to do then? My head is filled with thoughts. How am I going to get rid of them? They are there, I can't just make them go away", thought Irian to himself in a panic.

The temple wasn't far from the place where he had overheard the Light Creatures' conversation, and on the way to the temple, Irian was trying to change his thoughts and make himself think the sort of thoughts he imagined one of the Creatures would think. However, the more he tried to think like a Creature, the more his real thoughts would squeeze into his thinking space, without his permission. "What am I going to do? He'll realise who I am straight away!"

When they arrived to climb up to Arameen's temple, Irian realised that each step was as tall as one of his legs, and he realised another muscle-stretching lesson was awaiting him. Luckily, this time, there were not so many steps though. On the other hand, he thought that climbing them was a good thing this time. He usually couldn't think when he was too tired, so in a way, he wanted to exhaust himself just to chase his thoughts away before meeting Arameen. However, even when he had reached the top of the steps, his thoughts were still disobediently wandering around in his mind.

'Don't keep the master too long' instructed the Light Creature. 'I'll come and look for you after a while.'

Irian decided to think for a little bit before stepping in front of Arameen, and he realised that his time was limited as the Light Creature was going to come and pick him up shortly.

'How long have I got?' asked Irian.

'The master will ring the bell when he has had enough of you' replied the Creature. 'Hey, you ask me questions as if you had never been here. I wonder what your creature quality is. Are you the Stupidity Creature?'

Irian wished so much that he were the Stupidity Creature because at least he wouldn't have to think.

'Wait here! I'll announce you to the master' ordered the Creature.

Irian had to wait in front of the temple before being granted permission to go in. He was struggling to look around and he kept his eyes closed most of the time, as all the light made his eyes painful and itchy.

'You can go in now' said the Light Creature. 'Don't forget to kiss the master's stick!'

The massive doors made of stone now opened in front of him and, as he entered the temple, the doors closed behind him making a loud bang. He found himself in a large room with an enormous clock set in the floor, with one of its hands reaching up to Irian's feet. There was a huge hole in the ceiling of the temple, which was positioned directly under the sun. Therefore, as the sun turned around the sky, its rays influenced the hands of the clock and made them move around too. It was like a silent agreement between the sun and that floor clock; a mutual cooperation, where the sun directed the time and the floor clock obeyed and followed the sun's movements. The clock's hands even looked like human hands with clenched fists.

'What do you want from me?' asked Arameen, and Irian recognised the voice that he had heard not that long ago in the Clock Room of the Amphitheatre, the fateful day he opened the Destiny Book by accident.

Irian lifted his head after observing the floor clock and

looked in the direction of the voice. There sat the ultimate leader of the Sudba and the Light Creatures and the being that everybody, including Queen Ranna herself feared. Arameen wasn't wearing a mask like the other Creatures, and Irian noticed that he was hairless, as if somebody had shaved him clean. He was about eight foot tall, but slender and looked very much like some kind of statue with such impeccable skin. If he hadn't been half white and half black, he would almost have resembled another person. Irian thought Arameen would have had a more monstrous appearance, but he didn't give a scary impression at first sight. He was wearing a silk robe, and both of his arms and legs were filled with jewellery and bracelets so that in Irian's opinion, Arameen would have served as a perfect but strange model for some jewellery shop window. His eyes were two empty balls that projected onto things around him like two mirrors, but Arameen didn't move his head when talking.

Irian, more than a little intimidated, went to kiss his stick as instructed, and he felt so tiny standing in front of such a gigantic Creature that appeared so cold despite all the light and heat around.

'Why have you come here?' asked Arameen, coldly.

'You should know' answered Irian. 'You can read my thoughts, isn't that right?'

'Normally I can' replied Arameen. 'But for some reason, I'm unable to do it today.'

Irian didn't know how to take this answer; as a trap or as a true fact. If Arameen could read his thought but was pretending that he couldn't, it meant that Arameen had already recognised Irian and was waiting for the right moment to destroy him. However, Peena had told him that if Arameen suspected anything, he would surely take Irian to the Mirror Room. Arameen, however, didn't seem to have any intention of making the slightest of movements and appeared relaxed, waiting for Irian to speak. Therefore, Irian decided that Arameen probably couldn't read his thoughts because he wasn't a Sudba or a Light Creature, so his mind space couldn't be controlled.

'I have come to ask you for help' lied Irian.

'Your voice seems young. Which Creature are you, then?'

asked Arameen, and Irian had impression that Arameen had even moved slightly from his static position.

'The hard experiences of my past have influenced my whole body and my voice too, making it weak to your ear' invented Irian on the spot. 'We need more Light Creatures in the town.'

'Why would I give you more Light Creatures?' asked Arameen, as if he was referring to some sort of objects and not his protectors.

'The Sudba Creatures don't have enough guards to protect themselves. They can't cope. Apart from that, we still haven't got any answer from the young descendant' Irian thought that he should have used some horrible name for himself such as "that little pest", but he didn't want to overdo it.

'That little pest!' said Arameen angrily, and Irian's face now changed colour thinking that Arameen could read his mind after all, though it was more a coincidence than anything else. 'Isn't the drink ready yet?'

'I beg your pardon?' asked Irian, confused.

'The drink, you know what I'm talking about. Don't make me waste my breath! The drink, to make him change his mind. Why isn't it ready yet?' screamed Arameen and his loud voice pierced Irian's eardrums.

Irian now wished he had been able to hear the rest of the conversation he had overheard while waiting to be accepted by Arameen because he would have at least known what to answer next.

'We still haven't got all the ingredients' Irian tried to make something up as quickly as he could.

'What are you waiting for? Why didn't you go and look for them instead of coming here to waste my time on such stupid and non intellectual conversation.'

Irian was just about to answer, stepping backwards slightly in order to escape a little further from Arameen's loud voice that was becoming unbearable to his ears. As he moved backwards, one of the clock hands happened to move towards him, so that he stumbled over it and fell down. As he fell forward, his mask dropped off and slid across the floor. Irian tried to crawl to get it, but Arameen was faster and he picked up the mask with his stick. Irian was completely panic-stricken.

'You are not a Creature! You have a strange energy' shouted Arameen, getting up from his chair. 'Who are you? Speak!'

Irian was kneeling there, unable to move, as if he had suddenly been paralysed. He knew that it wasn't a good time to panic, but he was incapable of finding a solution for what to do next to protect himself from the mighty Arameen.

'I think I recognise your smell' continued Arameen. 'You're the little pest that opened the Destiny Book, aren't you?'

'I'm not a pest! You and your Creatures are the pests in our town! You came to disturb our peaceful town first. We didn't come looking for you. So, you are the unwanted ones.'

'How dare you speak to me like that?' yelled Arameen. 'I can destroy you with a single wave of my stick.'

'Before you destroy me, tell me something. What did you give to the Glimmers to change them into Sudba Creatures?' Irian was trying to ask question to gain time until he hit on an idea to act against Arameen.

'Why would I tell you that?' asked Arameen in somewhat calmer voice. 'Well, I'm going to destroy you in a minute, so why not after all. The diamond powder can transform you into whatever you want, depending on the quantity of it you take. If you dose it properly, you can become literally anything you want.'

'But how did you know how much powder you need to create a certain human quality?'

'We can feel our feelings and emotions, can't we? Some of them are very heavy, some of them are light and some of them are both. I used my scales that are very accurate when weighing things. So, I put all my feelings and emotions on those scales and they told me exactly how much powder I needed. I spent a long time doing that, because I had to go through all feelings and emotions, and the scales measured the energy coming out of me to find the exact right dose for the diamond powder' explained Arameen.

'Why the Glimmers? Why not somebody else?'

'The Glimmers are born with a precious stone replacing their right eye, and precious stones contain different energies. I thought I could use their natural energy and develop it into a human quality. Therefore, I only exploited their potential to the maximum. We all have a certain potential for something but we don't always know how to make good use of it. This can be manipulated. They couldn't survive without their precious stone in their right eye because they had lost the income of natural energy, which I then replaced with an exaggeratedly high dose of a given human quality so as to keep them alive' revealed Arameen.

'So, what would they need to do to get rid of the spell?'

'They would need to burn diamond powder in this temple to undo the spell because its smoke destroys our energies. But they don't know that' laughed Arameen and Irian had the impression that the whole of Arameen's body was in fits of proud laughter.

Irian could almost have thanked Arameen for telling him what to do so easily. He went to open his bag to get out the powder and burn it. However, he realised that he had left the matches on the balloon! He couldn't believe he could be so stupid! It was like having an empty gun that was useless without bullets.

'I'm not going to waste my stick's energy destroying you' said Arameen, serious this time. 'Nothing can destroy this stick. It controls time and all things and it is as old as the planet we're living on. Everything around it can be destroyed but not the stick. The stick adapts to its owner, but one needs to know how to use it.'

'Who did you get it from?' asked Irian.

'I was born out of this mighty stick. I don't know who my ancestors were. It's the great stick that decides when we are to come or leave and we can only obey' explained Arameen. 'Guard! Quick! Destroy him!'

Arameen rang his bell hysterically and the Light Creatures came running in, looking like hungry beasts.

'He's not a Sudba Creature!' yelled Arameen. 'He's the town's young descendant. Destroy him at once!'

The Light Creatures started to spit streams of fire at Irian, who tried desperately to escape them. Just then, he had an idea –

he took his rucksack in his hands and waited for the flames to hit the bag. As planned, one of the flames struck his rucksack and the diamond powder started to burn, slowly but surely.

'What is that thing burning?' asked Arameen suspiciously.

'It's diamond powder!' answered Irian. 'Thanks for telling me what to do with it, and thanks for the light too!'

'No!' yelled Arameen this time louder than ever before 'You're going to destroy me. I already feel weakened by the smoke. Stop it! Stop it!'

'You had no right to control my people and my town' shouted Irian. 'People have the right to decide on their own lives and live according to their merits.'

The smoke coming from the diamond powder continued spreading steadily around the temple and even the Light Creatures stopped spitting flames. It was incredible to see how such a small quantity of diamond powder could cause so much smoke and have such an extraordinary power over Arameen and his Creatures.

A new Order in the Town of Destin

At that same moment back in Destin, the Queen was about to confirm the destiny of Maia and Petalber's child. Once the Sudba Creatures had cast their spells in the Destiny Book and she herself had decided on the baby's lifespan, luck and gender, she was to place her hand on the book to confirm their decision. When doing this, she would add some extra words to make the whole thing more spectacular.

> *"The qualities we bestow have carefully been selected*
> *This is our mighty effort and cannot be neglected*
> *How much luck, how much fear, how much love,*
> *how much hate*
> *The judgement is fixed; we now grant you your fate."*

The Queen was just about to place her hand on top of a new baby's page in the great book, when something very bizarre happened.

* * *

Back in Arameen's temple, the smoke from the diamond powder had reached Arameen's stick and activated the diamond on the top of it. All at once, the diamond started to shine like never before, flooding everything with the most dazzling light. It was so strong that Irian had to cover his face with his hands to protect his eyes from the pain. The light streaming from the diamond stick began to obliterate Arameen's temple with great flashes that left complete emptiness in their wake, annihilating Arameen and his Light Creatures as well as the huge mountains and leaving a gaping blankness in the space of the blink of an eyelid.

In Destin, the Amphitheatre was erased at once, while the Queen disappeared just like in a magicians' show. The Sudba Creatures immediately turned back into the Glimmers, exchanging their powerful forms for the finer bodies and sparkling eyes of the Glimmer race. Everything that had connection with Arameen's government seemed to have been swept away by the might light coming from Arameen's stick.

No trace of the Sudba Creatures' rule remained.

* * *

Irian woke up lying on the ground in the middle of nowhere. He had trouble remembering what he was doing there and how he had reached the place. Further away in the distance he spotted Grandfather and the Old Lady, so he began walking towards them, somewhat confused.

'Grandpa' said Irian, 'how did we get here?'

'I've no idea' replied Grandfather. 'It's strange, but I just don't remember. It must be age. Where is this place? It looks so weird. How on earth did we arrive here?'

'I can't remember either, it's as if somebody has erased something from my mind' answered Irian, bewildered. 'And this stick? Where has it come from?'

'Let me see!' asked Grandfather. 'It's extraordinary! Where did you find this? Look, it even has a diamond on it!'

'I don't know' replied Irian. 'It was lying next to me when I woke up. Everything seems so confusing.'

'Let's go home' said Grandfather. 'We must be miles away.'

It took them quite a long time to get back home. They flew against the burning sun and at times in the face of capricious cold winds.

In Destin, nobody was ever to remember anything about the Sudba Creatures or Queen Ranna again, as if they had never existed. It all seemed like the vaguest of dreams, that exist at the time, but which leave only a strange feeling behind when you wake up in the morning.

So, Irian had inherited Arameen's stick, a strange object he had found in his possession, as a souvenir of an unknown adventure that he had experienced but that he couldn't recall. It was to remain a mystery, a puzzle about which he had no memory, only a feeling; a feeling of strength, relief and happiness.

THE END